Titles by Liana Cincotti

Don't Be In Love

Picking Daisies on Sundays

PICKING DAISIES ON SUNDAYS

Liana Cincotti

For the hopeless, and hopeful, romantics who don't know they're noticed in a crowded room.

Her lips pressed against my cheek and her hand left mine. I don't even remember taking her hand. But just like that it was gone. And she was rushing down the stairs, her long dress dragging behind her like an ocean wave in a storm, leaving me stranded.

Prologue

My heart's been borrowed and yours has been blue
— Lover, Taylor Swift

I loved Levi Coldwell. I was *in love* with Levi Coldwell. My best friend of four years and counting.

It wasn't love at first sight when we met freshman year. Especially when we both had braces and hormonal acne that changed location on our faces every day. The first day of high school, we found ourselves in two of the same classes, one we were each struggling with.

One audible sigh from Levi as he tried threading a needle in Sewing, and a C minus in my first English assignment, was all it took to start helping one another.

I taught him how to sew and he helped me edit my essays. It was exclusively a business transaction two days a week, until we started talking about things that weren't sewing or writing.

We had a list of adorations in common: our love for films, dedication to academics, loyalty to family, and the grief we went through—we were *going* through. We both had experiences with losing a father, and I think that's what bonded us first.

When I had met him freshman year, my dad had passed three

months prior, while Mr. Coldwell had already been gone for two years.

Levi still carried grief with him like an empty wine bottle.

Fast forward four years and we were the best of friends, about to graduate high school together.

Years of texting every day, spending Saturday nights watching movies, and eating school lunches together had become habitual. They were my equivalent to having a morning routine or praying at night.

Months of seeing him in the stands as he cheered me on at my softball games while I hit foul balls, and nights full of tripping on that one cracked sidewalk on the way to each other's houses.

I'd witnessed him bake cupcakes for his sisters' school functions, pulled their hair into ponytails, and sat still as they painted our nails. Those moments revealed every aspect of a person. And God, have I enjoyed every single one of his aspects.

We had become the type of best friends who came over for dinner every week and whose Moms knew each other's most recent drama, gossiping over cups of coffee on the porch.

He lived down the street from me, so I'd walk over and have dinner with his family on Sunday nights, laughing as Trish recalled old stories and his sisters threw chips at each other across the table.

But it changed when junior year rolled around.

Levi had finally returned from being away with his family in Vermont during Christmas break. I had been bored all December waiting for him. So the day he returned, I rushed through the hall to the second locker on the left from our English class to see him.

Only to find him kissing someone.

My stomach clenched as I spotted him kissing Jennifer O'Brien. I was blindsided seeing him pressed up against that locker with Jennifer's hands crawling across his body like she was etching a sonnet into his skin. I couldn't remember how long I stared; I couldn't stop. It was like catching your celebrity crush in person. My throat dried up, my eyes filled with tears, and my feet refused to move until someone bumped into me, forcing me out of the way.

I had seen Vi—Levi—leave for dates and go to prom with other girls and I was always completely fine! There were always twinges of jealousy, but I brushed it off as protectiveness for my best friend. But I had never seen him *kiss* anyone before. That… that felt wrong—intrusive actually.

And when I saw Jennifer taking his lips in hers, I regretted it instantly, because every emotion I didn't know existed rose to the surface.

It'd been almost a year since it happened, and I still couldn't erase the memory. But it was Senior Prom tonight and graduation tomorrow, and I couldn't put this off any longer.

Scrapbooking didn't work; watching endless romance films didn't work; embroidering and quilting didn't work; and writing a list of all of his cons definitely didn't work because he had none.

The only con I could come up with was that he didn't try to kiss me after the homecoming football game in September. We had been sitting in his car outside my house, and I had glanced at his lips *at least* twice.

Anyways, none of it worked. I still loved him. And I couldn't pretend anymore like my heart didn't hit my ribcage when he winked at me in class or brushed my hand—and *especially not* when he twirled strands of my hair when we sat across from each other. I couldn't pretend that my throat didn't resemble the tightness of a twisted towel when girls flirted with him at parties. I couldn't pretend like it meant nothing anymore.

I had to tell him, tonight, before we graduated tomorrow and left for college at the end of the summer. I couldn't suffer another summer and then wonder *what if* when he went to college and possibly met the love of his life.

The problem was: tonight was here now and I was terrified. I had spent hours fixing and retailoring my dress so it fit perfectly, but now it was too tight as I downed my second glass of spiked soda—courtesy of the hockey team that brought vodka—under the twinkly lights hanging around the overpriced prom venue.

Please don't let that affect your opinion of me though because this wasn't me. Drinking was not something I found pleasing by any means, and I definitely wasn't someone who was known by the hockey team.

I saw Molly Ringwald do this in a film once for confidence so I thought it couldn't hurt. But as I watched Levi from a distance talking to a few friends, my stomach still clenched and pinched with anxiety. His dark grey suit clung to his long legs and made his dark hair and eyes look edgier than usual. He always had this cool look about him with his brown, curling hair, tall posture, and captivating hazel eyes.

My gaze must've been heavy because he glanced at me, catching me in the act. My heart stopped in a panic, but he simply mouthed, *hey punk,* and winked at me, continuing on with his conversation.

　　　　　　　　　　　　　　　　　　　　　　　　Liana Cincotti

Pushing my hand out to the concerningly mature-looking hockey player for another drink, I swallowed it all before my mind could register the taste. I did come here with a (platonic) date by the name of Jeremiah. He was helping me figure out what to say to Levi tonight, resulting in an incredulously long note on my phone. Speaking of, where was he? The last time I had seen my phone, it was in his hand.

Crap, crap, *crap*. I couldn't do this without him or the phone.

Why was my face wet? Running my hand across my cheek, I realized that I was crying. Of course I wasn't a relieved, happy drunk, but a sad, *anxious* drunk.

Clutching my dress to avoid tripping, I rushed into one of the side hallways to pull myself together. Once I found privacy, my body relaxed and my tears flowed. *Where was Jeremiah with my phone?*

Tap, tap, tap. The tears in my eyes blurred my vision enough that I couldn't see the person approaching me, just the sound of their shoes. Squeezing my eyes shut, I prayed they just kept walking. Maybe if I closed my eyes, it'd be as if no one saw the embarrassing mess sitting on the floor.

"Hey, hey, hey, what's wrong, Daisy?"

Only three people in my life referred to me by my middle name, and only one of them was here.

My eyes opened on command at the sound of Levi's voice, watching him crouch down on the floor in front of me with urgency. His hands immediately cupped my face. Tilting it up, forcing me to meet his eyes, I found that his own face looked distressed. My heart pounded harder in my chest, warming my cheeks at the feeling of his palms on my face.

This was too close; he was too close. Could he see my love for him painted across my face? Could he tell from the way I shuddered when he touched me, that every fiber of my being was made to be touched by him?

How did we go from friends to this?

Tears refused to reel themselves in. But when I registered the absolute devastation on his face, my heart refilled with the hope that he might feel the same way.

Ten minutes later, he broke my heart. And I didn't see him for four years.

1

How did I ever let time pass this long without seeing you?

"Jia, I'm not sitting at the table with them, I have no idea what they're saying," I whispered in a hushed tone from the coverage of the booth I was hiding in.

"Then what was the point of going!" Jia responded over the phone.

"To make sure Gabe doesn't get murdered, of course," I responded seriously, watching Gabe from across the restaurant on his date.

"You're in the West Village, Dani, no one's getting murdered. The only crime around here is the preposterous real estate prices," Jia said matter-of-factly.

"We're twenty-two, this is the prime murdering age." I turned back to Gabe as he began furrowing his eyebrows. "Gabe's giving me the look."

"*The look?* —Wait, why are you dressed like you're going on a date?" Jia said entirely off topic, commenting on my (apparently uncommon) blouse and jeans.

I turned around abruptly in my seat where I found Jia entering the restaurant. If you could call it entering; it was more like a hunched walk behind a menu to hide from Gabe's date. I raised a discrete waving hand above my own menu to catch Jia's attention. "Where did you go?" I asked. Switching my phone off, I moved over to make room for her in the booth. She had a maxi skirt on, leather boots, and a small top that just covered her chest. Her hair was naturally black, but it'd been dyed every color of the rainbow, changing every season. It didn't matter what she colored her hair, though, because everything complemented her thin face and tall frame. This spring it was blonde. Her parents hated that she colored her hair, but her response was: "I work in fashion, it matches my job description." A very Jia response—to me, of course, as she reiterated the conversation to me. No way in hell would she talk back to her parents.

"I had to pick up fabric for the devil and drop it off to her," Jia said, exhaling, as she rested her chin on her fist.

"Why don't you just quit? You have enough experience at this point," I insisted, worrying about the last of her energy.

"If there's any chance she can get me into the Met Gala next year, then all of the work I've done would be worth it," she said with a matched urgency and concern.

Before I could reply, Josh, our waiter, arrived at our table with a look of scorn. Rightfully so. I had been sitting at this table for thirty minutes without ordering anything other than water. But there were about ten other open tables and no one waiting at the door to be seated, so I didn't feel *that* bad.

It was fine though; I left him a really nice tip every time and I'd bring him flowers in a few days.

This was our love-hate relationship. Jia, Gabe, and I used the table at the restaurant once in a while for scoping out dates in case we needed a reason to get out of an awkward situation (and to avoid being kidnapped), annoying Josh a little, in which I then brought him flowers that he swooned over.

He mentioned wanting peonies before seating me.

"Ladies, you need to order something if you're going to use the table—"

"Two waters," we responded in unison.

"And a basket of fries, please, Josh," Jia added in. Josh rolled his eyes, walking away with the order.

"What's happened so far?" she asked with curiosity, bringing the menu just below her eyes.

"Gabe has laughed twice, checked his phone once—"

"Good, good."

"—and finished four glasses of wine," I finished, pressing my lips into a solemn line.

She smacked her palm against her forehead in disappointment, "And he did a look?"

"*The look*, yes."

"Yeah, it's over, let's wrap this up," Jia said, putting the menu down and getting up from her seat. As quickly as she got up, she was turning back around, pointing a finger at me with a threatening glare. "Don't forget the fries."

Here we go, the funniest part of the night.

Jia made her way to Gabe's table with her hands in fists at her sides, mustering up her performance.

"*How dare you,*" Jia shouted with seething anger as she slammed her hands onto the table in between Gabe and his date.

"I tell you I'm pregnant and you decide to go on a *date?*"

Gabe clutched his chest, choking on his shrimp at her abrupt appearance. The blonde guy across from Gabe was washed with horror, his cheeks turning pink and his eyelashes practically reaching his eyebrows.

Gabe pressed a hand against his throat, now clear of shrimp, with feigned earnestness, "Darling—"

"I thought you were gay!" Gabe's date interjected with horror.

I have to say, *that* would not have been my first concern when hearing the word pregnant …

Gabe's head tilted at the audacity of his date's concern, obviously mirroring my exact thought.

Jia grabbed Gabe's collar. "This is the last time I let you out of my sight," Jia raged, trying to get Gabe out of this— apparently—horrible date, pulling him out of his seat.

As if on cue, Josh placed the basket of fries on my table while Jia and Gabe rushed out of the restaurant. I swiftly picked up the basket, left cash on the table behind me, with an apology wave to Josh.

Scrambling out of the restaurant, I found Jia and Gabe outside waiting for me, laughing. "*Pregnant?*" Gabe asked, practically wheezing with laughter. "We agreed on you being my *girlfriend*, not my baby mama!"

My own laugher spilled out at Gabe's comment. "If you ask me, that was an award-winning performance, Jia."

She bowed at the waist and said, "I would like to thank my mom and Daniella for their support, and Gabe for his horrible taste in men."

Receiving a slap on the shoulder from him, she only erupted in more laughter. "You owe me a drink for that performance," Jia stated, pointing at Gabe.

"Yeah, yeah," he responded. "It's on its way." He rolled his eyes and scrunched his button nose. It made him look like a kid. His height alone gave him a child-like appearance, standing two inches shorter than me, meaning several inches shorter than Jia. You could never tell though because he wore platform sneakers, a gift from the company he interned at as a marketing assistant.

Turning another corner, we made our way to the bar down the street, entering into the usual crowd.

"A beer and a Dirty Shirley," Gabe asked the bartender, squeezing in between those also asking for drinks as Jia and I shouted our thanks.

Turning to me, Jia took another fry out of the basket, "You never explained the cute outfit." Her gaze swept over my clothes, from the well-fitting jeans to the low-cut, long sleeve top that accentuated my chest in a way I knew she commended, but I opposed. It was a stark contrast from my usual attire which often consisted of overalls, flowing linen pants, midi dresses, et cetera— anything that didn't stick to my body.

I pulled at the top, trying to cover more of my chest, but then it exposed my belly button.

I sighed. "I needed a silhouette example for the dress I'm sketching. I wasn't sure if I liked the combo of this cut with a bodycon style frame towards the bottom."

Was she listening? Because she looked more focused on how I couldn't stop touching my shirt. Then suddenly, she was pulling at the top too, trying to fix the mess that was me in fitted clothing.

"What did you end up deciding?" Jia asked, apparently listening.

"To keep the dress fitted in the waist and hips, but have it flare from there. If the neckline was higher, I would've decided otherwise, but I feel like it's too much all together, right?" I asked.

Talking about design-thoughts wasn't good for my mental health after class hours—it made me stress-sweat—but it had to be done because it was all I could think about. If I didn't figure it out now, then it'd knock on my glass window like a desperate Romeo visiting Juliet tonight. And I liked my sleep uninterrupted.

I rummaged for my flower hair clip in my purse and then twisted my short brown hair up.

Jia continued, "Nope, I totally—"

"Oh crap," I exhaled, my hair clip falling to the ground. Squatting down, I searched for the bright clip. As soon as I reached the floor, I was standing back up with the clip in hand—*shit*. Was that the bottom of someone's beer that just hit the top of my head?

"*Shit*," I said in unison with the person holding the beer. Standing up, I ran a hand through my hair (no beer, thank god) as I went to apologize to—

How hard did I just hit my head? Because there's no way this is actually happening right now.

"*Daisy?*" Levi asked. Levi Coldwell. Levi Coldwell was standing in front of me.

2

I never understood why anyone spoke poorly of the color brown,
it was a dream on you

Short, curling hair—shorter than I remembered—in the most perfect shade of brown, along with his hazel eyes and melting smile.

How did he get more handsome?

The Levi Coldwell that I loved in high school. The boy I spent nearly every day with and watched every girl swoon over him in the process while my heart was shattered into pieces. Roaring started in my ears and the room began to sway as past memories flooded my vision. The last time I had seen him was when he walked across the graduation stage our senior year of high school four years ago. I had been silently wiping tears as I avoided his gaze in the crowd, thinking of everything he said to me the previous night.

"*Levi?*" I was trying to hide any state of panic, but I couldn't relax my shoulders or lower my blood pressure as I took in the man in front of me. I rushed to fix whatever the beer glass just did to my hair as I absorbed that he was real.

"Levi?!" Gabe and Jia whispered from behind me, reminding me that we were in public, not in a dream.

"You cut your hair," Levi said in astonishment as if we had been speaking for the past four years. His hand reached toward my face to touch it, but then, his hand moved down to his side quickly. My breath hitched in my throat like a hormonal teenage girl.

Don't blush, don't blush, be cool, be cool. He mentioned your *hair*, not the shape of your lips in a romantic way.

I suppressed my numerous questions about why he was here. Like where he'd been the past four years, if he'd thought of me at all, if he was doing okay. Instead, I said, "I did. Kind of gets in the way while sewing."

That wasn't a complete lie, but it also wasn't the full truth. I cut it short the day after senior graduation because that's what all the heartbroken main characters I watched did when they needed a change. It seemed like a good next move after finding out the person I was in love with didn't feel the same way.

His face lit up. "How's that going by the way—designing?" he asked, sincerity in his eyes and smile.

"It's good," I said. "I love it." Trying to keep myself from rambling, I stopped there, unsure of how much longer I could hold this discussion without asking him a million questions and sounding insane. Not my best quality while I tried to discretely adjust my top in the process.

Did my boobs look okay?

"I'm sorry, by the way," he winced, referring to his beer hitting my head, as he reached for my forearm to enforce his sincerity. The small touch sent goosebumps up my arm, something I hadn't experienced in what felt like years. It felt more intimate than any of the sex I had in the past four years. "Let me buy you a drink. Dirty Shirley, right?"

My lips parted in surprise as I said, "Yeah," despite the drink in Gabe's hand that was waiting for me.

I followed Levi up to the bar as he made room for us, trying my best not to stare at his long stature as he walked. Or at his lips as he ordered our drinks. Or at his hands as he touched his hair. It was like I was back in high school; my mind reeled as I stood in his presence.

"Are you still going to NYU?" I asked as he leaned against the bar.

"You remember?" There was a flicker of surprise in his face.

"Of course, you don't give me enough credit, we were best friends," I said softly. But I was fully aware that he heard me from the look on his face as I said *best friends*, despite the rowdiness of the people drinking around us.

"We were," he said, nodding his head at the memory. "Are you still living with your mom and aunt in the West Village?"

"How do you know I live in the West Village?" I asked with confusion. The last thing I expected was Levi to remember anything about me, let alone where I was currently living.

He laughed as if he was trying to prepare himself for what he was about to admit. "I called your mom the day after graduation to find out if you were still moving into the city. She gave me the address in case I ever wanted to stop by."

My chest tightened. He had never stopped by.

I wasn't sure how to respond to that information, and honestly, I wished I hadn't known it at all. I'd already struggled the past four years wondering what he was doing, so knowing that he'd had this information all these years and did nothing with it … It left a pit of anxiety growing at the bottom of my stomach. With the old feelings rising to the surface, I refrained from responding and waited for him to continue.

"How are they—your mom and aunt, I mean," he asked, tripping over his words. Was he nervous?

"They're good," I said smiling. "Aunt Mandy is running the flower shop and my mom is designing, as usual. How are your sisters?"

His face lit up with joy. "They're great. Claire and Rhea just entered the third grade, and Sarah's getting married, actually."

I gasped, "*To who?* Don't tell me it's Jeff," covering my mouth with anticipation.

"You're not helping the situation," he said dreadfully as he ran his hand over his jaw with a groan.

"Oh my gosh, it is Jeff," I said urgently, trying not to laugh at this *horrifying* news. "Why would she ever agree to that?" I asked with intense curiosity.

I was always invested in his sisters' lives. I still remember going over to his house in high school and being sucked into their rooms to catch up on all the gossip happening in kindergarten for an hour before I even saw Levi. Sarah was only a year below us, so we usually talked about the cutest guys in class. I never admitted to her that I thought it was her brother.

"Because she's tired of the dating world—those were her exact words," he said shaking his head, obviously stressed over the engagement.

"Are you dating anyone?" The words were out before I could

process what I was saying.

His eyebrows raised. He hesitated before answering. "No. Are you?"

"Not at the moment," I said. *Not at the moment? What was that supposed to mean?*

He obviously didn't think much of it because he responded casually, "That's good."

God, this conversation was going into a territory I wasn't dressed properly for. I think this was the type of conversation I needed to be prepped on before I was allowed to speak freely.

The first time I saw my childhood crush in four years, and I was wearing ill-fitting clothes. Someone please save—

"Levi?" Our heads turned at the sound of his name.

"Bella," Levi said, color coming to his cheeks.

"How are you?" she—Bella—asked as she practically jumped onto Levi in a warm embrace. This was *not* the kind of saving I was looking for.

"I'm good, I'm good. How are you?"

Should I leave? Honestly, what would you do in this conversation? I obviously had no clue. I stood there for a moment debating my options, watching as Bella and Levi talked, his hand on her arm the entire conversation and her hand on his.

Her hair was the color of the homemade blondies I made on Sundays before working at the flower shop. It had this strawberry blonde tint and was the perfect length, hitting the middle of her back. It made me wish I had never cut my hair.

"I'm here with one of Sarah's friends, she'll be at the wedding with us."

Us?

I glanced at Levi in surprise. She was invited to the wedding? I hated to admit it, but I couldn't watch him be invested in every word Bella said. It felt like senior year all over again. And hearing about how involved she was in his life—how I used to be that person—was too much.

I stepped away from them before I could do anything pathetic, they wouldn't notice me blending into the background—but then I was pulled back within one step, a hand in mine.

"Bella, this is Daisy—Dani," he said, correcting himself in a flustered manner.

Hearing the sound of my name coming from his lips affected my body in a way that other men couldn't even do when kissing me.

I refrained from looking down at my hand in surprise like a love-obsessed stalker, and instead looked at the girl across from me, who was now climbing off Levi at the sight of our interlocked hands. Now she was looking at me as if she knew me. Did she?

"*Daisy?*" Bella asked Levi, rather than asking me, with an appalled look on her face.

At the nod of Levi's head, Bella continued, "I've heard a lot about you." The way she spoke made it sound as if she regretted it.

Before I could speak, Bella kept going. A flirtatious smile painted on her face as she touched his thigh, her body in between his legs. "Did Levi tell you we're together?"

The comment hit me like a slap in the face, my heart instantly faltering. Did he lie about not being in a relationship to make me feel better about my poor excuse of a dating life? My reaction must have been evident because he spoke up immediately.

Liana Cincotti

"We're not together anymore," he said.

"I was just testing you, calm down." Bella rolled her eyes and then flicked one of his loose curls.

Catching her hand, he said, "Unnecessary."

I couldn't help but notice how when he said my name it sounded sweet, but when he said hers, it sounded seductive. Probably the perfect way to describe how the two of us were different; she was all glamour, and I was all … vintage.

"Oh, come on, Levi, everyone knows you're obsessed with me. No hard feelings. I promise it won't affect my mother's decision about the job. Maybe." She spoke with wit, finishing it off with a wink.

"That's not true."

She continued, not caring for his refusal to agree with her. "Being obsessed with me? Oh, *come on*, Levi, everyone can see it, it's nothing to be embarrassed about. You haven't even dated anyone since—"

"I'm dating Dani."

The only thing that kept my jaw from dropping was the satisfaction I got from her shocked face.

"Excuse me?" she asked, her voice iced over with an intensity I only ever heard from my aunt when they messed up her takeout order.

He didn't miss a beat. His eyes went straight to my face to drive the point home. My knees locked up as he looked into my eyes and said, "Daniella and I are dating." His words were seductive and determined, like I was his and he wouldn't sit there and be told otherwise.

I stared back in awe; the moment being broken up by Levi as he returned to Bella. "So no, it shouldn't affect your mother's decision."

Coldness wasn't something you'd see from Levi often. I could count on one hand the number of times in which he raised his voice or cut someone off in the four years I spent with him. Seeing this side of him was like witnessing a tsunami in a landlocked country.

"I didn't think you'd ever do the boyfriend thing," she speculated. "I assume she'll be coming to the wedding then," she stated formally, still ignoring me.

"Yes, she will be," he said.

He was upset. She had the ability to make him upset. Levi liked this girl. It was obvious from the way his face lit up the second he saw her. He had always attracted girls though; it was no surprise. From his flirtatious charm to his hazel eyes and dark hair. It was like the angles and structure of his face were made to be replicated by artists and stared at by beautiful girls.

Just the way he would look at you with this absolute intensity let you know he was paying attention to every word you said like you were an addictive drug. Everyone desired to be with him and be around him. But I had never seen Levi reciprocate those feelings for the girls that followed his movements.

I was going to vomit.

"I guess I'll see you both at the game tomorrow then," she said.

Game?

"See you tomorrow," he finished without looking at Bella, his hand now catching mine as he pulled us out of the bar and around the corner. Before he could walk any further, not having any clue where he was headed, I came to a halt.

"You need to explain, right now." I let go of his hand so I could think clearly.

The sky was only just darkening as the sun made its escape. The streetlights clicked on and illuminated the brownstone townhouses and shops.

As Levi turned around, I realized that it was the first time tonight that I saw a look of distress sweep over his features, his hand pressed against his temple. "I did not plan for that to happen," he said leaning against the wall, not far from my home and the flower shop.

"God, I would hope not, because you should know that I am the worst person to pick when it comes to lying. So, explain to me what just happened," I said.

"I panicked." He rubbed the back of his neck.

"You *panicked?*" I asked with astoundment. "If that girl looked at me one more time, I'm convinced it would've been the last thing I saw before she knocked me out!"

He laughed, a smile appearing across his tan face. As our eyes met, all the anger in my body extinguished.

"What happened?" I asked, expecting some horror-filled break up story based on the way she reacted to him dating someone else.

"She's a friend of Sarah's. We went on a few dates throughout the year, but it didn't turn out how she wanted." It sounded like there was more to be said, but he looked conflicted.

As much as I wanted to reach out to him, similar to the way we used to hug one another every Thursday night before I walked back to my house or when we passed our dreaded Friday physics exams, I kept my hands together. We weren't those people anymore.

"Why would you tell her we're dating then?" I asked, genuinely curious.

He shook his head. "I'm trying to stay on her good side, and she knows that. Her mother runs the Arts department for *The New York Times* and has the power to hire me. She's convinced that I'm a loose cannon though."

"What? Why? That makes no sense," I shook my head, even more confused than before.

"She thought I was a qualified candidate for the position before finding out about me dating Bella. She's convinced I won't stick around in the city—that I'm not serious about my future because I can't commit to a relationship with her daughter."

"She said this to you?" I asked in disbelief; my face hurt with surprise. This sounded … illegal?

He had something to say, something that he didn't want to share. The reason … I didn't know why. But often he held back when it involved his personal feelings. There was something about this relationship, or lack thereof, with Bella that he wasn't saying.

"She's her mother. I couldn't blame her for putting her guard up."

Protective, caring Levi as usual. "And I come into this how …"

He groaned with embarrassment. "I promise this was not planned. I panicked. First, I saw you" —my heart swelled at those three words— "then her. I know if Bella sees me in a relationship, she's likely to tell her mother."

"I don't know. We're talking about pretending to be a couple here, and I haven't even seen you in *years*. The last thing I want is to deceive your family and intrude on Sarah's wedding." This was much easier to say than explaining my unrequited feelings for him, even as fizzled as they were after all these years.

Pushing off the wall, he strode across the wide sidewalk in one fluid step. "What are you talking about?" he asked, shaking his head, perplexed. "Sarah would die to see you again; my family has always loved you." The confession made me nostalgic, missing the large family dinners and chatter of his siblings. And that quick memory must've appeared on my face because the tension in his shoulders relaxed. How was I supposed to say no? This used to be my best friend.

"You'd be doing me a huge favor." He gave me a childish smile that made me snort with laughter.

"It's not fair," I said like a child.

"What?"

"I've never been able to say no to you," I said, knowing that he would take it as a sign of our friendship and nothing else.

Kissing me on the head in excitement as if nothing had changed, he said, "You're amazing, Daniella Maria!"

"You owe me, Levi Coldwell," I replied with a finger in his chest, trying to recover from the ghost of the kiss on my forehead.

"Free strawberry shortcake for the rest of your life," he cheered with joy as I pulled his hands from my face.

"How do you remember this stuff?" I laughed in response, surprised that he would remember something so specific.

"Friends, remember?" he spoke nonchalantly, having no idea that those were the last words I wanted to hear.

Friends.

"Now, how is this going to work, and what is this game?"

3

It's all you loved, but never yourself

Three hours later and I was back home—Aunt Mandy's home specifically. A brownstone townhouse that used to belong to my mom before she moved to the suburbs and started a family. When her career in wedding dress design took off, she bought a home in the most expensive, but beautiful, area in New York City. Years later when she got married and moved, she sold it to Mandy, my dad's sister.

I moved in with her once college started. Mom often jumped between here, our home in the suburbs, and the five-star hotels of the cities she had work in for photoshoots, fashion weeks, and so on. Mandy and my mom were only a year apart, so they acted more like best friends than sisters-in-law. It made for a very sitcom-like environment when we were all together.

Walking up the stairs with an immense amount of knowledge about Sarah's wedding and how this plan was going to work, I found Gabe and Jia sitting on Mandy's couch.

"Well, hello there," I said, not expecting either of them to be here. They did have the keycode though, so it wasn't the first time

I'd found them waiting for me.

Both of them flew off the couch once they spotted me. They asked questions at the same speed, only taking breaths for the other to ask the next one.

"What happened?" Jia asked.

"Was that *the* Levi?" asked Gabe.

"Who was the blonde chick?"

"Why did you walk out holding hands?"

"Did he walk you home?"

"Whoa, whoa, whoa. Sit down and I'll answer your questions, after I take off these clothes," I spoke in a rush, running down the hall to change into sweats.

Coming back just as quickly, I explained what happened at the bar: how I hit my head off his beer—"Yes, saw that already," Jia said aggressively, wanting to know the parts she didn't hear—and then what had caused Levi to say we were dating.

"I'm sorry, he said what?" Gabe asked, almost falling off the couch.

"Yup." I nodded my head, crossing my legs on the couch across from them like a child in kindergarten. "They used to date, but it sounded like it didn't end well, but her mother works in the department that Levi is trying to get a job in, so Bella has an influence on who gets hired—"

"So, nepotism," Gabe reflected.

"—therefore, I'll go to the wedding and all the events leading up to it so that Bella sees that he won't be leaving the city and will report back to her mom, and then Levi can get the job."

Jia stared at me with narrowed eyes, the way she always did when she was trying to figure out a problem. "Let me repeat what you just said. Levi has a hot ex whose mother can either hire him or not, and you've been assigned as his personal cockblock to make sure he gets this job."

I pursed my lips. I knew she would be too pessimistic.

"That's not fair, that's not who Levi is," I said, because that'd never been who Levi was. He dated girls, but he never led them on. It was always a few dates, and then it fizzled away the way dreams from the night before were forgotten throughout the day. It simply seemed like he wasn't interested in being a boyfriend. He always put his family first, spending every waking moment with them. Tying Claire and Rhea's shoes before school, helping Sarah edit her English papers, and cooking dinner the nights his mother tutored at the school nearby.

"Levi was my best friend," I explained.

"And he broke your heart, Dani. What kind of friend does that?" she asked. But if she was expecting an answer, she wasn't getting one. Levi *was* my best friend for years; I couldn't just say no to him. Not when I had the chance to be friends with him again and be part of his life. Not when we had gone through the same trauma, and he helped me climb out of the hole I had dug.

"You do realize that this is the complete opposite of a rom-com, right? As in, you're the other woman in the story—the one the writers add in for extra drama, not for the happily ever after," she spoke matter-of-factly.

I had seen almost every cheesy romance movie; I knew what she was talking about. And it wasn't the first time I had envisioned myself as the side character. But it hurt to hear it from her.

"Do you still love him?" Gabe asked, leaning forward on the couch across from me.

"I—no, no, no of course not," I said quickly. It'd been four *years.* Yes, my heart pumped blood fast enough to burst out of my shirt when I saw him. But that was from surprise and nostalgia.

"That was a lot of no's," he said warily.

"I'm going to need ice cream for this," Jia said, getting off the couch.

"Do you?" he asked again in a hushed tone, as if my answer would be different without Jia in the room.

He was right though, it usually was. Jia always had a strong opinion.

"No," I said with frustration. Frustration with myself. I ran a hand through my hair hoping the feeling would bring some type of serenity.

"Does he love her?" Gabe asked hesitantly, knowing the sensitive waters he was treading.

I bit my lip. "Yes." I knew that Levi said he wasn't trying to get Bella back, but that didn't mean he didn't want to. I saw the way he held her in the bar. I'd watched enough romance films to spot desire from a mile away.

"Have you ever thought that maybe he has feelings for you too. That after all these years, maybe he regretted saying no to you in high school?"

I had thought about it constantly, wondering if Levi had ever missed what we had. If he ever missed what we could have been. That maybe his longing gazes, unexpected gifts, and late-night calls were a sign of his returned affection. But no, they never were.

I shook my head. "You know the story; he couldn't have regretted it."

"I don't know, Dani. I saw the way that man grabbed your

face," Gabe said with a *I know what I'm talking about* look.

"How long were you watching us for?" I asked suspiciously, laughing.

"Long enough to make sure he wasn't an ax-murderer. But back to the subject: I saw the way he looked at you, and a man doesn't look at a woman like that if it doesn't mean something," he said with the tap of his finger in the air.

"Gabe, what do you know about men?!" Jia shouted from the kitchen.

He twisted in his seat, shouting, "Just because you watch k-dramas doesn't mean *you* know anything about men!"

"*Yes it does!*" Jia practically screamed.

I was laughing so hard that my stomach began to hurt. It was enough to subdue the nagging feeling in my belly after what Jia had said.

Was Levi really just using me? Or was Gabe right, and maybe Levi did regret what happened?

It didn't matter now. Because tomorrow I'd officially become Levi's girlfriend. Just not in the way High School Dani had dreamed of.

4

The wallpaper above her bed frame was glued in my brain the way it was glued against her walls. I got so close to running my fingers against it.

A wedding party softball game was what Levi had told me last night. Goosebumps had risen on my arms at those words, because to play softball in front of a group of people I didn't know was one thing. But to play in front of *Levi?* Well, I was screwed.

You would think this situation would be ideal seeing as I played softball in high school. But you would wrong. Because when it came to doing anything in front of him, I was a complete disaster. Anytime there was a chance of impressing him, my body failed me.

He used to try to come to my games every Saturday morning and I'd have to create some elaborate lie as to why he couldn't, because I'd only ever hit foul balls when he was there. Every time he came, I felt this intense pressure to be good, which made me *horrible*—like I wasn't leaving *home base* type of horrible. The only reason he knew I was good was the other players cheered me on in class the next day after I'd hit a home run for us—a game he wasn't there for, obviously.

Looking back at myself in my bedroom mirror, I sighed. A white tank and an open navy-blue button down that met the ends of my denim shorts felt like a sufficient outfit for a softball game while large cherries dangled from my ears—something I had picked up at the flea market weeks ago after leaving the fabric store.

My hair was just long enough to sweep into an elastic and through the back of Dad's old baseball cap. Moving closer to the mirror, I searched for any rogue eyebrow hairs and put lip gloss on, praying it'd keep me from gnawing on my bottom lip.

My mom always said that was a bad habit. She was like that; always wanting to make sure that she fixed every aspect of life, making up for the lack of a father figure the past few years. Her fixing ranged from convincing me not to get bangs to holding my hands when I cried on the kitchen floor over a ruined dress.

As stressful as it was to be a Type B raised by someone so Type A, she dedicated every free hour to me when I needed it. Did it often involve a mountain of sticky notes, putting plans in her Google Calendar, and creating to-do lists that I didn't think were appropriate for certain situations? Yes, but I loved her for it.

The sound of a car horn made me jump from the mirror and toward the window. Lifting the window up with a grunt, I leaned out to find Levi getting out of his car.

Sticking my head out the window, the greenery that climbed the brick of the home brushed my head as I tried to get a peek of his figure. I admired how the sunlight shined through the hanging trees, highlighting his brown hair, and making his eyes look like a mixed paint palette of shades of green. His eyes were this special hazel that could go from greens as vibrant as ivy to the deepest of browns. Curse my perfect eyesight.

"Coming!" I shouted, causing him to look up in surprise. A smile effortlessly spread across his face. Closing the window, I ran down the stairs right as I began to panic. Could I do this?

I could do this. I've made an entire dress from a pair of jeans in one night before. Was it ugly? Definitely. But did I do it? Yes, and that's all that mattered, so maybe I could handle this too.

But as I pulled the door open and saw him standing there—backwards baseball cap and a T-shirt with rolled up sleeves that clung to his biceps and all—my ability to speak expired. He looked so perfectly toned; you could see it in the way he gripped a drink or picked up his sisters. He had enough muscle that would allow him to pick you up, kiss you, and carry you over his shoulder. His dark, loose curls were just spilling out from under his hat, and his lips looked darker under the shade of the trees and townhouse awning.

I watched as his lips formed a small smile because—oh my gosh—I've been staring at him. How long had I been staring at him? *Speak, Daniella, speak.*

Trying to regain any possibility of looking normal, I said, "I'm almost done, I just need to finish my make-up." I led him out of the townhouse foyer and into Mandy's unit.

"Daniella Maria wearing makeup? To think I thought you hadn't changed," he teased as he took in the eclectic apartment around him. Windows that were ambushed by ivy; flower arrangements on every surface that stood; corduroy mauve couches decorating the living room we stood in. As well as the fashion magazines Mom and I shared, dancing along the coffee table.

"I haven't seen your family in a long time, I want to impress them," I shouted back in defense. Applying makeup and parking a car were one in the same to me. They were two difficult things that I only did when necessary. Parallel parking and applying eyeliner were not natural things. But if I was going to fail at softball today, then I at least needed to look presentable.

I jogged up the stairs to the bathroom, creating as much distance as I could between us to let my body return to a normal internal temperature.

"Especially when I have no idea what you've been saying about me the past few years," I said laughing, leaning over the sink, applying mascara. It was supposed to be a joke, but I kind of wasn't joking.

He laughed, the sound of his voice becoming clearer as he appeared in the doorway of my bathroom. "It's nothing bad, don't worry," he said shaking his head. I felt tempted to ask him what he had been saying. But as he leaned against the doorframe, I refrained from asking.

I had so many questions that I yearned to ask him, so many things I wanted to share with him. Every bone in my body wanted to revert to high school habits when we held hands and stood a footstep away from one another when speaking. But my present self was too nervous to even look him in the eye, let alone try to start a conversation about our past.

"Dani Daisy, we're home!"

"*Crap,*" I muttered, my lashes brushed mascara into my eyebrows because they reached so high. My mom and Mandy were supposed to be at the farmer's market for at least another two hours.

"Is that Linda?" Levi held a mischievous smile, obviously excited. Of course he would smile, my mother loved him, *everyone* loved him.

"I didn't tell her or my aunt about this," I said stressfully, referring to this fake dating plan we had.

"Mandy's here too?" he asked with even more excitement.

"What are the chances you'll go out the window?" I asked with a *I know it's a slim chance but please* look.

"We'll just tell them the truth, don't worry," he said nonchalantly.

But I was definitely worrying because my mom and Mandy watched me talk and cry over Levi for months after our high school prom. If they knew I was pretending to be his girlfriend, they'd be *horrified*, and an intervention would then be staged to address my sanity shortly after.

"We can't," I said quickly, grabbing his shirt to keep him from leaving.

"Why not?" he asked, his eyebrows knitting together.

Pulling together the first lie I could think of that would make sense, I said, "Because I just got out of a relationship."

"You did?" he pulled back. It was a partial truth. I had been on more than enough dates with this guy who was a TA for one of my classes. But it wasn't serious, and I was the one to end it. He never cut his hair and didn't wear enough deodorant; it was never going to work.

"Yes, and if they knew we were pretending to date, they would think I'm delusional and heartbroken." I spoke so swiftly that it didn't give him a moment to question it.

I left the bathroom hastily, trying to get as far away as I could from my bedroom and him before the two women downstairs would find us. Maybe he would stay in my room until I found a way to sneak him out.

"Hi, Mom, hi, Mandy," I said with a smile, finding them in the kitchen. "What happened with the farmer's market?" I asked, trying not to sound suspicious as I hugged them both.

Mandy sighed, waving her hands in circles as she spoke, "*What didn't happen*, is what you should be asking. Hal didn't have my cucumbers, your mother forgot her wallet here, I wore two different shoes"—yup, two different shoes were on her feet—"and then I—"

"Where are you going?" My mom cut Mandy off, noting the baseball cap and sneakers I wore like she was collecting evidence. Her tone was serious and motherly enough that Mandy didn't interrupt her.

Apparently, I didn't wear athleisure often.

I did my best to remain casual. I drew out my words until I knew what to say: "I … am …"

"Coming to play softball with my family," Levi spoke up behind me in the doorway of the kitchen, finishing what I definitely *did not* plan to say. A heart melting smile pressed into his sharp cheekbones with his hands in his pockets.

So much for waiting in my room.

"*Levi!*" My mom and Mandy jumped from their seats, running past me, enveloping him in a hug only women with motherly bones in their bodies could offer. He embraced them, his arms stretched around them with nostalgic love.

I couldn't help but admire the sight, but I also didn't want them to crush him any longer. "Let Levi breathe please," I said with an embarrassed smile.

My mom backed up, gripping his arms. "How have you been? How long are you staying? Are you going out?"

"As much as I would love to stay, Dani and I are actually going to Sarah's softball game—it's one of the wedding festivities." He put air quotes around the word *festivities*, followed by a laugh.

"*Sarah's getting married?*" Mandy asked hopefully, clasping her hands together.

"She is," he said with a smile, "end of May." Turning his head to focus his attention on … me, oh no. My face flushed as he said, "Dani will be there."

My eyes widened in the least discrete way possible. *Why* did he have to bring that up? The best option possible would have been to let them think we were just friends. Now—

"Oh, will she?" Mom looked at me pointedly for not keeping her in the loop. "Why is that?"

He glanced at me; a light smile and romantic look swept over his face as he said, "We're dating."

Oh god. This was a lot of feelings for only day one of fake dating. I would've believed him too from the way his eyes darkened, and voice softened. It felt romantic and intimate, as if we shared secrets before getting ready for bed together and knew what each other's lips tasted like.

If only it weren't for the image of Levi's hands on Bella last night.

"You're *what?!*" If my mom and Mandy were excited to see him, then they were over the moon about this. I hadn't seen her this happy since her dress was featured on the cover of *Vogue*.

"I never gave up hope on the two of you getting together! I knew you'd come around Levi!" Mandy shrieked as she gripped his arms in excitement.

Would I be overreacting right now if I walked into the first moving vehicle outside?

Instead, I avoided eye contact with him as he faced Mandy.

"When did this happen?" my mom asked with a smile on her face, but not nearly as loud as Mandy, who obviously questioned the circumstances of this situation.

But Levi and I hadn't planned this far, and she knew that my ability to lie on the spot wasn't the strongest. Fortunately for me though, lying about liking Levi wasn't a lie at all. And he also knew how to act in on-the-spot situations.

"We ran into each other a few weeks ago at the bar down the street and started catching up," he said effortlessly. "And then I invited her as my date to the wedding. Today is the first day of the pre-wedding events, but I'll make sure to have her home right after—"

"No, no, no. As long as you keep her safe, she can stay out for as long as she wants," Mandy squealed, like I was sixteen rather than twenty-two, with a smile bright enough to charge a solar panel. But it reminded me of how Levi and I *did* have to ask about curfews when we made plans in high school. I took it as my chance to rush us out before they could say anything else about my unrequited, embarrassing love life.

Leaping forward, I gave them each a kiss on the cheek, and grabbed the hem of Levi's shirt to drag him out.

5

Neck stiff, legs weak, eyes set on what we could've looked like
if you hadn't left

I watched Levi's left hand rest on the bottom of the steering wheel and his right extended over the shifter; his knees almost hit the wheel because his legs were so long.

"I'd have you drive if I had any confidence that you'd been practicing while in the city," he said with a child-like smile on his face, referring to the way he wasn't made to fit into such a low car.

"There's nothing wrong with being a bad driver," I said defensively. Why would I drive when there was the subway and taxis? I *hadn't* driven a car since moving into the city four years ago. But that was beside the point. He laughed as if he could read my exact thoughts. "At least I'm not a hoarder!" I shouted in defense.

For effect, I turned in the passenger's seat to wave at the abundance of books in the back seat, all stacked up like an unsteady, makeshift bookcase.

"Hey, hey, hey, don't try comparing my choice of storage to

your lack of human ability to drive," he said.

"I *can* drive, I just can't drive *well*. There's a difference and I have the license to prove it."

"I have no idea why though!"

But when he saw the unbothered look on my face, he came up with an example. "Do you remember the time you had to drive us to Junior Prom because I had a broken wrist? You saw a ladybug on the dashboard—screamed—and then took out half of the mailboxes on the street," he repeated, erupting in laughter at the look of shock on my face that he remembered. I hated ladybugs after accidentally eating one as a kid, finding a polka dotted wing in my teeth.

I instantly covered my face in embarrassment: *how* could I forget that day? Levi had held my face as I sobbed (because I just wrecked his passenger-side mirror), worried that I was hurt, not even concerned about his car. Along with the fact that one of those mailboxes was Cora Messing's; the girl he was dating at the time and going to Junior Prom with.

Cora not only gave him an earful about the demolished mailbox the next day, but for deciding not to go to prom because of how worked up I was. I felt horrible that he missed prom, but I also secretly hated Cora. She used to go out of her way to step on the toes of my leather shoes when talking to me.

"Don't remind me, I felt so horrible that night," I said shaking my head thinking about how much I cried that day. The tears were partly from the fact that I was going to have to watch him dance with another girl at prom. I also didn't look great in comparison to Cora after proving that I couldn't even drive.

"*I* felt horrible that night!" he urged with a hand against his chest, evidently trying to make me feel less embarrassed.

"I knew you hated driving, but I thought if I was in the car with you, you'd feel more comfortable. But I shouldn't have pushed you, and then I made you miss prom too, *God.*" He groaned.

I struggled not to focus on the curve of his jaw and the way his tongue slipped out to lick his lips.

"My dress looked so bad that night anyways, if anything, you saved me from embarrassing pictures and having to deal with Jared Miller trying to kiss me." I shivered at the thought, thinking about the goatee he was trying to grow and the pink dress I had tried designing.

He laughed in response to my verbal shiver. "There wasn't a guy at that school that deserved you," he said, briefly glancing at me before returning to the road.

Every cell on my skin warmed at his small look and sweet sentence. Gabe's statement returned to my head and made me wonder if maybe Levi cared about me now.

I changed the topic before I could say anything I'd regret. "I can't believe you still keep books in your car," I mentioned.

"Well, actually, I'm a TA now," he said with an introverted smile.

"Levi that's *amazing!* What's the class about?" I was eager to hear.

"It's 'Reading Jane Austen,' so I've been trying to read her entire work to have a broader perspective on the themes and voices that aren't solely *Pride and Prejudice*, ya know? For example," he mulled over an accordion of thoughts before a light bulb went off, "the way moral judgement is highlighted in almost all of her protagonists. The whole class is women who I assume love Austen, so I want to know what I'm talking about." He moved his hands across the steering wheel as he spoke.

"The professor has given me a lot of say which has been incredible; I'm allowed to run portions of the class, along with evaluations. It's really, really great." He beamed warm light that a summer night sunset couldn't have even crafted. He always had this overwhelming respect for literature. But it made me question his interest in the journalist position with *The New York Times*. If he was dedicating all this time to becoming a teacher, then why would this position matter so much to him?

"That's amazing, Levi, you deserve it." I spoke with my entire heart, trying to escape any sadness. To know that I missed out on the day he was told he got the position, and not being there to hear about his first week, gave me an anxious stomachache. But that was my fault. I was the one that decided to distance myself.

"I want to tell you more about it, but we're almost at the field, and I think we need a game plan," he said.

"A game plan?"

"In case anyone asks us questions, about us dating," he said, turning to me for confirmation.

"Wait, did you not tell your family that we're dating?" My voice iced over with the same alarm that arose in high school right before we got into an argument.

I assumed that he had told his family beforehand—how we rekindled our connection, where our first date was, how I was the same person he knew all those years ago but better—all of the lies I would fail to uphold and make up! The last thing I assumed was to be waltzing into this party as an unexpected surprise.

"Well, Jeff does. I had to make sure that I could bring a plus-one to the wedding—it was an easy yes," Levi rushed apologetically.

"No one knows I'm coming ..." I repeated with a horrified look.

He must have registered my concern as I finished my sentence because he looked regretful, trying to explain his intention. "I thought it would be a fun surprise, they could use it, especially with Jeff there."

The comment made me laugh despite my anxiety. It's not that Jeff was necessarily bad, he just wasn't ... great. I felt guilty for even thinking of this—I swear I'd never said it aloud—but he was the type of guy who couldn't hold a conversation longer than five minutes and would choose football every Sunday before you and knew he could because he had dreamy eyes.

"So, we need to catch up on the past four years of one another's lives in ..."

I checked the ETA on his phone.

"Five minutes?"

"I know you that still love strawberry shortcake and hate ladybugs. Your driving skills are not listed on *any* resume. You're studying design, and I'm going to take a wild guess here and assume you still listen to ABBA like a Christian listens to the Bible," he said with a hint of a smirk. His eyes darted to mine for a moment before they returned to the road. The brownstones and burly trees with their delicate pink flowers flew by.

"You love 'Waterloo' too!" I fired back. I wasn't the only ABBA fan in this car. I've seen him almost lose a vocal cord screaming to 'Dancing Queen'.

"Well, obviously, who doesn't love 'Waterloo'?" he smirked. "What else did I miss?"

"I'm working at Mandy's florist shop." It was called Daisy's, a tribute to my middle name. Daisies were never my favorite flower though. That'd be a bit cliché, wouldn't it? It felt arrogant to enjoy something that had to do with myself. I preferred cornflower blue hydrangeas, quartz pink tulips, and crimson red bleeding hearts.

"I'm in the middle of applying to grad schools, and I'm finishing up my capstone." *Finishing up* was a slight exaggeration. It was more like rushing to get the last five dresses completed before the runway exhibit because I'd had zero inspiration.

"You're TA'ing and going to NYU, meaning you ended up majoring in English," I repeated.

"And secondary education."

I assumed he wanted to go into journalism because of the job Bella's mom was offering. But he was always great with his sisters, and kids in general. It made perfect sense; it was so undeniably Levi. His mother taught elementary while we were in high school as well.

My heart skipped a beat. When had he become such an adult? It seemed like yesterday we were applying to colleges together.

His jaw tightened as he focused on the road and the turn ahead. His hands brushed the wheel; two thin gold rings decorated his middle and index finger, and his typical watch rested on his wrist.

"Are you still studying French?" I remembered in high school that he was teetering on being fluent. He wanted to get into French literature because the translations into English lost a lot of the important underlying meanings in the original French versions.

"Bien sûr." The words fell from his mouth like melted chocolate dripping from fresh fruit. I wanted to wake up to that voice and listen to it while I sewed and draped fabric. I wanted him to whisper to me in French as I put together bouquets of bleeding hearts, like a protagonist in a black and white French film.

That was a bit much, apologies.

"And we're here," he said as we pulled into a sandy parking lot, baseball fields extending across the area.

I got out of the car and watched as he pulled out two softball bats and threw one over his shoulder likes he'd played the game his whole life. The worst part of this was that *I* had played this game my whole life, but there was no way it was going to look like that.

There was a reason I never let him come to any of my softball games.

6

*Do you hear that? That's the sound of my heart knocking against
my chest at the sight of you*

"Levi!" Levi's younger sisters screamed with joy, running across
the field into his arms. Their ponytails bounced in the wind and
their sneakers lit up pink as their small feet stamped the ground.

I knew four years meant a lot more to children than to adults,
but it was proof in how they looked. They were not only four
inches taller from the last time I had seen them, but they had
grown into the shape of their noses and lost the extra fat around
their cheeks that clung to them as kids. They were thin like their
older sister but had darker hair. Rhea had brunette bangs and
chopped hair at her shoulders, while Claire's was parted down the
middle and much longer.

"My girls!" Levi shouted back as he crouched down to
anticipate their hugs. As they ran into his chest, his left arm
wrapped around Rhea and his right around Claire, lifting the girls
in the air with a spin. Their giggles were quickly followed by
Rhea's shriek to slow down in between fits of laughter.

It was like looking into a picture frame from the outside. His
love for his family was so abundant that I wished I could bottle it.

But despite the overwhelming warmth I felt my heart swell with, I stood to the side by the car, not wanting to interrupt.

He placed them back on the ground, crouching forward to talk to them. Each of his hands were assigned to one of their small ones as he spoke.

"I brought someone special with me," he said with an ounce of excitement, as if he'd brought the girls a small horse topped with a bow rather than an old friend from high school.

Kneading at the bottom of my shorts like dough, I waited for the end of his sentence, nervous for the girls' reactions, or highly possible lack thereof.

What *were* the chances of the twins remembering me? They were four the last time I saw them. I didn't know what reaction he was expecting from them, but there was no way—

"Daisy!" the girls shrieked as they turned their heads and followed his gaze towards me.

At the sound of my old nickname, my cheeks hurt from the smile that spread across my face as the girls ran into my arms.

There wasn't much crouching involved seeing as the elementary school-aged twins caught up to my height. But as I leaned over, and squeezed them like they'd disappear if I didn't hold on tight enough, all the memories from high school rushed back.

Taking the girls to soccer practices on Thursday nights with him; baking cupcakes together for the movies to hide in their backpacks; letting them paint my and Levi's nails when they were sad.

This was why I'd bottled up my feelings for him for so long, because if, and when, he rejected me, this would all go away: Levi and everything he came with.

And it did. It had all gone away.

"I missed you both *so much*." Their arms wrapped around my torso in a bone crushing hug. "I didn't think you'd remember me!" I said honestly. We were always honest with one another. I never understood the point of lying to kids. I wanted them to know I was there for them, through thick and thin, and that they could tell me everything. I cared for them as much as I cared for Levi.

I remembered when they used to tell me that Levi and I should get married—they'd made it very known that they didn't like his girlfriends. I'd always held that information close to my heart, knowing that his family liked me so much. But I never dared to share that with him, despite always secretly hoping he'd feel the same way.

"We couldn't," Rhea whispered as she pulled away, a sweet smile on her face. "Levi talks about you *all the time*." I must've not hidden my surprise well because Rhea laughed so hard that it made her nose crinkle.

"Did you meet Bella?" Claire asked quietly, for obvious reasons, even turning to look at Levi. He cocked an eyebrow at the suspicious look from his sister.

I tried to hide any look of surprise, wanting to stay neutral on the topic of his love life. "I did," I said. "She's very pretty." My heart squeezed with jealousy at the statement.

Rhea tipped her head in thought, considering my statement. "Yeah, I guess," she settled with a sigh. She brushed away her chestnut-colored bangs in the process. The two girls weren't identical twins, but they had the same brown hair and heart-shaped faces.

"I apologize to break up the reunion." Levi's voice came from behind me making me jolt, especially as his clasped onto my shoulders. "But we have a game to win."

He had explained in the car that the game was between the two wedding parties: Jeff's family and groomsmen versus Sarah's. Jeff's party consisted of his two brothers, his parents, and his six groomsmen. Sarah's included her mom, Levi, six bridesmaids (including Bella), and ... me, unfortunately. (The girls were too young to be put in the line of fire of thrown softballs, so they would be watching from the side.)

I could already feel my hands clamming up as we made our way to the field, the girls leading the way. It's not like this game was a big deal, I knew, trust me. It's the fact that I was playing in front of Levi and his past—present? —lover.

I may have just gagged a bit.

You can't blame me for being worried. Who wouldn't want to impress someone they're interested in? Especially when I'd possibly be compared to Bella the entire time.

As if on cue, I watched her come into view. She was sat on one of the benches in the dugout lacing up her sneakers. She wore denim cutoffs, a baseball jersey, and blonde hair in an elastic. She looked like one of those models on a baseball costume package.

Bella snapped her head up, spotting Levi's presence I assumed, giving him a big smile and wave before she got up to walk towards us—him. It was like watching the star of a romance film make her entrance.

I immediately looked down at my tank top and linen button down, its fabric shaping my short torso but doing nothing for my boobs. I looked back at Bella's full chest to compare, as if that would help my case—worst idea ever.

Was this some sick joke? She had to have big boobs? Really? *What is it like to be that beautiful?*

Guys didn't care that much about boob size anymore, right?

I already imagined Jia and Gabe's responses: "Why the hell would you think *that? Do you not know the male population?*"

It shouldn't matter; it's the 21st century and I shouldn't look at my body as something to satisfy a man.

But then I looked up at Levi as Bella approached him. All dreamy gazes and sensual smiles as he watched her.

There was a pinch that clung to my heart. I instantly wanted to curl into a ball; my hand instinctively went to my shorter ponytail before my arms held each other in front of my chest. Maybe I should've put on more makeup or worn a thicker bra.

"Hello Levi," Bella said as she embraced him. Did her voice always sound sensual?

Levi returned the embrace, but his words were much more formal, as if he were trying to keep emotional distance. "It's nice to see you. You remember Dani," Levi said kindly as reached his hand out for mine, where I stood several feet away, trying to stand out of the way.

I subdued any look of expression that my face was prepared to make at Levi's outreached hand as I placed my hand in his, and allowed him to pull me forward, the plan already forgotten.

"Hi …" I paused for a moment, unsure of how to refer to her, "Bella, it's nice to formally meet you," I said as nicely as possible, and reached out with my free hand.

I watched as she looked at my hand, assessing the gesture. I expected her to reach out with a hand as well, but instead she bypassed my hand and leaned in for a hug. *Not what I was expecting.*

"How old are you, sixty-five? Who shakes hands anymore?" Bella said with her arms around me and laughing, which somehow making it sound like less of a dig.

I responded the only way I knew how to: laughing with her.

"Ready to play some ball, *Dani?*" Bella asked, a smirk on her face that made her look like she could take a good picture at any angle. But the way she said my name felt like the way a kid mocked an adult when you told them to do something.

"Oh, she's ready," he said confidently. "Dani was the best on her team when we were in high school."

"We'll see about that," Bella said.

Oh yes, we will definitely see about that.

Fortunately for me, my body hadn't lost the ability to catch a ball. Specifically, because Levi was too busy standing at first base to see me. But unfortunately, my body did as I expected, which was lose all ability to hit a ball.

My team made the decision that I would only be allowed to bat one more time, seeing as the first three times I did, I couldn't even make contact with the ball. Which wouldn't have mattered if there weren't last minute stakes added to the game by Jeff's wedding party.

"The winning team gets their own rooms at the beach house, and the losing time has to share the rest," one of Jeff's friends had said—or shouted more like, with a beer in his hand. I didn't think that—whatever *that* is—would have anything to do with me, but it must've for the rest of the wedding party there, because I had never seen a group of men get so competitive before.

"Let's go, Dani!" Levi cheered from the dugout, a huge smile on his face, beads of sweat on his temples. His curls stuck to his forehead from the two homeruns he'd just made.

Whereas I stood on homebase; the only one with softball experience, and nothing to show for it.

I smiled back at him as I positioned my hands on the bat. *Come on, Daniella. Dad would be disappointed; you can do better than this. Just one good hit, that's all you need to save yourself.*

As I lined up the bat up, one of Jeff's groomsmen threw the ball and I *finally* made contact with the ball. But not good enough.

"Foul!" another groomsman shouted from behind me.

As they retrieved the ball, I lined up again. If I'd hit the ball once, I could do it again.

As the ball flew towards me, I swung and the bat came into contact with the ball again, the pressure increasing against my closed fist to follow through with the swing.

Now, the next thing that happened felt as if it took place in slow motion. But if you asked Bella, she would not have said it happened slowly.

As quickly as the ball approached me, it just as quickly flew away from me after I hit it … straight towards Bella.

I don't think any of us realized how closely it was getting to her, especially since everyone on my team was cheering because of how high the ball went in the air. But there were two seconds suspended in the air where we all realized where it was going.

And then the field was filled by Bella's screams.

I wasn't sure if she was screaming before it hit her, but all I knew was that Levi's ex-girlfriend was currently lying on the ground because I'd hit a ball off her head.

I threw my hands over my mouth in shock—I did not just do that, I did not just do that, I did *not just do that.*

Everyone ran towards her, except the twins, who I saw laughing from their seats.

Well, at least I know two people won't hate me after this.

My physical reaction was delayed compared to everyone else's, so as I started approaching, everyone was already swarming her. With Levi at the center of the crowd, holding up Bella's head, where an egg-like bruise was already beginning to form.

"I am so, *so* sorry, Bella, I had no idea that was going to happen," I uttered with sincerity. I waited for her response, filled with sheer fear for her reaction to my presence.

She shook her head, and began to sit up with Levi's support, her hand clutched to her brow. "It's alright, don't worry, I should've moved faster," she said with a small smile. "Looks like my chance at modeling is over." Everyone laughed at the joke, which lightened the tense mood.

"I am so incredibly sorry," I repeated, truly feeling horrible.

"I think I'm done for the day."

"Is that defeat I hear!" another groomsman of Jeff shouted.

Crap.

"I think it is!" another responded.

"Looks like we'll be sharing a room," Rhea said, as she suddenly appeared at my right.

"Oh, no, I don't think I'm involved in that," I said.

"You're part of the wedding party though, aren't you? That means you'll be coming to the beach house," Rhea explained.

"No, no, I think I'm just invited. I'm not a bridesmaid."

"But you're dating Levi now!"

I watched as heads turned around us like dolls in a horror film as a reaction to Rhea's words. *Double crap.* Levi hadn't told everyone we were dating, let alone that I was going to be here today.

I was instantly crushed in a hug by Sarah as she shouted, *"Finally!"*

As happy as I was that Levi's family approved of me this much, I was beyond embarrassed. I could only imagine how pathetic I looked right now. Each of our families had been hoping we would date for years, especially when they all knew how I felt about him, and they were finally getting that wish.

But Levi was still uninterested.

7

Blue hydrangeas, pink tulips, red bleeding hearts

Hi Dad. Remember my first month at fashion school when I was so nervous that I accidentally sewed that girl's dress into a pair of denim pants I was making? Well, today was somehow so much worse.

I began freshman year of high school incredibly depressed. I know what you're thinking: wasn't the depression supposed to start during high school, not before it? Well, a month before my first day, Dad passed away from cancer. The wake, funeral, and pity greetings the nights after felt like some nightmare I couldn't wake up from.

It was the hardest year of my life to date. I know that's not saying much for someone who has only been alive for twenty-two years, but it felt like I had cried so much over Dad's passing that I no longer had room in my heart for any other sadness. My body couldn't imagine any event or moment being any worse than that, so the tears slowly ran out and I only knew grief.

Until I met Levi.

Levi became a major part of my grieving. He hadn't turned my life around the way Prince Charming transformed Cinderella's life, but he taught me how to look for the positives again. How to cope and move on without forgetting. Because that's what everyone wants you to do after you lose someone: move on. But how were you supposed to just move on? How were you supposed to simply pretend like they never existed and try to be happy when they were no longer here?

I met Levi the first day of high school; we ended up in two classes together, one we each dreaded. Levi thrived in English, which, to this day, I still hated writing papers. While I thrived in our sewing elective, which he claimed to have chosen the class because it looked good on a college application. Two months later, he confessed that it was really to help his mother with fixing his sisters' sports uniforms.

The first week of class posed to be an issue for the both of us, and that's when we realized we could help one another with our weaknesses by providing our strengths. Afterschool sewing lessons and essay editing sessions slowly became eating lunch together, celebrating birthdays, and Sunday family dinners. We were best friends, and we only got closer when we realized we were both grieving.

Levi had lost his dad a few years prior, so he understood what it was like. He understood that fear of forgetting and the struggle to be happy as if it were betrayal. He told me something a therapist taught him to do when he was sad: to write. To just write out everything on paper that was going on in your head as if you were writing an autobiography.

I told my mom about this advice Levi had given me over dinner at his house that day—I think that's the day she fell in love with him like I slowly did.

Ever since then, I typed emails to Dad anytime I needed him.

The first few years of writing the emails were often followed by a string of sobs. I remembered getting an email from the fashion university I applied to, accompanied by an acceptance letter senior year. The happiness quickly disappeared once I realized that I wouldn't witness him shout with excitement or lift me up with a hug because I'd never be able to tell him. He would never get to know.

So, I wrote him an email about it, like he was a pen pal that would respond back.

Knowing that he wouldn't be there and would never read these emails often brought on another wave of sadness. But it's the only way I could remember him.

Something that no one talks about when a loved one passes, is that when the years go by, it feels as if they never truly existed, like it was another life. My memories had been slipping away like chapters in a good book with each passed day. No one tells you that the reality of them actually being gone doesn't kick in until you try to call them and realize … you can't, that you can never call them again. That they aren't just gone for a moment, but they're gone for the rest of *your* moments.

Those years also brought peace though, as much as the sadness lingered. I slowly felt content because it was no longer a surprise when he wasn't home; time had healed that pain. He was happier this way, not having to undergo chemo and sad looks from visitors. Now when I wrote emails, it wasn't a way for me to get out my thoughts, but a way to share them, almost like a diary.

Sitting at the desk in front of my window, I swatted away the moths that tried coming into the room, attracted to the strawberry lamp lit beside me. The warm night air of May in New York was too beautiful to pass up, so I kept the window open as I continued typing on my laptop, wrapped in blankets like an overdecorated couch in Pottery Barn.

I managed to hit Levi's ex—Bella—in the head with a softball today. You would've laughed because it was a really good hit—it looked like a homerun—beside the point, I felt horrible. She was so understanding after, but I could feel everyone's eyes on me as the bruise started forming on her forehead. I was so embarrassed that it took every muscle in my body not to leave the field and grab a cab. Meaning I had to get back into a car with Levi after all of that. You can probably guess how that went: awkward silence, reassurance, pity, and more silence. Just wait though, it gets worse! When we got to Mandy's, he dropped me off, got out of the car, and as I opened the door, it hit him in the head.

I hit Levi in the head with the car door. I will now proceed to jump out of the window in front of me.

I've never apologized so much in one day. I hadn't realized he was going to come around to open the door for me! I'm praying to every Skin God out there that he doesn't wake up with a bruise tomorrow. I practically ran into the house after that, especially when he turned down my offer to come in for a bag of ice.

Three hours of softball, two (possibly) bruised heads, and one sob fest later, I'm seated questioning: how on Earth am I going to handle Sunday dinner tomorrow?

Love, Daisy

8

I got so close to running my fingers against it

"Wear that top, it makes your boobs look better," Gabe recommended as he lounged on my bed.

I hadn't exactly asked for his and Jia's help on what to wear. They somehow ended up here an hour ago after a group call went from "Can you hang out?" to "What do you mean you're going to Levi's tonight and don't know what you're wearing yet?" Ten minutes later and they were at my door with bags of Trader Joe's chips and Pinterest boards.

Thirty-five minutes left to figure out what to wear and put in my purse before I needed to head to Daisy's for a shift, so time was dwindling here. I made a face at Gabe's suggestion; bringing attention to my boobs was the last thing I needed at a family dinner.

"Stop objectifying her." Jia threw one of my embroidered pillows straight at Gabe's head.

Gabe argued, "I'm not objectifying her. If anything, this is an FU to the world because she has such nice boobs!"

"What do you know about boobs?" she asked with skepticism.

"Don't act like we didn't watch *Burlesque* together." Gabe silenced her with narrowed eyes.

Despite my stress, I laughed, failing to stay on track. Jia got up and shoved her arms into my closet as if she was parting the sea. "Let the professional do her job. And while I do that, you're going to pack your purse and put on the best tasting lipstick you've got."

I thought I was going to vomit with anxiety after Jia built up the idea of Levi and I kissing tonight. It was the last thing I had considered. But once she said it, it made sense. Couples did that, obviously.

But not in front of the families, right?

Ringing out the last customer at Daisy's before switching the sign to *Closed*, I finished wrapping a bouquet of white roses in brown paper as I spotted Levi walk in.

Three times. That was how many times I'd seen him this week. The only three times in the past four years, yet I still couldn't keep my nerves together when he entered the room. He wore a white button down with short sleeves, a few buttons left open at the top, with navy blue trousers. His usual watch gripped his wrist, which led your eyes to the muscles in his forearm and bicep. If I didn't have 20/20 vision, I would think it was in slow motion, the way his bicep flexed as he opened the door, and ran a hand through his thick, short, Hugh Grant-like brunette waves.

I pressed my damp palms against my pale blue midi skirt, decorated in small peonies, paired with a white tank that covered the tips of my shoulders and edges of my collarbones.

"Hey," he said in a soft voice.

"Hey, thanks for picking me up," I smiled, turning around while folding excess brown paper.

"Of course," he said, and put his hands in his trouser pockets as he gazed around the small store.

"Your mom likes hydrangeas, right?"

"How do you possibly remember that?" he asked with surprise.

"Knowing everyone's favorite flower is my party trick," I shrugged my shoulders with a smile like it was as cool as being able to open a beer bottle with your teeth.

"Can you do mine?"

I looked up for a quick moment. "You're the exception."

"Am I?"

When wasn't he the exception?

After a moment of silence, he spoke up. "Can I help with anything?"

As I finished tying twine around another group of flowers, I asked, "Would you mind grabbing my bag?"

"Of course." He lifted my crochet strawberry bag—a purse I made during my crocheting phase in high school—and eyed it. For a moment, I questioned if he recognized it, but no. "What's in this bag?" You would think he asked *are there bricks in here?*

The way the purse slumped under his hand, the yarn carrying the weight of its contents, did make it look fairly heavy. "Umm, just my Kindle, an apple, a few scrunchies, my water, a sandwich, a sewing kit—"

"A sewing kit?"

"—and a second pair of earrings in case I lose mine."

Liana Cincotti

"You know we'll feed you, right? I won't let you starve. We are going over for *dinner*."

I rolled my eyes. "I told Sarah I'd show her my Kindle after trying to convince her she needed one; Rhea said she's never seen a scrunchie before; Claire said she had a hole in her skirt; and I get extra hungry," I finished reading off my mental list from yesterday's conversations at the game.

When I was relieved of having to remember everything, I looked back at him. His lips were partly separated with … surprise? Like I'd perplexed him.

"You do perplex me," he responded. *I said that aloud?* I watched as he put the purse over his shoulder and walked to the car without another word.

9

And that kiss ... I think about it
all the time

My top was starting to feel tighter as we arrived at Levi's house—not the one I grew up going to after school though. After we graduated, Trish, Levi's mother, had completed her real estate license, left teaching, and became a real estate agent full time in the city. Based on the front of her new home, it must have been a success.

I made sure to take a moment before opening the passenger door, knowing that he was going to open it this time. Don't worry, there was no bruise on his forehead after yesterday's *other* incident.

The front door to the large townhouse was black, matching the lamp posts lining the quiet street tonight. His tan skin had a golden hue under the dark sky and moonlight. It was as if the moon followed him everywhere he went simply because he was more beautiful than the sun.

"Do I look okay?" Levi asked with concern, evidently because of the way I looked at him. I needed to learn to stop staring at him and train myself like some conditioned dog in a Pavlov experiment, because apparently, I couldn't contain myself.

"Yes? Yes, of course you do! You always do," I rushed to answer.

He laughed and his face lit up at my enthusiasm. "I appreciate the reassurance." Thankfully, he didn't realize just how genuine I was being in that response.

Reaching the door, I clutched the hydrangeas to my chest with my teenage-level anxiety. Levi stood at my side as he knocked on the door with pastries in hand.

Before anyone reached the door, Levi leaned down towards my ear and whispered, "I know you didn't ask, but you look okay too. Beautiful, actually."

My heart sprung forward through my chest the same way cold rain hit asphalt on a stormy night.

Tonight was going to be more difficult than I had expected.

After I'd sewn Claire's skirt—"Dani, I can do it," Levi argued apologetically—shown Sarah how Kindles worked, and given Rhea my new, unused pack of scrunchies, we were finally sitting down for dinner. Levi's mother's dining room was massive, but not in the way that it felt rich. Rather, it was made for a family that invited over loud cousins, social aunts, friendly neighbors, and playdates that involved table space for crafts. From the hardwood to the mismatching plates and family members talking over one another. It was what one hoped for in a Sunday family dinner.

I sat with Levi on my right, and Rhea and Claire on my left. There were a few different conversations taking place around the table; Levi was currently talking with a cousin about grad school.

But I sat distracted, looking around the room to find a head of strawberry blonde hair. I hadn't asked Levi about whether Bella would be here tonight because I didn't want to come off concerned. When I came up empty, I released a breath I didn't realize I was holding because she wasn't here. Only Sarah's other bridesmaids sat with us: Nicole, Delanie, and Aparna.

My peace didn't last long because someone said my name from the other side of the table.

Swallowing the food that I'd just stuffed into my mouth, I squeaked, "Excuse me?"

"I was just telling my sister how gorgeous the hydrangeas are that you brought me." Trish wore a warm smile the way a figure skater wore skates; the two were meant to go together.

"They're very popular this time of year," I responded with a smile, hopefully as warm.

"I hope you don't think that you have to bring them over just because you're dating Levi."

My cheeks heated, especially because everyone chose to stop their conversations to hear this one since Trish was speaking to me from across the length of the table.

"I really don't mind." I shook my head.

"I'm just happy Levi has finally come to his senses," she said, exasperated. "I never approved of any of the other girls he was with."

Oh my gosh, this could not get more embarrassing.

"Alright, Mom, I think we get that you haven't approved of my dating life," Levi intervened casually, trying to save me.

"I'm done, I'm done," she said, placing her palms up in surrender. "Has he told you about the book he published?"

A book? I couldn't hide my look of astonishment. This was a dream of his for years. "You did *what?*"

His angular jaw turned pink as he shielded his face with his hands and shook his head. "I did no such thing," he argued as his voice came out gravelly under his palms. I had the sudden urge to pull his hands off of his face and kiss his embarrassed face. My spine tightened—*stop*—I pressed down harder on those teenage thoughts.

Trish rolled her eyes at her son's lack of ability to boast. "Yes, he did."

"It's nothing groundbreaking." Finally pulling his palms from his face, he nursed the back of his neck. He used to always do that when he was stressed or embarrassed. I saw it whenever we watched his sisters together; nervous that they were going to trip or fall or combust into thin air.

"What is it about?" I asked with excitement and curiosity all in one.

"*Love*," Rhea rushed to say from beside me, evidently excited to embarrass her older brother even more. But now my cheeks were as pink as my nails.

"It's only a few poems, that's all," he said casually, as if it wasn't something to be proud of. I itched to ask him if I could read them. But I didn't want to overstep.

"You wrote a collection of poems? That's incredible," I said earnestly, extending my hand to his knee. It was only a quick gesture to show my amazement, nothing else. But his hand briefly landed on mine in a friendly manner, and the pad of his thumb ran along the back of my hand, sending goosebumps up my arm.

It was like no time had passed in that quiet moment.

"Thank you, Dani," he responded. It was only a few words, but I could feel his heart in them.

Before I had the chance to have heart palpitations, I asked Trish, "Have you read them?"

But it wasn't Trish that responded. "They're in French," Levi interjected shyly.

My jaw dropped. "You wrote them *in French?*" French. Love. Poems. Written by Levi. You've got to be joking.

Well, that confirmed my curiosity on how well spoken he was in the language.

He nodded in response. I sat there in disbelief. "You're amazing." I said it with my whole heart. I didn't ask to read them, as much as I was even more intrigued now. I didn't want to push; he'd offer if he wanted me to.

His eye lit up, accompanying his bright smile. I felt seen in that moment, and I would've slept in that feeling if it weren't for the fact that it was all pretend.

The night from there was smooth; I answered several questions about myself for various family members of Levi's, ate more food, and witnessed Levi be Levi. It was like having déjà vu all night; watching him pick up the twins, clean up after dinner, and take care of his mother. The same moments I had witnessed when we were younger.

With his dad passing away so long ago, it made him a father figure to all the women in his life. He became the constantly moving gear that kept everyone working together. But as much as it made him independent, it also turned him into a puzzle, made of pieces of each woman.

He had Rhea's silliness, Claire's thoughtfulness, and Sarah's tenacity. He supported and cared for them all, but they gave away pieces of themselves to him over the years.

As he made his rounds through the house, saying goodbye to the family members spending the night here, I got a text from Gabe.

Gabe: How's it going?

Dani: Good! About to leave now.

Gabe: Perfect, I just caught you. Leave your purse.

Dani: Excuse me?

Gabe: Leave. Your. Purse.

Dani: Yes, I can read, thank you. Why would I do that???

Gabe: I saw this thing in a movie once where the girl left her purse at a guy's house on purpose and if the guy brought the purse back to her the next day, it meant he was into you. But if he doesn't, then it's a lost cause. Bam. Mission How To Find Out If Levi Is Into Dani complete.

Dani: You're insane.

Gabe: You're saying you don't want to know?

Dani: I do know! Levi's not into me.

Gabe's name appeared on my phone, flashing. I accepted the call. "Yes," I sighed.

"Leave the purse then if you're so sure," Gabe said on the other side of the receiver.

"And if I don't?"

"Then I'll tell Levi about the tongue story."

I snorted; he'd caught me off guard with his serious tone. *"About the thing I did with my tongue?"* I quoted, laughing. Now Gabe was just making fun of me. The tongue story was an inside joke; I kissed a guy sophomore year of college who, unexpectedly, had a tongue ring. And I may have possibly touched his piercing with my tongue ... I thought it was going to be hot! But instead, it made the guy cry because the piercing had been so new. Jia and Gabe thought it was hilarious, so anytime one of us kissed someone, they always asked if we, "did that thing with our tongue?" It was a habit for one of us to laugh at the joke.

"You'd never tell him; you want this relationship to happen more than High School Me. But I'll leave my purse to make you happy."

I ended the call and pulled my keys out of the bag, reluctantly leaving the bag on the couch near the foyer.

I didn't know where Gabe was getting this idea of Levi being interested in me when Levi had been writing love poems the past four years about the numerous women he'd dated. But fine, I'd humor him to prove a point.

On the drive back, we chatted about his family and plans for the week. It was nice. It was always nice talking to him. But I had this nagging feeling behind my rib cage; my mind continuously going back to the love poems.

He walked me up the steps of the brownstone in the darkness, every light in every shop nearby turned off. That didn't change as we reached the top of the stairs since the motion sensor light was still broken from the time Gabe tried throwing something into my window, and instead smashed the light.

As we stood there in the dark, the nagging got heavier. It felt like there would never be a better time to ask. "Levi," I prompted, looking up at him.

He looked at me in wonder, his brows slightly furrowed. His eye contact made my nervousness rise. I turned away for a moment and pulled my hair to one side over my shoulder. Which was useless because the length was just short enough that it missed and fell back.

His loose curls fell forward, getting in the way of his eyes as his head was tilted down to meet mine. Without thinking, I brushed the hair out of his face, grazing my finger against his skin. His hair was as soft as it looked. His eyes followed my hand as if I was going to do more.

I was thankful for the shield the night sky granted me on those steps because I couldn't stop staring at his lips. The way his tongue ran over them, and the deep color they took in the dark, like he was in a black and white film.

"Sorry," I whispered. Apologizing for touching him, I reiterated, "I should've asked."

"Don't say sorry, you don't ever need to ask," he whispered in a husky voice. My skin hummed at the tone of his voice and the closeness of our bodies.

I didn't know how to react. Luckily, he picked the conversation back up. "What were you going to say?"

If it weren't for the complete darkness we stood in and the intense awareness of no one else around, I think I would've just said that I had forgotten. "Were the poems about Bella?"

He must've not understood what I was asking about at first, because he didn't answer immediately. After a moment that felt like minutes, he said, "Yes."

My heart folded in on itself like the air was ripped from my gut. I shouldn't have asked. I shouldn't have asked. Who did I think was?

I wasn't sure how he took my lack of response, and I didn't care in that moment because I felt so much sadness for thinking he had thought about me all of these years.

He placed a hand on my bicep as he leaned in and kissed my forehead, sending a chill down my spine. "Good night, Daniella."

It felt equivalent to a rejection.

10

Don't worry if the flowers pass, I'll be right there to plant you more

The next morning, I was a pile of bones trying to lift myself out of bed. A headache knocked on the front of my forehead from last night's events as I got ready for the day.

I know, this was profoundly dramatic; I'd only seen Levi three times. But that's what made it dramatic: I'd seen him three days in a row for the first time in four years. And I hadn't stopped thinking about him at all these four years.

Seeing him again had brought back every fiber in my body that found him attractive in high school. But I needed it to be different now. I needed to realize that this was not going to end in a romantic happily ever after. Levi and I were meant to be friends, that's all.

So, I took an Advil, washed my face, refrained from writing Dad an email, and left for class. The walk to the university was too long, so it required a train in between. But the walk from there was beautiful this time of year. New York in the springtime was ethereal. It's why all the best romance movies were set in New York during this season, i.e., *How to Lose a Guy in Ten Days, Maid in*

Manhattan, Enchanted, et cetera. With its flowers and parks full of greenery; trees lining the cozy neighborhoods that you see on your walk to the bagel shop around the corner.

Which is where I was headed now. Every Monday morning like clockwork.

"Hi Marty!" I greeted the older gentleman rolling dough behind the counter.

"Dani! How are you? Are we getting the usual?"

"The usual would be perfect, please."

"Half a dozen French toast bagels it is." He quickly moved to the glass case that separated us, pulling out six bagels and bagging them.

Classes ran Monday through Friday, and I had 9 a.m.'s every one of those mornings. Ironically enough, the classes tended to be pretty small, so each of my 9 a.m.'s had the same five girls. So we each assigned ourselves a day of the week to bring something for everyone. Mondays were my day with bagels as my go-to. Some of the girls brought egg sandwiches, some did pastries, and others even cooked us breakfast. I was always eager to see what Daya cooked—last week was strawberry pancakes.

You'd think coffee was a go-to, especially since we were at the end of senior year, crippling under procrastination and exhaustion. But the coffee Vera had spilled on a dress she spent two weeks working on was so traumatizing for everyone that we only drink water in the room now.

After dropping off Josh-from-the-restaurant's peonies, and a subway ride later, I was immersed in the heart of the city. I walked by Central Park, admiring its forest green trees, its bright dog walkers, and picturesque grass. Even the smell of the fried food sold on the sidewalks wasn't bad enough to ruin it.

My campus building was a block away, made of the red brick many of the homes in the West Village were made of. It was quaint compared to the financial buildings and hotels that surround it.

Walking through the entrance, I showed the receptionist my student ID, and made my way up the stairwell to the second floor. I felt like a pack mule going up the staircase because I was not only heaving, but was carrying three different bags: the bagels, my tote bag filled with fabrics I had experimented on, and my backpack which held my laptop, notebook, and sewing supplies.

Before you even have the chance to ask why I was bringing my own sewing supplies to a place that already had everything, it's because I was particular.

The sewing kit I used religiously was a gift from Dad for my twelfth birthday. He said that when he first started dating Mom, one of the things he loved most about her was her ability to overthink and color code and schedule absolutely everything, except what she loved. She never overthought her work, not a single stitch in a single dress.

I would sit on the hardwood and watch her for hours as she ran seam lines through her sewing machine. She'd glimpse at me every once in a while, to see if I'd nodded off—which did happen on occasion. But when it didn't, she'd tell me to grab my sewing kit and sew with her.

A year later, they bought me my first sewing machine—a John Lewis in peppermint green. It was the most gorgeous pastel green color. I loved it so much that I carried it around the house with me like a doll. I still used it every day.

"Dani!" the five girls shouted as I walked in the door with the bagels.

"French toast bagel time!" Vera shouted with excitement, squeezing my shoulder as she relieved my arms of the bagels and cream cheese.

"I brought you a lactose intolerant pill, Sandra, in case you forgot again," I mentioned as I put my bags down on the large table.

There often weren't desks in the design rooms, but rather large, wooden tables each made for multiple students. That way we had room for cutting and measuring fabric in the same space without getting in one another's ways. My designated space was with Vera and Daya. While Sandra, Lexi, and Camille sat at the table beside ours. The rest of the room was pretty messy; there was a spot for the professor to sit at the front at their desk, while the walls had cork boards with sketch designs. Numerous sewing machines were lined against the left side of the room, followed by dress forms—mannequins—piled in the corner like a set from a horror film.

"Poor Sandra, she'll never truly be able to appreciate cream cheese," Camille said, moaning as she consumed her bagel.

"I appreciate cream cheese!" Sandra said defensively to Camille. I turned around as Sandra walked in a hunched stature towards me. *"I just need a little extra help,"* she whispered as she approached me with an open hand, presumably for the pill.

I handed it to her like we were doing a drug exchange. She played along, stuffing it in her mouth so quickly that I thought she missed her mouth, making me snort with laughter. *"Thank you,"* she whispered before she left to grab her bagel from the table.

"Here you are, my dear." Daya spoke as if she were a duke,

handing me my bagel.

I briefly noticed her neon plastic rings, accentuating her dark skin and bright nails. Today she wore blue-rimmed glasses, a watercolor midi skirt, and a short sleeve top that's cropped just enough to show her belly button ring. She always had this ability to look cool, but without making it look like she was trying. Like when a supermodel leaves their million dollar apartment to grab milk or walk their dog.

Despite our different wardrobes, we agreed on most celebrity fashion looks, hence why we started a club together on campus: *Look of the Week*. We'd spend an hour debating the best, and worst, celebrity looks of the week. For a meeting that usually only included fifteen women, you'd think we were hosting fight club because of how intense it gets.

We don't watch the time for when class starts because it's so laidback. Our Monday 9 a.m. was designated to our senior capstone project, so the professor always arrived late since they were only here for feedback. The project was due in four weeks, and then they would be showcased in a runway show to the whole school, along with friends and family.

When we finished speaking and eating our bagels, we collected our garments from the side tables to start working. I reached my hand into my bag, wiggling my fingers around for my sewing kit.

Where was it?

Okay, *now* I was getting frustrated. I continued moving my hand around. When I still didn't feel it, I picked my bag off the floor to look inside it. But it wasn't there.

I reached for my backpack and pulled out each item like a

pissed off TSA agent—headphones, student ID, peanut butter and jelly sandwich, lip gloss, various rings.

I needed this sewing kit. It had the specific color thread I had to go to three different fabric stores for and the needles Dad bought me that created all my pieces.

Don't panic, don't panic. Maybe it fell out when I grabbed my strawberry lip balm earlier—

Oh my gosh. Strawberry. My strawberry crochet purse. My sewing kit was in my strawberry purse because I needed to fix a hole in Claire's skirt. Which I left at Levi's mother's …

I was going to kill Gabe.

"What's wrong?" Vera asked, noticing my panic.

"I forgot my sewing kit," I huffed with frustration. Everyone here knew of my weird habit, as well as the oddly specific thread I'd been buying for my projects.

The two hours I had here to utilize all the equipment in the room, and the extra eyes and opinions I could get on my work, were vital. My dresses were due *at the end of this month,* and I could not be more behind. I had one completed and one that I didn't even like, when I was supposed to have *five* in total. Was that my fault? Yes, totally. But was I still allowed to panic? *Yes.*

If I left now, it would take me about forty minutes to walk to the train, take the train, and then walk—

A knock sounded at the door, followed by a, "Hello?"

Our heads snapped to the direction of the door behind us. If I weren't panicked before, I was now, because Levi—*my Levi,* Levi Coldwell—was standing at the door.

Liana Cincotti

11

*I would've gone down on my knees just
to hear you say yes*

A leather satchel sat on his shoulder while his arm held a stack of books. He wore black trousers, and a grey sweater with the sleeves rolled up. His short, dark waves rested above his ... glasses? *Glasses.* The man was wearing glasses. The dark-rimmed glasses rested on his small nose that was pink from what I assumed was the morning spring air.

I looked down at what I was wearing, immediately flattening my baggy button down with my hands. He maintained a nervous look until his eyes found me among the mess of fabric and girls in the room.

"Levi, hi, sorry!" I said in a rush, realizing how long I took to respond.

His face bloomed with a smile that caused his shoulders to loosen. My legs felt wobbly as I stood abruptly from my seat to meet him at the door.

The girls whispered behind me as I pulled him into the hallway. They were all fully aware of who he was from our taco and wine nights where you couldn't help but share all of your embarrassing, childish secrets because they were sharing theirs. As if the admittance to having a good time was to relish in the hilarity of being a woman with a crush.

I didn't miss how Levi waved at one of them in confusion. I was almost positive it was Sandra.

When I looked back, Daya and Vera were pretending to make out like middle schoolers. This was what you got when you shared your love life with your friends.

As I shut the door behind me and prayed that I looked presentable, he started speaking.

"I didn't mean to show up like some parent of high schoolers—you just had left your purse at my mom's last night," he explained as he handed my bag over.

Gabe was going to go absolutely feral when I told him this.

I stood there speechless momentarily, taking the purse. But then it hit me: "How did you know I was here?"

He looked away and scratched the back of his neck, which caused the hem of his sweater to rise up … It was too early for this.

The tone of his voice brought me back to reality. He almost sounded embarrassed. "I called Linda." Oh my gosh, he called my mom. "I hope you don't mind; I wasn't sure how important it was that you had everything in there," gesturing to my purse.

I shook my head in disbelief. It was 8:30 a.m. on a Monday morning in the city, or in other words, the equivalent to a Macy's on Black Friday. "Levi, you didn't have to do that—"

"I really didn't mind. I was on my way to class anyways," he replied with a soft voice, nodding towards the window where we could see the street.

"Oh, what class do you have? That's a lot of books …" I murmured in thought.

He laughed. "It's because I'm teaching the class," he responded as if it was no big deal. But it was most definitely a big deal. This was actually the *epitome* of a big deal. You could put it under the dictionary description as an example because that's how ideal it was.

The Jane Austen class he was TA'ing, that was filled with college women, got to see Levi—academic, shy, sweater, glasses-wearing Levi—*who knows* how many times a week? Attractive Levi, with attractive forearms, attractive hair, and attractive glasses.

I pulled at my button down, trying to straighten it out again. Why did I stop ironing my clothes? In the process of trying to fix my shirt, my bag slipped off my shoulder and fell, causing all of its content to spill out with it.

I was a mess. He made me a mess.

I squatted down immediately to grab everything, but he followed, pulling up the pant legs of his trousers before kneeling, then picking up twice as many things with his larger hands.
"Have I completely ruined your morning yet?" I exhaled.

"My whole day actually. Maybe even my entire month, despite it being May first." When I tilted my head back, he had a smile. His sarcasm made me laugh. "I'm going to think about how I was forced to stop at a much cooler college than mine, drop *one thing* off, and then talk with my friend."

My heart felt a pinch at the word *friend*. "I guess my college *is* a bit cooler than yours," I said, shrugging my shoulders, feeling more comfortable—more *us*.

"*Much* cooler," he corrected me. As we knelt on the ground, we were close enough that the warmth of his breath felt like the whisper of a kiss on my cheek. "I would love to see what you're working on at some point."

"Only if you'll recite me Jane Austen like we're in a period piece," I requested.

"Only if you'll be my seamstress," he argued.

"Yeah, yeah," I rolled my eyes, standing up and straightening out my jeans.

He stood with me, fixing his slacks, and situating his glasses. "I'm serious, I need my suit tailored for the wedding, and I rather pay you than someone else."

Surprise waved through my shoulders. "You want *me* to do it?"

"Well, I definitely wasn't going to ask Claire."

I disregarded his joke because stress reverberated through my spine now.

"You haven't even seen anything I've sewn in like … four years—"

"Yes, I—"

"—and you could probably find a professional that could get it done quicker—"

He looked confused. "But that's not what I'm—"

"—and better and—"

"Dani, I want—"

He was not understanding.

"—and cleaner and—"

"*Daisy.*"

My mouth stopped moving, and I could tell by the exasperated look on his face that he was as taken aback as I was by his words. His cheeks were flushed, and some of his waves had fallen forward over his brow, as if we had just pulled away from a kiss.

It felt like our years as friends were being peeled away slowly to reveal what was left: my past romantic feelings for him, and the lack of his for me. But hearing that nickname—my nickname— one that was only used by a select group of people, felt so much more intimate coming from him. And I knew, *I knew*, that he thought so too from the look of surprise that mirrored my own.

He looked away for a moment, collecting his next words presumably, with a clenched jaw. "I know that you don't think you have the skills to do it, but *I* know you do. If you don't have the time for it"—I definitely *did not* have the time for it—"then I won't mention it again, I promise. But if you do …" He left his unspoken question hang in the air.

If I took this on, it only added more work for me to do when the wedding and runway exhibit were in four weeks, and my graduate applications were due in two. I'd have to make sure it was perfect and not a thread out of place because I couldn't afford to replace a whole suit.

But it was Levi … Even four years later, he had gotten more handsome and more mature in a way that I wish I could've embroidered into fabric.

It's exactly why I said: "Okay."

His brows lifted with surprise and a glimmer exploded in his eyes. "Are you positive?"

I nodded. "But I'll need you to come over as soon as possible so I can get your measurements, and have it finished early enough," I said. I'd need to have him try it on again to see if any other adjustments were needed, which was going to require a few fittings…

I should not have put on liquid blush today.

"How's Friday?" he asked.

I paused, realizing what Friday was. "I have a date."

There was a look that went across his face, but quickly disappeared, not giving me a chance to understand it. "Who are you going on a date with?"

"Jia—I have to watch her date."

"Oh, of course, normal. Why?" he responded with a light laugh that made him sound like a confused dad.

I smiled. "To make sure her date isn't an axe murderer, obviously."

"Obviously. Has there been a past run in with an axe murderer?" he inquired, his glasses and light academia outfit only making him look more serious.

"If you would count the southerner Gabe once went on a date with that chopped trees for a living."

"Doesn't sound like a run-in at all, but that does sound slightly exhilarating. Need company?"

"Oh, are you sure? I don't usually buy food or anything, I kind of just sit there, watch, and commentate."

"I can buy us food," he responded, gnawing on his bottom lip, fully aware that food was the way to my heart.

"And the fitting after?"

"Or before, whichever works best for you." He almost sounded shy. Like I was a professor, and he was my student nervous to speak up. Jesus, his glasses were doing something to me.

"After. I have a meeting on campus beforehand that won't end until seven."

"I'll pick you up here then, on Friday. Maybe you can Introduce me to your friends," his eyes flickered to the door behind me where … *Oh my.* Discretion was in *none* of their vocabulary. All of the girls had their ears or eyes peeking out of the crack of the door. I tried my best to not turn the color of cherry pie.

"It's been many years since any of them have been with a man, let alone seen one." A choking noise, or several choking noises, sounded from behind the door.

He laughed, which caused a beautiful smile to sweep across his face. "It's a date. I'll see you Friday." And just like that, he was walking down the stairs and out the door.

I turned around slowly, hoping to make myself look like a possessed doll in a grungy horror film. "You couldn't have at least *closed the door?!*"

Instead of the five girls running away or shutting the door in my face out of fear, they ran towards me with questions.

"*That* was Levi?" Lexi shouted in shock.

"Did he say he was a *teacher?*" Camille asked with amazement—to which I quickly clarified.

"Those *glasses!*" Vera uttered.

"He came all the way here just to bring you your purse," Lexi cooed.

Sandra began, "That was one hot piece of—" before I cut her off. I didn't need a reminder; I was fully aware.

Daya wiggled her brow like a mischievous matchmaker. "Friday's meeting will be *really* interesting now."

12

And when the soil grows old, I'll comfort it in
the chaos of the storm

"I *knew* he'd bring the bag!" Gabe shouted, standing from his seat, his arms in the air like he'd scored a goal.

Jia shook her head. "That doesn't mean anything, Gabe."

Gabe sat back down, slightly more composed. "That man has feelings for you, Dani. He offered to stalk your friend's date with you *on a Friday night.* Do you *know* what men that look like that like to do on Friday nights?"

Jia and I looked at each other, sharing a look of *do you know what he's talking about?*

Gabe rolled his eyes. "Strip clubs." He shrugged his shoulders and placed his hands on the table in front of us, as if he'd dropped the mic at a groundbreaking TED Talk.

Jia and I looking at each other was all it took to burst into laughter. "Levi's not a forty-year-old man, Gabe!" I uttered in between of tears of laughter.

"It's true though!" Gabe said, trying to defend himself.

Jia began waving her hand in front of her. "Just stop talking, my stomach hurts too much!" She was hunched over in tears of laughter.

Pulling myself together and wiping the single tear that made its way down my nose, I told Gabe, "I appreciate your support, but Levi and I always hung out together on Friday nights. I doubt the past four years has him paying to see half-naked women and drinking overpriced beers."

Gabe shook his head, evidently horrified by my ignorance. "He's a man now, Dani. I doubt he's at home every weekend watching his sisters still. He's *hot*. Hot men don't just go through life not taking advantage of it."

I didn't know how to explain to Gabe that that wasn't who Levi was. He was the person to be at home every weekend and take care of his family because that's what he wanted. He wanted to see with his own eyes that they were okay and happy.

But I knew how idiotic it would make me sound, especially when Levi had grown up these past four years. It *was* possible that he went out clubbing on the weekend, and drank, and kissed women he didn't know the day before. He had pretty much admitted to something like that, hadn't he? Wasn't that the point of this set up between us—to make him look committed?

It didn't matter anyways. His love was the type to be shared, not to be owned.

I knew Jia and Gabe were peering at me as I processed all of my thoughts. Instead of saying anything though, I went back to writing. We were currently in our usual restaurant at our usual table—our spot for date watching—filling out grad applications, sans Jia who was updating her resume. I'd be back here tomorrow night for her date.

"How's your essay going?" Jia asked.

I was thankful for the change in conversation. With there only being two weeks until grad applications due, it was crunch time. "I still feel like everything I write isn't good enough."

"Read me the question again."

"*Write about a pivotal time in your life that sparked growth.*"

"What have you written about so far?"

"Moving into the city ... entering university ... learning to sew."

I already knew what she was thinking by the hard look she was giving the table in deep thought. I could hear her unspoken idea hanging in the air: to write about losing my dad. It was the first idea Ethan had come up with too. I wasn't doing that.

"What'd your advisor say?" she asked.

"Ethan thinks I should write about the first time I saw one of my mom's runway shows."

I'd been seeing Ethan twice a week since grad applications were released. He'd helped me narrow down my options for applying, and review which schools offered the best fashion design and haute couture programs. I was applying to each fashion university in New York, as well as a few in the UK and mainland Europe. I was hesitant to apply somewhere that far, but Ethan said there was no harm in applying anyways. I was only interested in one master's program though, and that was the one at Lazaro here in the city.

It was the only application I hadn't submitted yet. Ironically, it had the second lowest acceptance rate, second to ESMOD in Paris. Ethan got his master's at Lazaro only two years ago, but worked in the industry throughout that time, so he had a lot of stories about working for A-list designers and celebrities.

He was also pretty cute, but it did make the backs of my knees sweaty and my cheeks flame during every conversation we had.

Not Levi-type-of-cute though.

Levi had a sharp angle in the curve of his jaw, charm in his smile, and way with words that made him different than everyone else. Whereas Ethan was attractive in the way that made you do a double take if you walked by him on the street. Not stare at him from behind his desk and wonder what it was like hold his hand from across a dinner table.

Levi was the man that women wrote their romance novels about, while guys like Ethan were shadow replicas of them in real life.

And as professional as Ethan's work experience made him, it was like he had this high school football player ego at times.

I'd had a meeting with him earlier to go over the essay topics again. Jia didn't have to ask why I didn't go with Ethan's idea to write about my dad.

"Give it time, it'll come to you," she reassured me. I didn't argue with her because I was too defeated. Instead, I went back to my laptop, and tried to figure out how I was possibly going to answer this question when I hadn't experienced inspiration in years.

13

*Was it wrong of me to think of you
when you were never mine?*

"If you think that skirt with those shoes makes that a *good look*, then it's a good thing you're not trying to be a stylist."

Everyone in the room gasped—even me, which said a lot because I'd heard them *all* say something spiteful at this point.

Gabe was currently looking at Vera in disgust from behind his desk—the one that was placed at the front of the classroom by the projector, where a supermodel was projected from Gabe's laptop. The rest of the club was seated in chairs facing Gabe at his makeshift podium, as he tried to explain why this was the best celebrity look of the week.

Vera very much did not think so.

Who would've thought people could get this passionate about celebrity fashion? Well, me, and everyone else attending fashion school here.

"*Low-rise mini skirts are in!*" Gabe shouted so passionately that he added a little hop in his stance.

"Not with those shoes they aren't!" Vera shouted back with an unnerving level of passion.

I stood up before Gabe had a chance to leap over the desk—we didn't need to witness that again.

I clapped my hands like an elementary school teacher to get everyone's attention. "Raise your hands if you think Gabe's pick is the best look of the week."

Daya and I counted the raised hands, but when there were none to be found, we all erupted in laughter.

"If any of you ever need help with your marketing, you can all go *screw*," Gabe huffed with frustration and a middle finger in the air, as he took his laptop and returned to his seat.

The funniest part about it was that he'd be incredibly drunk with all of them in about an hour. No one took each other too seriously once they left this room.

"That means Cassidy's pick is the best Look of the Week!"

Everyone began collecting their things and moving their chairs back to their designated places. But as Daya and I cleaned up the snacks and shut off the projector, some of the girls' voices rose.

As if reading my mind, Daya and I turned at the exact moment to find six of the girls at the doorway giggling. *What were they looking at?*

"I'm just looking for Daniella." The muscles in my body jumped at the sound of Levi's voice saying my name.

"Dani!" all six girls called, turning around to face me, revealing Levi who was hidden behind them in the doorway. His hair was soaked and pushed back. There were rain drops sitting on his clothes like sparkles. He wore a canvas jacket, a black T-shirt, and jeans.

He had a backpack pulled over his shoulder, and in his free

hand, an umbrella that looked like it had been mauled by a dog.

I gulped.

The room felt incredibly silent, and maybe that was because it was. Was everyone watching us?

"I'm sorry I'm not dressed nicer," he said with a shy smile. I couldn't figure out if it was because we were going out on what was a date but not really a date, or because he was in a fashion university, where everyone was dressed for a night out.

"No, no," I rushed to say. "I'm not wearing anything special," trying to reassure him. It was true though; I was dressed in a mini dress that I'd made years ago from extra satin fabric that was polka-dotted with vintage pink flowers, paired with a sweater pulled over it, disguising my dress to look like a skirt.

The only thing that looked partially nice was my hair, which I had straightened, making it appear slightly longer than usual. But that was about to go out the window based on how his hair looked.

I couldn't tell if I imagined his eyes wondering over my fairly bare legs. But he cleared his throat and spoke, sounding slightly flustered. "It's raining."

I released a small laugh, still unsure of how my voice was going to sound. "Oh really? I thought you had visited the car wash." He laughed. My heart squeezed.

Why were we standing at opposite sides of the room? I couldn't tell you. All I know is that if I got any closer to him, I'd lose the ability to breathe.

"Is it possible you have an umbrella?" he asked with speculation.

"Unfortunately, I'm not that prepared." There was a

moment of silence, where I think we both realized that we were about to be alone for the first time since high school. Every instance we'd seen each other in the past week had been in the company of his family.

This was going to be the longest amount of time where it was just us—and Jia from afar, of course.

"Is this your *boyfriend, Daniella?*" Amelia, a freshman studying international business who joined the club last year, cooed.

I'm kicking her out of the club.

My face grew hot like the embers of a fire. My mouth immediately opened to say no, but our plan came to fruition in my mind like a stop sign. What if I said no and it somehow got back to someone in his family? Or if someone here knew Bella or her mom? This one instance of embarrassment would ruin everything.

I sucked up my embarrassment and practically whispered, "Yes." Instead of looking for Amelia's reaction though, I looked for his. I expected him to look horrified or confused, but rather I was met with the most beautiful thing I'd ever seen.

He was blushing. His cheeks were pink, and his eyes were turned down, while everyone else's were glued to him.

"Dammit," someone muttered in the group, making us laugh. If I told them no, at least one of the girls here would've given him their number.

On that note, I collected my bag, said my quick goodbyes, and walked us downstairs to the exit. After opening the main door in silence, I started walking outside until a wave of rain came pouring down. I immediately stumbled backwards, directly into him.

Whoa. His hands caught my arms as my back hit his chest,

which kept me from tripping over my feet. Some form of apology escaped my lips as I ran from his grip, trying to suffice any dignity I had left. I hadn't accounted for how close we were, or how perfectly tall he was that if I pushed onto the balls of my feet, my lips would meet his.

I turned back to the rainstorm outside, and then down at my delicate clothes and bare legs, mentally swearing at myself for not wearing jeans or at least bringing my umbrella.

Without having a chance to form another thought, a jacket—his jacket—wrapped around me. It smelled of sandalwood and cinnamon, and was heavy on my shoulders, like a workman's jacket meant to protect his skin.

"Are you sure?" I asked.

"Positive." He lifted the collar of his jacket over my shoulders, trying to create a shield from the rain for my hair.

As gracious as the gesture was, my hair ended up almost as soaked as his by the time we got to the train. And as much as I was disappointed that my hair was ruined and probably made me look like a wet rat, it helped break the tension between us because we were more focused on dodging puddles and cabs, rather than trying to talk.

Josh was standing behind the hosting podium when we entered the restaurant. He pointed out where Jia and her date would be sitting, and then let us seat ourselves.

"You weren't kidding—you really do this a lot," Levi commented, nodding to Josh's figure.

"Almost every other Friday night," I laughed, because there was no point in trying to lie about it at this point.

"Do you go on a lot of dates?"

My eyes left the menu instantly. I didn't need the menu since I knew it top to bottom, including every price and calorie, but it felt like the normal thing to do.

I looked at him, but he was focused on his menu. I must have imagined the weight of the question, seeing as he didn't look concerned by any means.

"I wouldn't say a lot. Once every few months." I loved the idea of dating: getting dressed up, meeting a person outside a restaurant with a shared nervousness. Then sitting at dinner together for hours talking, knowing there was a mutual attraction when they looked at your lips or bumped your foot under the table.

Not that any of that happened though. Only in the movies I watched.

That's why I only dated once every few months—not that men were constantly hitting on me. I wasn't the girl that men gravitated towards or even wanted.

Every few months, I opened the dating apps back up. It was how my dating cycle started. Only choosing to date every few months gave me (one) time to build up my love for romance before I met someone cute for a date, and then (two) be disappointed by how the date went, and finally (three) grow worried that I'd never find love. I then entered into my romantic-comedy and love-storyland hibernation, where I tried to remind myself that if love existed in films and books, then those stories must've been inspired by real love stories too. Right?

He responded simply by nodding. *What does that mean,* you may ask? Absolutely no clue. I hadn't seen men in rom-coms do that.

I tapped my phone screen to read the time. Jia should be here with her date in about fifteen minutes. I guess our sprint to the train station through the rain got us here early.

"Do you walk to the train by yourself every Friday night?" Levi asked, as if he was reading my mind.

"Sometimes I skip there," I joked, trying to make him laugh. But I answered too quickly, not understanding the concern in his voice.

"Dani," he asked in his authoritative, big brother voice, the one he used with his younger sisters. It made me feel worse. That was the last way I wanted him to talk to me— like I was another sister.

I matched his tone, putting the menu down. "Some Fridays, not all. The girls usually go out after club meetings, so the nights I don't go out with them, I walk back by myself."

He adjusted one of the rings from the matching pair on his index finger. "Call me next time you decide not to go out, I'll walk you back."

"I've been walking back to the train by myself since freshman year."

He ran his hand through his hair. "Just call me, okay? I'm only a few blocks away."

I pursed my lips in thought but nodded in agreement.

"How's trying to get the job going?"

"I had an interview yesterday with a team of journalists, but Bella's mom stopped me. Bella must have brought us up because she congratulated me on my new relationship."

"Wow, that's a bit condescending. I'm surprised you want to work for someone like that."

"It's not that I *want* to. I want to teach, that's why I'm studying it, and student-teaching with every free hour I have. But the journalist position pays well. It would give me the ability to help out with the girls." There was no morsel of exhaustion or regret in his voice, only matter of fact. As if he had no idea how selfless he was being.

"Levi," I sighed, my heart aching. "I thought real-estate was going well for your mom?"

He nodded. "It is, it is. But it's not a job that has a constant flow of income. It all depends on whether she's making sales. I want to make sure that there's money available during off seasons for her."

I wanted to tell him that he should be following his heart by teaching. I wanted to explain that his happiness and well-being should be more important. That there could be really great paying positions in those roles depending on where he went.

But those weren't guaranteed unlike this position with *The New York Times*. I could see how badly he needed this job from the way his shoulders slumped forward during this conversation. To tell him to give up on his family and leave them when Sarah was already states away was unrealistic.

I remembered the years when his mother struggled to make ends meet and he would grow with tension every time his mother opened a bill. That fear didn't just go away.

"We'll get you the job. I promise," I reassured, leaning over to squeeze his hand.

Our conversation was cut short by Jia's sudden appearance with her date.

"It's gametime," I said with the passion of a football coach. He laughed, showing off the contrast of his white teeth to his tan skin. I almost lost my next words, but then I spotted what her date was wearing. "*That's* her date?"

He glanced at her date, and then back at me with confusion. "What's wrong with him?"

I pressed myself close to the table, trying to lean towards him in order to be discrete. I placed the menu beside me as a shield in case her date was somehow incredibly good at reading lips.

Levi watched my movements, mimicking them. But he forgot how much taller he was than me because our noses were only inches apart when he leaned across his side of the table.

Pull yourself together, Daniella. "He's wearing a shirt with a *Rubik's cube* on it," I whispered in horror.

Levi narrowed his eyes. "What's wrong with Rubik's cubes?"

"It's not that it's the Rubik's cube itself, but the fact that he's wearing it *on a first date.*"

He thought on it before agreeing. His tongue ran across his bottom lip so quickly that I wanted to pinch myself for even noticing. "What should he be wearing then?"

Sitting back up and putting the menu down, I pondered it for a moment. What would I want a guy to wear on a first date?

"A clean pair of jeans would be nice. A plain shirt, and maybe a nice jacket," I answered.

He looked down at his own clothes, and then it clicked. *Mortification.* I was a ball of mortification, containing every embarrassing word a girl could utter to her crush. I may as well just put my heart on the table for him because I could not make my attraction for him any more obvious.

He smiled a kind smile though, halfway through fixing the bottom of his plain, black shirt.

I knew I shouldn't, but I couldn't help it. "Do you date a lot?"

His eyes meet mine in surprise, his lips partially parted. He cleared his throat.

I crossed a line that I wasn't supposed to cross.

"Not often, no."

I nodded. I've changed my mind; I don't want to talk about his dating history.

The rest of the time moved slow. We watched Jia chat with Rubik's Cube and have dinner. There were no alarming looks or handwaving in need of help, so we continued to talk, even after Jia and her date left.

We avoided the topic of dating the entire time, and that seemed to be the sweet spot because we had fallen back into a comfortable rhythm of banter and teasing.

The joy that swelled in my chest to have this friendship back couldn't be explained. But it didn't cover up the hole in my heart that was getting wider. And I knew it wouldn't get better when we left for my apartment tonight.

14

"My mom and Mandy are gone for the weekend," I told him as he shut the townhouse door behind us, switching on a few of the lamps.

I always loved the look of the apartment at night. The dark sky outside and yellow lamp light inside brought a coziness to the soft furniture and flowers that only autumn carried. But not even the coziness of the apartment at the moment could calm the anxious nest in my chest.

"Um. We could go in my room if you want?"

He looked at me with hesitation, sizing up the question. "It's fine with me," he replied, his tone sounding similar to my own.

I nodded since I had no words, letting him follow me up the stairs towards my room.

I don't know why I was making this weird, this didn't have to be weird. It wasn't weird!

We'd been in each other's bedrooms before—not this specific one since we all moved after high school, but still. I couldn't help but let that one distinction make me feel nervous. Somehow letting him enter my room that had never been seen by him and had only been lived in by Adult Me rather than Childhood Me felt like we were crossing into the multiverse.

He walked into my conjoined bathroom to change as I collected what I needed for the adjustments: a small ruler, several safety pins, tape measure, and pencil. They weren't difficult to find seeing as my room was so spotless that I could host a dinner party on the floor.

I'd made sure to clean this morning, knowing that he was coming. I'd tried hiding some of my childish trinkets, like bracelets with glass daisies on them and frames I made out of guitar picks. I'd almost considered cleaning the walls—my mom said that everyone should clean their walls at least once a month—but since half of my room was covered in green and white baby's breath wallpaper (horrendously applied because it was left over from our old home), I think I got a pass. But once I'd started shoving my strawberry lamp under my bed, I'd realized there was no point in hiding everything.

Just because I enjoyed colorful décor didn't mean I wasn't an adult. At least that's what I told myself.

But I did hide the vase that was in the shape of a fairy with flowers protruding from its head.

The flowers were currently resting in the neighbor's bushes outside.

"Don't laugh." I instantly turned to find him standing in the doorway in his suit. I fully expected to laugh, but no such thing happened because he looked incredible.

Yes, the suit could fit better in a few places, but the dark navy on his skin did him wonders. The jacket of the suit looked about an inch too big on each side of his torso, along with the length of the pants.

"Well don't look at me like that! Is it that bad?" he asked.

My eyes darted to his face after being glued to his body. My cheeks were warmer than the chocolate croissants I ordered from Marty. "Oh—no, no." I cleared my throat. "I've seen much worse actually."

His eyebrows arched, making me panic for a moment, but it was swiftly paired with a friendly scoff. "And what would that be?"

I put on my most serious face as I said, "What you were planning to wear to Junior Prom?"

His face was riddled with complete surprise, but a moment later, he was hunched over laughing. In moments, I was hunched over with him.

"It wasn't that bad!" he insisted, choking on a laugh that only made me laugh harder.

"It just *really* was," I insisted, thinking of the hideous floral pattern in the interior of the jacket as I wiped a tear. The smile on my face was making my cheeks sore.

As our laughter came to an end, his face grew melancholic.

"Why did we stop talking, Dani?" The question was like a slap in the face. Any form of a smile on my lips was erased.

How was I supposed to answer that? Where would I start? I couldn't just say, *I was in love with you, and you weren't in love with me.* Did he not already understand that? Did I simply imagine everything that happened senior year? Because the night of prom when he was kissing Cora Messing like she was supplying him air was melted into my brain since the day I saw it.

I knew I hadn't imagined it.

The day I saw that happen was the day I realized I needed to cut myself off. If I wasn't allowed to love him, then I shouldn't be allowed to be his friend and torture myself any longer.

Unable to muster up the courage to speak up for myself or talk to him the next day, I had shut down. There wasn't a bone in my body that was confident enough to approach him.

As much as I wanted to believe that I was no longer that insecure, eighteen-year-old girl in high school, I couldn't even muster up the courage now in front of him.

"I—I don't know," I shook my head, looking down at the ground to keep the truth from appearing in my eyes. I watched as his feet moved closer to mine on the hardwood floor, his suit pants dragging. Swallowing, I said, "I'm going to take your measurements."

He said nothing as I stood in front of him, eye level with his chin. His breath grazed my forehead as I measured his torso. Pinching an inch on each side of the jacket at his waist, I asked, "How does that feel?"

"Much better."

I nodded at his response.

Leaning backwards to my desk, I grabbed two safety pins, opening them, and placing them between my lips carefully.

I was fully aware that it wasn't the safest method to hold something with a sharp edge, but it was the most efficient way. Turning back around, I pulled the fabric at one side to measure it and confirm it was an inch, but suddenly, the fabric was pulled from my grasp as he raised his arm. His fingertips brushed my bottom lip in what felt like slow motion. Glass could have fallen from my bedside table, and I wouldn't have heard it for another two minutes.

As his fingertips left my lips, he took my safety pins with him.

"I can hold them," he said, his voice sounding husky.

I couldn't form a response because my lips burned from the shadow of a touch his fingers left. I was almost tempted to grab new safety pins, just so he would do it again.

I shook my head in disbelief as if I had found that as an annoying remark, rather than a turn on.

I went back to measuring and pinning, now retrieving the pins from his hands. When his jacket was pinned, I moved to his pant legs, bending down to lean on my knees.

I've had male models to work on clothes for before, so this wasn't the first time I'd run my hands against a man's legs to get a feel for the extra fabric. But, oh my, they never looked nearly as heartbreakingly beautiful as Levi's. I'd never thought I'd be so close to him before, let alone on my knees in front of him. And while I was doing my best to suppress every dirty thought that knocked on my head, I knew that it was appearing in the blush of my cheeks.

This was pure torture.

I folded the bottom of the pant so it was no longer covering his shoe. "How does that look?" I asked.

His eyelids jumped open as if I had shaken him from a nap.

"Perfect," he commented.

I grabbed more pins, measuring and pinning the bottom the pants.

"How are grad applications going?" he casually asked. Okay, I guess we were speaking like humans again.

"I had a discussion with my advisor about them today,

actually."

"How'd that go?"

"Well, they're all due in a week and a half, but I'm still stuck on one. So, I went to talk to Ethan—"

"Ethan?"

"My advisor," I explained. "He said that if I included my full name on my app, that I'd have a better chance—"

"What?"

"He thinks I should include my mom's maiden name on the application and in the essays." When my parents got married, my mom kept her maiden name because it's what she was known as in the fashion industry. All of her interviews, the labels on her dresses, and her runway shows included that name.

When I was born, they decided to hyphenate my name, putting my father's first. Growing up, I just didn't write my mom's in at all because it came second. But now, as someone who was trying to get into the same industry as her, I'd completely avoided the name, wanting my work to lead me to my success and nothing else.

"Dani, that's horrible advice. You've been listening to what he says?"

I pressed my eyes closed. I knew that Levi was studying to be a teacher, but Ethan had experience only few had. "I understand why he says it. He's been in the industry for a few years—connections are the way to break through."

"He's—" He cleared his throat and paused. "Can you stand while we have this conversation?" I looked up at him and realized that I'd been pretty much talking directly at his … crotch.

Oh my *gosh*.

I whipped my head away. It wasn't often that I thought about my minimal sexual experience—actually, I tried to never think about it. But it was almost impossible to avoid it in moments like these.

I stood immediately, holding my skirt to make sure it didn't rise. I didn't need another thing to be embarrassed about.

He looked at me without a lick of mortification. "He's asking you to change your name to get accepted, rather than trusting your work to get you there." He searched my eyes for a reaction, obviously surprised that I would listen to Ethan's advice.

But something he didn't realize was that my work *wasn't* impressive. I worked day and night and poured my heart into pieces, but that didn't make them revolutionary or groundbreaking.

He continued when I didn't disagree. "I'll help you with your application, anything you need."

I bent back down, realizing there was a pin out of place. "We're done."

"Excuse me?" he asked as if I had told him I'd stolen his firstborn.

"The suit. It's all pinned—you can change now."

"Oh, okay." I watched as he walked into my bathroom, trying to avoid staring at his butt. *God*, I hated myself for thinking it, but it looked amazing.

"This conversation isn't over by the way!" he shouted humorously through the door. I laughed. "This guy doesn't know you."

"It's not that big of a deal, Levi," I shouted back.

"Do you remember Jack Huntington?" he asked through the

door.

I processed the name for a moment, trying to remember. Then a switch went off in my head and Jack's face appeared in my head. "Oh my gosh, *the kid that made the comment about my ass?*"

He groaned. "Yes, him."

"He was such an asshole!"

"You didn't think so at the time. You didn't want to tell anyone about what he was saying to you because it wasn't 'a big deal.'" I could practically see his air quotes through the door.

"Well, he got detention like a week later for something he said to another girl."

I heard the bathroom door open as I placed my pins back into the box under my bed.

"He got detention Dani because I punched him."

"You *what?*" But I kind of choked on the words because he was half dressed in the doorway when I turned around.

He was in the middle of pulling a shirt over his head, where I watched the muscles in his stomach flex.

"I punched him," he shrugged, perfectly satisfied with his answer as he pulled his shirt on. "He kept saying things like that about you. I told him to stop, then he made another joke about it, so I punched him. We both had detention, his was just longer than mine."

"You're insane." I stared at him with wide eyes, trying to process what he'd just told me. *He punched someone?*

"I would've done it for any of my sisters."

The comparison to his sisters melted all of my muscles into the ground. I was slack with nostalgic sadness. He didn't punch a guy for me out of boyfriend-like protectiveness, but because he thought of me as one of his sisters. I hated how gutted I felt.

He continued, "So this does matter, just like that did."

I swallowed my thoughts and asked, "What would you recommend?"

"The Met."

"The Met? As in the art museum?"

A small smile perked up on his face. "For inspiration. It's where I go for writing when I'm stuck. We could go on Sunday if you'd want? I'll even let you make fun of what I wear."

I suppressed a laugh, but I couldn't suppress my smile. "I can't, I'm supposed to have a meeting with Ethan."

"Screw Ethan! We don't need him."

I laughed. "Maybe I could move the meeting."

He couldn't hide his sweet, nervous smile. "Does four o'clock work? A few hours before dinner?"

This realization of habitually being invited to everything again, of being desired and wanted as company, caused my face to bloom into the color of bleeding-heart flowers. It was a nostalgia stronger than middle school summers.

Saying yes was as easy as falling into bed.

15

Because you look at me with conviction when I don't even know
the crime I committed

The train ride and short walk to The Met was peaceful and romantic. It would've felt like I was living in a romantic comedy if Levi and I weren't trying to pick out all the ways someone could get murdered in New York—other than the most obvious ways.

"Death-by-sewer-grate," I stated confidently.

"If you think that tops death-by-neighbor's-feral-cat, then I'm going to need an explanation," he responded in an official manner, both of us very serious over this argument.

I'm not sure how we got to such graphic scenarios. But this started when I was frantically demanding that he tie his shoe before stepping onto the train because I saw something on the news once about a person getting their shoelace stuck in the door of a departing train.

He laughed at the story but seconds later he registered that I was genuinely concerned and quickly tied his shoe.

We were only a block away from the museum, and I was doing my best to meet his long strides. He had already slowed down twice, realizing that he had most definitely grown in height and strength during college, while I remained eight inches shorter.

"Imagine you're walking along the sidewalk, and then someone comes up behind you and pushes you." I tilted my head to make sure he was following. But when I glanced at him, he was looking back at me. I had forgotten what it was like to be watched when speaking—not stared at, not looked at, but *regarded*. From the way his chin dipped to fully consume my vocalized thoughts to the precise manner of his gaze never leaving my lips in order to catch every word. It almost made me trip on the smooth pavement.

"I—uh—then there happens to be a sewer grate in front of you, that happens to be open, and you fall in."

"This seems extremely circumstantial," he speculated.

"But your neighbor's feral cat attacking you isn't?"

"*You've* never been attacked by Marty's cat."

Walking up the grand stone steps of the museum, Levi paid for our tickets, pushing away my wallet before I could pull out any cash. I insisted that he let me pay him back, but my words were cut off when I felt his hand on my lower back, leading us into the building. The thick denim of my overalls felt thinner than flower petals under his hand. I wanted to lean into it, but my habit to avoid any physical contact with him was glued to me like a curse, keeping me standing straight.

Keep it together, I reminded myself, it was just a hand—*hands that could cover the entire surface area of my backside; that could grab my jaw and tilt my lips upward; that could embed themselves in my hair and make themselves at home.*

Oh Jesus.

We passed through galleries of paintings and sculptures,

where most of the rooms were dimly lit, only shining light on the paintings themselves. Walls were painted dark mauves, decorated in paintings that were hugged by gold frames. The people that walked by us were quiet, as if there was a silent agreement between everyone to enjoy the art silently.

That's why the sound of a high-pitched laugh made me jump. I twisted to find a young girl being picked up by her father. He was lifting her in the air, making airplane noises that resulted in a fit of giggles. Bringing her back down to his chest, he brushed her hair out of her face.

I swallowed and stared up at the ceiling. Mom always did it whenever something went wrong at a shoot or show to hold back tears. Something about tilting your chin up.

"How often do you think of him?"

He didn't look at me when he answered. He stared ahead at the father like he was replaying a tragic dream. "Every single day. I see him in every room I walk into, like he'll be there waiting for me on the other side of the door. Sometimes, I swear I hear his voice in the morning calling me downstairs. And there are instances when I run down and don't realize it until I'm halfway down the stairs." He shook his head and made a sound similar to a laugh but resonated it with defeat. "I don't even live in the same house that he raised me in either."

His words caused the tears in my eyes to form again. "So it hasn't gotten any easier?"

He blew out a breath. "It's not that it hasn't gotten easier, but rather my eyes and heart refuse to believe what's real."

Could I live like that forever? Waiting for my heart to catch up with reality? I had grown accustomed to what life was like without Dad, but that didn't mean I felt okay.

"I have to show you something that reminds me of you." As we approached another room of statues, he brought me to a tall marble statue of a man that was missing his lips and nose. It was as if someone sculpted him in the middle of a rhinoplasty procedure that he wasn't put to sleep for.

I slapped his arm. "I'm not going anywhere with you again."

His laugh reverberated his words and chest. "I'm kidding, I'm kidding, I promise. I just wanted to see your reaction. The painting is down here."

My disappointment diminished as he wrapped his hand around my fingers to propel me forward into another hallway. It was only a friendly gesture; we used to hold hands in high school as we moved through the crowded hallways together. Pria from Anatomy always glared at me when she saw us.

I tried not to overthink the feeling of his palm in mine, because this was who he was and always had been: flirtatious. He showed his love for you through words and touches. His love for me was just not the type I desired.

I couldn't help but glance down at our hands where his sleeve grazed my wrist—oh. I swear, I swear that was my old bracelet—the one made of glass yellow daisies. It looked exactly like the one he made me for my eighteenth birthday. But I left it sitting at the bottom of my fairy vase, covered by peonies in my windowsill. No, there was no way. It'd been years since I'd looked at it anyways.

"This one," he said, stopping me in front of a grand painting that covered the wall.

It was a painting of a pale, well-dressed woman. She wore a voluminous dress that overtook her plush chair; seated at a desk in front of a window, she clutched flowers and a note. It breathed of sunlight; each color used in the painting had a yellow or orange hue. Reading the plaque on the wall, it said: *Love Letters* by Jean Honoré Fragonard.

"Why?"

He hesitated for a moment. "When I look at it, all I see is you."

"I'm most definitely not this fashion forward."

"I completely disagree. Everything you wear is perfect."

I tilted my head down at my overalls for effect.

"I love your overalls most of all, especially when you fill your pockets with ridiculous little things."

My cheeks grew warm with embarrassment. "I don't fill them with ridiculous things."

"Hmm," he hummed, knowing he wasn't wrong. It made me unreasonably frustrated.

"I would think most men enjoyed mini skirts and low-cut shirts." The second the words were out I regretted them. *Completely unnecessary, Dani, we didn't need to argue with every person that complimented us.*

"I never said I didn't like those." His gaze moved to the side of my face. He cleared his throat. "Let's write." He gestured to the empty bench in the middle of the gallery where we could still see the painting from our seats.

Instead of pulling out my notebook for ideas on my essay, I grabbed my sketch pad. He watched as I took out a pencil and drew the silhouette of a woman. He didn't say anything, only watched for several minutes.

I was unsure how much time had gone by when he asked, "I never understood how you did that." He sounded like a child filled with wonderment. I popped my head up, partially forgetting that he was seated beside me.

"Draw?"

He shook his head, trying to reword his question. "Yes, but no. How do you come up with so many designs?"

It wasn't the first time I had been asked that question, but it had gotten harder to answer. "Actually, I've been struggling to come up with anything for a while. It's like I've been drained of all creativity and now all that's left are numerous quilts made of pieces of past projects. I haven't created anything original that I love in a while."

"The Hepburn films don't work anymore?" he asked casually, but it felt *anything but* casual. How did he remember that I used to rewatch Audrey Hepburn films when I needed inspiration? This was the same person who forgot his locker combination every day, and it *never* changed, but he somehow remembered this.

I used to turn to Hepburn films the way a 9-5 real estate agent turned to *Million Dollar Listing*. Her movies were filled with dated fashion trends, but they were made by classic designers that used elements of fashion that were timeless. It made my heart tremor.

"Not as well as they used too. I've bled every idea out of Audrey Hepburn's discography. My heart still stops, though, during the scenes where she walks into a crowd with a breathtaking dress on and everyone turns and watches. *Those* were the best scenes, the ones with a gala or ball."

"Have you ever been to one?"

"A gala? God no," I laughed.

"I wasn't going to say anything, because I didn't want you to feel like you had to say yes, because I know you'd feel like you needed to say yes, and I know how busy you are and—"

"Levi, spit it out," I laughed with eagerness.

"There's a gala, next week, at the Plaza to celebrate Sarah's engagement. Jeff's father set it up."

"Oh. That's awfully nice of him."

His Worried Older Brother Look appeared in the lines in his forehead. "It's a political thing; his father is running for District Attorney. Something about publicizing the wedding will show a 'strong family front.'"

"A *fancy* gala then, that's fun. If you're trying to rope me into stealing a suit for you from my school, then you owe me a lot more than strawberry shortcake." I narrowed my eyes in the way I knew would make him laugh.

A shot of laughter left his lips. It was so loud in contrast to the quiet museum that I gripped his arm, shushing him. It didn't help that I was also laughing.

His laugh settled. "Be my plus-one, come with me."

My heart shuddered. That was the worst possible idea for how I should spend my Saturday. I should be pulling a mini skirt over my ass to go out to a bar and get plastered like most college students—not go out with my high school best friend.

"Will Bella be there?" If I was going to go to this gala, then it would be for this deal, and this deal only, in order to get a grip on my sanity. I couldn't convince myself that this was him asking me to be his date.

"She will," he responded. The furrow of his brows made me realize he was going to ask why so I opened my mouth.

"Sounds like the perfect place to convince her that you're in a committed relationship then."

16

I think I'm falling

"Yes, Thursday works," I responded over the phone.

"Have you thought more about my idea?" Ethan asked on the other side of the line.

With my phone wedged between my ear and shoulder, I collected my things around Daisy's, knowing that Levi was going to be here any second.

"It just doesn't feel right." I had thought more over Ethan's idea to include Mom's maiden name in my grad applications and essay. But all I could hear was Levi's reassurance in the back of my head that I could get in with my work.

Levi walked in as Ethan responded, but his words became background noise. Levi smiled this brilliant smile as he walked in, catching my attention. He had a different pair of glasses on today—wire frames and slightly circular. They held up a curl that was brushing his forehead. A dark hoodie complemented his denim jacket and black jeans. If I didn't know him, I'd think he played in a band.

"Daniella? Did you hear what I said?" Ethan asked. I definitely did not just hear what he said because I was too focused

Liana Cincotti

on the model of a man that just walked in the door as if he was shirtless and pouring water over his chest.

"Yes, yes, sorry!" I held up my hand to Levi to give me a second. Rearranging the phone on my shoulder, I locked up the cash register, turned off the lights, confirmed that the floral fridges were plugged in, and grabbed my bags. "Could you repeat that, I think you cut out," I told Ethan.

Levi attempted to take the bags off my shoulders as we left the store, but I pulled them back like a game of tug-a-war.

Give me the bags, he mouthed, trying to be quiet over my call as I locked the door to the flower shop.

I pulled the phone away from my ear, leaning towards him. *"I can do it,"* I whispered back with determination.

"Dani, is someone there?" Ethan asked with even more confusion. *Crap.* I looked up at Levi in panic, but he was staring at my phone, offended.

"Um—no, no, sorry! I'm just ... ringing up a customer!"

I wouldn't be so stressed about where Ethan thought I was if it weren't for the fact that I had canceled our advisor appointment to spend the day with Levi. He currently thought I canceled because I had to work.

I did have to work, just not during the time of our meeting ... I practically had to beg for this call with him so there was no way he could know that I lied.

I shifted the phone away from my mouth and shouted across the street, "Enjoy the petunias, Marjorie!"

Levi burst out with laughter at my performance. He shoved a hand over his mouth, but it wasn't enough to hide his wondrous smile. I whacked my hand against his shoulder to be quiet before he blew my cover.

He used it as his opportunity to pull the bags off my arms, knowing I couldn't argue, and put them in the car. One eye roll later and I followed him into the car.

Ethan sighed. "Daniella, I don't just say yes to anyone for a meeting over the phone, you know how packed my schedule is." The use of my full name gave me flashbacks to high school. Embarrassment filled my throat. "Why don't we just have this conversation at my place tomorrow, that way there's no interruptions."

Guilt lingered in my sternum for canceling on him when he'd dedicated so much time to helping me. But my schedule was filled this week trying to finish my gowns and Levi's suit. Finding time for another meeting would mean another all-nighter to finish my last two dresses. It wasn't that I didn't trust him either—I wouldn't be having this conversation with him if I thought he was secretly a murderer—I just didn't have the time.

"I know, I feel terrible, I apologize. What about Thursday? I'll be on campus all day," I said with hope.

He audibly sighed, again. I hated this; I hated being an inconvenience. "Don't think that I just do this for anyone, because I won't offer this favor again, even for you." His words were stern, but it sounded like he was smiling. I let my shoulders sag with relief.

"You have *no idea* how much I appreciate it."

"My office, 7 p.m." And the call cut. Dropping my phone into my lap, I leaned into the seat and closed my eyes. Talking to people was so draining, but over the phone, it was even worse.

A phone call with Ethan was often worse because he rushed

through conversations like he was timing himself, never giving me a chance to prepare my responses.

"You're going to be coming home late?" Levi asked, sparing me a quick glance before turning his gaze back to the road.

"Not too late, I should be done around eight."

Another glance towards me but accompanied by a furrowed brow. "That's late."

"Not as late as previous instances." I expected a humorous eyeroll or a laugh, but instead, silence. His silence was never a punishment though, it was just his way of thinking things over. He used to do it in high school when the teacher called on him for an answer or his sisters asked logical, complex questions, like *why did dogs exist?*

But his mother's brownstone townhouse came into view before anything more could be said. Now it was time to pretend. Hold hands, smile, look at one another lovingly.

I grabbed my purse from the floor of the car when he came around to open my door. "Thank you."

He nodded, took my hand, and led us up the stairs. My hand was stoic in his, trying not to move or else every part of his skin would be embedded in my brain. But when he knocked on the door, turning to look at me and silently check if I was alright, I clutched onto his fingers, trying to remember the feeling of his hand before I had to let go.

Bella was sitting at the other end of the table and had been running her eyes across Levi's body like she was undressing him for the past twenty minutes.

I couldn't blame her—I spent four years enamored by his presence, let alone his appearance—but Jesus, I was *right here*. This was more painful than the time I stained the wedding dress Mom designed the day before it was photographed for the cover of *Vogue*. It was as if I wasn't sitting right beside him, our hands interlocked on the table for everyone to see.

Pretending, pretending, pretending.

I hadn't stopped repeating it since his hand caressed mine. It sounded like a hospital monitor in my head on repeat, but the sound went up an octave when the pad of his thumb rubbed my index knuckle. I think I jumped slightly, but everyone seemed too wrapped up in wedding conversation to notice.

"How was The Met today?" Sarah asked. I had a mouth full of pasta in my mouth, so I turned to Levi at my right to answer.

"Busier than usual for a Sunday morning," he responded.

"That's one of the things I miss most about the city, there's always people around," she emphasized.

"You could always move back."

Sarah rolled her eyes. "I rather not live with three roommates in order to afford it."

I couldn't tell if she was referring to her mother, Rhea, and Claire, or the fact that Levi lived with three roommates. But either way, she wasn't wrong. A closet-size apartment with a monthly rent the price of a car down payment wasn't exactly ideal for newlyweds.

He didn't look up at her when she responded, dropping the conversation altogether.

Sarah and Jeff moved back to the city just to prepare for the wedding, but Levi had explained to me that they had been living in Vermont the past two years. That was the only time we had talked about it, and I could tell he had no interest in talking about it further.

Trying to change the subject, I asked, "Are you saying you *don't* want to move in with Levi and his roommates? I'm sure they'd make room for you in the cabinets."

Sarah laughed, earning me a shooting glance from Bella down the table. "Have you *seen* their apartment? There wouldn't be room for me in the cabinets!"

"The cabinets are not that bad!" he defended himself with a laugh.

"You need to move out of there, they live like pigs. You could always move to Vermont, you know."

"I'm not interested in leaving New York, we've talked about this."

"Have you considered moving in together?" she asked. Everyone at the table went silent, forcing me to look up from my plate to see that "you" meant me and Levi …

Oh my. There wasn't a lie my mind could come up with in a seven mile radius.

I couldn't answer questions about our fake relationship, let alone our fake future! Obviously, no one at this table knew that because they thought we were childhood friends to lovers, when in reality, we were just two adults who had a past friendship that was presently filled with awkward moments and a one-sided crush.

"We haven't even graduated yet," he replied, shaking his head in a dismissive way.

"So," she said, shrugging her shoulders, "you guys have known each other for years. You're perfect together!"

"You guys are going to move in together?!" Claire shouted from the end of the table, obviously only just joining the conversation. Her toothy grin was wide as she leaned over the table with joy.

"Does that mean you're going to get married and have babies!" Rhea screamed.

"Um"—*cough*—"I"—*cough, cough, cough. I think I'm choking.* Probably the most convenient time to drop dead.

"Levi and Dani sitting in a tree! K-I-S-S-I-N-G!" Rhea shouted.

"Kiss! Kiss! Kiss!" Claire began chanting. I looked to Levi for clarity, but Trish caught my eye. She was smiling with pure joy; something I rarely ever saw when I had met her.

And he was noticing the same thing, gazing at her with equal surprise.

When I had met her eight years ago, she wore a sad smile and tired eyes, walking in late from work before climbing into bed. That was life after her husband died. Seeing a genuine smile from her was like spotting a hummingbird in your garden—wondrous and rare.

I was happy to hear that her career in real estate had been successful. So successful that they moved to the city. But there was still a lingering sadness that rested in her posture and the creases of her eyes.

My heart swelled with guilt, and I couldn't suppress it. She was happy because Levi and I were together. How was she going to feel when I stopped coming over with no explanation?

Trish began chanting with Rhea and Claire, causing the entire table to join in. *The entire table.* I think I even heard Grandma

Coldwell chanting.

On my right, Levi didn't look nearly as panicked, but instead curious, as if he was actually thinking about kissing me. His eyes were focused on my face with a quiet clarity, and his head was tilted down at the perfect angle.

My mind was like a radio with a broken nob; nothing changed no matter how much energy I put into pushing down my loud thoughts.

This couldn't be happening.

17

I'd be lying if I said I never thought about where my hands would take me across your body

My thoughts were coming out quicker than the end credits of a film: I couldn't kiss Levi; I couldn't have the first time we kissed be in front of everyone; I couldn't let him kiss me when he *didn't even have feelings for me.* That was the equivalent of getting addicted to a drug that wasn't prescribed to you in the first place.

I'd pay millions to know what he was thinking as he stared back at me. His gaze was so heavy that it pushed mine away, right towards the glass of wine in front of me.

My next movement was so impulsive that I was thankful I didn't give myself time to think through it.

"I'm so sorry!" I gasped.

Levi jumped out of his seat, his chair screeching against the hardwood. He whipped his head up at me in surprise before an audible light bulb went on above his head. A whimsical smile grew on his face, despite the glass of wine I just purposely spilled onto his shirt. His reaction made me burst out with laughter, while everyone else around the table was muttering their concerns or covering their gasps.

Between the look of surprise on his face and the way the wine managed to only hit his white shirt; I couldn't keep in the giggles. And the way he looked at me ... It felt like I had my best friend back by the look of awe on his face as I laughed with joy. The two of us were in our discrete bubble of understanding.

"I think that's going to stain," I commented.

He scoffed and grabbed my hand, swiftly pulling me away from the table. "Oh, you're helping me."

I shrieked as he tugged me out of the chair, presumably pulling me towards the bathroom. My laughter began dying down as my brain digested the feeling of his hand in mine, and the fact that we were about to be in the—

He opened the bathroom door, pulled us in, and shut it behind us.

"You punk, I liked this shirt!" he shouted, joy evident in the way his hair was disheveled.

He waved a hand at his white shirt; it was soaked with swirls of red wine, as if his heart had been cut open.

"What did you want me to do?" I leaned against the bathroom door catching my breath. Thinking on the spot wasn't my best skill, but I was patting myself on the back for this one.

He rolled his eyes in amusement. He closed the toilet seat, sat down on it, leaned back, and spread his legs, unbuttoning his shirt.

Oh my *lord*. I pressed my hips hard against the bathroom door like it was going to keep me from falling. I observed how his long fingers flexed around the buttons, undoing one at a time, staring at each one with precision. One, two, three buttons undone.

Wow, the ceiling looked really nice, did they repaint it

recently?

"Would kissing me be that bad?" His voice sounded husky with his face tilted down.

I rushed through an awkward laugh, still staring upwards. "That is not what I signed up for."

"That's not what someone else told me."

My head jolted.

He laughed at my reaction. "Calm down, calm down. One of the bridesmaids told me what you and Gabe talked about the other night over the phone."

What Gabe and I talked about? What did Gabe and I—*oh my god*. When Gabe had me leave my purse and he brought up *the thing with my tongue* story … My face fell as embarrassment filled my gut. "You're joking," I stated mortifyingly.

He registered my embarrassment and softened his voice. "Delaine told me when she was drunk the other night with Sarah; said she was really impressed by the details of our *intimacy*," he air-quoted. "It made my week." He laughed.

The next noise that came out of my mouth resembled a dying cat. I shielded my face. "I'm going to kill Gabe," I announced, but it sounded more like *hmgoingtokillGabe* because my hands were pressed against my face. "I'm absolutely mortified and I'm going to need you to leave the premises so I can die in peace."

"Hey." His voice got louder.

I shifted a finger away from my eye to find out why, and was greeted by him standing up, with his shirt half-unbuttoned, coming closer to me. I quickly covered my eyes again. I shouldn't see this.

"You never have any reason to be embarrassed with me. Best

friends, remember? Now let me see your face."

Light reentered my vision as he nudged one of my fingers out of the way, slowly peeling each one off my face.

A new hospital monitor tune kicked on in my brain: *we are friends, we are friends, we are friends.*

"Hi," I whispered once all my fingers were pushed off my eyelids. Still absolutely humiliated, I tried my best to push mine and Gabe's sexual conversation about Levi from my head as he looked back at me, partially shirtless.

"Hi," he whispered back. His eyes were doing that seducing, charming thing where they were narrowed in on my face and his lips were parted. If I tore my gaze down even a few inches, I'd see the muscles in his chest that hid beneath the cotton of his shirt.

"Hi," I repeated.

"Now, what's the tongue thing?"

I made a sound that resembled both a broken sewing machine and a grunt at the same time. I shoved his shoulder backward. "You *suck.*"

He laughed at the push, sitting back on the toilet seat to finish unbuttoning his shirt. A blush was tattooed to my cheekbones.

After finishing, he stood back up, letting the shirt slide off his shoulders and down his arms. Without moving my head, I directed my eyes back to the ceiling. The last thing I needed was an image of him fully shirtless existing in my brain forever.

"For your information, it's an inside joke, that I will never tell you now." The sound of his laugh bounced off the tile walls as he turned the sink on, running the shirt under the water.

"Oh, come on! I want to be part of the inside joke."

"Not happening."

"What do I have to do? You want me to get on my knees and beg? I'll do it." My face flamed—*keep your eyes on the ceiling, keep your eyes on the ceiling, you will not look at this man shirtless as he says the words* beg *and* knees. He continued, "I'll—"

"I'm taking it to the grave with me, Vi!"

My words cut through the air leaving us both silent. As I looked at him for the first time, I realized what I had just said.

He was looking at me like he had seen a ghost, and that's exactly what it felt like—a ghost. Anytime we got a glimpse of who we used to be together, it was like the ghost of our past entered the room and reminded us that there were four years of time separating us for a reason.

We weren't Vi and Daisy anymore. We'd never be.

"Can I ask you something?" he asked.

"Always." I listened to him turn off the sink, wring out the shirt, and open the linen closet to my right. I caught the flash of material out of the corner of my eye and watched as he finished pulling a shirt over his head, sitting back down.

He was quiet for a moment, evidently thinking over his question, maneuvering his two rings around his fingers. Sliding one ring up and over his knuckle, and moving it onto the next finger, doing the same with his second ring; the pair moved in synchronization the way a figure skaters danced with one another.

He finally lifted his head up to look at me. "Are you interested in Ethan?"

"How so?"

"Are you interested in him romantically?" His question was clear, but I still struggled to piece the relevance of his question together, because what did Ethan have to do with any of this?

"No. Why would you think that?"

"The way you both sounded on the phone. It sounds like his opinion matters a lot to you."

"Well, of course it does, he's my advisor. He has experience in the field I want to work in. But that doesn't mean—"

"That he's interested in you?"

I stood there dumbfounded. Was this his protective brother instinct or his concern for our fake relationship being tattered?

I shook my head, laughing in disbelief. "Ethan's not interested in me."

"He asked you to go to his place, Daniella," he stressed. The use of my full name made me jump—he was serious.

"That was the first time that's happened."

"It'd better be," he emphasized. His Older Brother Look was back in place.

"Levi, that's how Ethan is; he's friendly."

"It's not his *job* to be friendly. Has he always been like this?"

"Oh my gosh, Levi, *no*. He asked me out *once*—"

He stood up from his seat like a lit spark. "He *what*?"

Shit. I rushed to get the words out. "It was before he was my advisor—"

"Dani, *that doesn't matter*. I've only been working in a teaching position for a few months, and I still know how wrong that is," he stated, emphasizing his words with his hands and leaning down to meet my gaze. "I *swear to God* if he ever tried to touch you—"

"No! No, that's never happened!"

"Was he working at the college when this happened?"

I cringed. "Well, yes—"

He scoffed, looking up at the ceiling and running a hand

through his hair, tugging on the strands. Anger was radiating off of his skin, yet I still couldn't help to notice the way his muscles tensed and how absolutely *attractive* it was. "Jesus. You need another advisor, right now."

"Oh no no no." I shook my head. "He's the best one there is."

"That's exactly the problem. He knows you need him."

"I don't need him; I just need his help." I appreciated how Levi always cared, like no time had passed between the two of us. But I hated when he acted like this—*I hated it*—when he thought he had a say in which men got to like me and who should find me attractive.

I was twenty-two years old and graduating from college in just a few weeks; I was an adult. I didn't need him treating me like another sister out of pity.

"Exactly! I heard the way he spoke to you over the phone."

My own frustration began to grow the more he rebutted what I said. This was *ridiculous*.

"Is this why you were being weird in the car? Why you're acting like my brother?" I shot back.

But the second the words were out, I wanted to pull them back in. My mouth was trying to catch breaths I couldn't hold. I didn't know what to say.

He looked at me like I'd slapped him in the face, and my body was shivering with anger as if I had done just that.

"Well, I'm sorry if you think I'm acting like your brother, but that's been my job for the past ten years without any choice, so it isn't exactly easy to not interject when I don't think you're being careful. I care about your safety and well-being and need to know that you're okay at all times. So, if I don't think you're safe, I'm not going to be quiet about it for one goddamn second."

I was completely gutted when he finished talking. His chest was rising and falling. You'd expect anger in his tone based on his words, but all that lingered was sadness. He looked as defeated as I felt regret. I reached forward to apologize but his exhale cut me off.

"If you're not going to drop him as your advisor, then I'm picking you up after your meetings with him."

Oh. "That's not necessary."

"Maybe you don't think so, but for my sanity it is. Now let's go back out there before Rhea thinks we're actually making babies."

18

My heart was so full of our memories that it painted
my body like a scrapbook

"I royally screwed up, guys."

"Yes, that's obvious."

"Gabe!" I shouted over the phone, mimicking the tone of a child.

"Well, Dani, you told the boy he's acting like your brother when he's been forced into a father role for the entirety of his life because of his dad's death," Jia exclaimed. "Your words, not mine," she added quickly.

"Agh, why did I open my mouth?" My hair clip snagged on strands of my hair as I pulled it out in frustration, redoing it.

Sitting face down over my sewing machine, trying to finish the last of my dresses while my hair got stuck in my mouth, wasn't the most convenient scenario. I'd called Gabe and Jia in desperate need of social interaction, putting my phone on speaker while I continued to work on the pleats.

I would've called them sooner, but when Levi dropped me off last night, I just wanted the comfort of my bed, a blueberry milk candle, and to send an email to Dad in peace.

"Because you need to voice how you're feeling or else it'll all build up, babe," Gabe reassured me. "Why don't you just apologize?"

"Because I'm beyond embarrassed," I groaned.

"What did you usually do when you guys fought in high school?" Jia asked.

I almost ran my finger under the moving needle. "Jia, you're a genius! I've got to go, I'll text you!" Hanging up before I could forget, I started writing the letter.

When Levi and I fought in high school over me not showing up at his sixteenth birthday, I wrote him a letter. I knew how much he loved the way words strung together into a sentence could sound like a song without the music. And he knew I lacked the ability to form coherent thoughts, so if I took the time to write him a letter, then he'd know I was serious.

I wrote him a three-page letter explaining that when I was half up the walkway to his house for his party, one of the guys made a comment on my clothes and body, laughed, and then walked into the house. It only took me thirty seconds to process his words, another two for the tears and shaking to start, and then sixty for me to run down the street back to my house. Tears painted my face like excess make up that refused to come off. Mom and Mandy—who had been living with us for a year since Dad died—rushed to me with glossy eyes.

I didn't tell Levi what the kid had said or which kid it was—*Brad Harris, you suck*—but that it was enough for me to feel embarrassed and leave. I definitely didn't want to see him then, with puffy eyes, and apparently, prude clothes. So, I walked back to my house with his present in my arms.

That was the first time I'd ever told him something like that.

I was always nervous that if I shared the unkind words people threw at me, then that was all they'd associate me with. That they'd begin to notice that my skin *was* too blemished, or that the clothes I made *were* too cliché, or that I *did* dress like a seventy-year-old woman who'd given up on life. If I were to tell them what others said, then that's all they'd see.

So, I never told anyone when I was criticized or mocked. Those memories became skeletons in my closet on every date and every interview and every first impression, knocking on my door to remind me of my flaws. Keeping them in was a protective instinct.

I had dropped off the letter the next day when he had sent me a text over how upset he was that I hadn't shown up.

He showed up that night teary eyed at my front door, pulling me into a hug, telling me how sorry he was for getting upset. In which I apologized for not telling him what'd happened in the first place.

He, of course, told me to stop apologizing.

Then started our letter exchange.

When my phone began ringing Wednesday night while sitting in the kitchen with Mom and Mandy, I froze up. Flipping the phone over, I saw his name.

"One second," I said, leaving the kitchen island, taking my phone with me. Exhaling, I clicked answer. "Hey."

"Hey." He sounded tired.

A moment of silence passed before I pleaded, "I'm sorry, Levi.

So sorry."

He exhaled with what sounded like relief. "Dani, I know, it's alright."

"It isn't though. I am so sorry, I was overreacting. I was——"

"Dani, it's alright, it's alright. No more apologizing. I think you wrote 'I'm sorry' twelve times in this letter already."

"Twelve times too few."

"Twelve times too many. You were right the other day though; I overstepped, and I don't have the right. I'm sorry too. But I did enjoy the letter. The strawberry parchment paper was cute."

I shrugged my shoulders in relief. "I don't use that paper on just anyone."

I could hear his smile on the other side of the line. "Daniella Maria, are you saying I'm special?"

"The specialest," I said, making up my own word.

He laughed. "As long as you think so."

"Friends?" I asked.

"Best friends."

The happiness that flooded my chest was enough for me to ignore the lingering crack in my heart. But it wasn't enough for me to ignore how he held onto the pieces that were missing.

19

She lives in between the pinks and yellows of the world, where a beautiful color is unknown to others

Filling out applications for master's programs had driven me to excessive peanut butter eating. I hadn't stooped that low since my last bad date a year ago when this guy tried to tell me that the idea of women in positions of power was ridiculous because they were too emotional. That should've been my villain origin story but instead I cried on the couch with a tub of peanut butter in my arms like I was cradling a baby, watching Audrey Hepburn's *Sabrina*. Mandy said I could've gotten the words, "I'll never find a boyfriend," stitched onto a pillow because of how much I said them.

And to say that today's meeting with Ethan about my applications didn't go well was an understatement.

For my essay to Lazaro, I'd written about the first fashion show I went to freshman year and how it inspired by major. After emailing him the paper this afternoon, I'd come to his office around 7 p.m. for his feedback.

His office was impressive in size because it was the same as some of the professors here that were on tenure. An oak desk, a few bookcases, and numerous photographs of runway shows, editorial photos from fashion magazines, and him with celebrities dressed in his work, hung on the walls like a gallery. He looked up from his desk as I opened the door, his blonde hair and freckled nose looking up from his laptop.

"Have a seat," he said, skipping any greetings. It wasn't the response I was expecting, but I sat down, with a smile nonetheless, across from him. "I read your paper," he continued with no emotion. The unimpressed look on his face triggered a familiar emotion of queasiness in my stomach. I didn't think the paper was perfect by any means, but I also didn't think it was necessarily *bad*.

He pushed himself up in his seat, clasping his hands together on his desk. "I read the paper. It wasn't bad." A genuine smile grew on my face. "But," I retracted my smile instantly, feeling like an idiot, "it lacked emotion and sounded immature. Lazaro is going to think that you chose this career on a whim, whereas the rest of these students have been working for this since middle school. You need to sound aspirational and decisive—Lazaro doesn't want a dream; they want a hard worker."

Tears began pricking my eyes at the word *immature*. By the time he was done speaking, I was digging my nails into my thigh, trying to keep myself from falling apart in his office.

Even just the way he phrased the sentence made it sound like I wasn't a hard worker.

This was the fourth essay I'd written for Lazaro *alone*, and yet it still wasn't good enough. I'd submitted the rest of my applications last week—even the Paris program.

I briefly said my thanks, repeated that I'd work on it again (for the fifth time), stood up, and escaped the room.

Nudging my long sleeves down with my thumbs, I brushed the spilling tears from my eyes and moved into one of the empty classrooms.

Despite the air outside being that ideal temperature that only occurred when the sun was halfway set, I waited. I also didn't feel like crying in public or being kidnapped; this night was bad enough already.

Only ten minutes had passed since the meeting, and I'd spent half of them trying to suck the tears back in and the other half trying to figure out what I was going to do about this paper.

When the door clicked behind me, I expected to see a student, but instead Ethan walked in, making me jump. I rushed to blot my eyes, praying that they didn't look as puffy as they felt.

He shut the door behind him and walked towards my table. The tension in his forehead consisted of three lines, while his eyebrows were directed in a sad gaze; completely different from the emotionless stare I'd received ten minutes ago.

My body was riddled with anxiety as he walked into the room and perched onto the table I was seated behind.

Was he going to tell me to give up on Lazaro? To not even apply? It was the only the guess I could come up with as he continued to look at me with pity.

"I apologize for what I said in terms of your paper, that was harsh," he said.

"It's okay, you were just being honest, it's your job." It wasn't a difficult response because it was true. He didn't come to apologize because he was wrong, but because he didn't dish it out nicer.

"No, it was harsh, and unnecessary. I want to make it up to you." *Make it up to me?*

"Oh, no, don't worry." I tilted my head up because of the way he was seated on the table.

"What are you doing tonight?" The orderly whiteness of his teeth was intimidating. Everything about his appearance was neat and clean and professional. If he had a suit on rather than a T-shirt and thousand-dollar cargo pants, maybe I wouldn't be as intimidated. But something about him appearing like he didn't care, made me really care in a really stressed way. Even his cologne emanated luxury.

The longer I sat there with him perched a foot above me, the more it felt like I was leaning into him. Or maybe he was leaning towards me? I swore I could smell what brand of cologne he was wearing.

"Um—I—well not much but—"

"Perfect. Why don't you come over for dinner and we can go over how to work on your paper."

I sat there mortified. The paper was bad enough that he wanted to spend the rest of the night going over how to fix it? I took a quick glimpse at the vintage watch on my wrist—similar to the one on Levi's because we bought them together junior year—and found that the time was 7:49 p.m. The last thing I had left in my social battery for was dinner and a paper review.

"Yeah, I, I'm not sure—" The sound of the door swinging open cut me short and caused us both to turn. But Ethan didn't move from his spot above me. Turning to look at the door, I saw—

"Levi," I said in surprise, a familiar pang hitting my heart that only happened with him in the room.

His entering presence mimicked the nostalgia of coming home for Christmas; his name like mulled wine on my lips as I watched him enter. He smiled at me in response, the precise sweetness of his face and joy in his eyes warmed my chest. It felt like it was made for me. But he quickly darted his eyes to the figure above me, and any look of peace or happiness was wiped from his eyes.

Levi's words about Ethan and I being interested in one another rang in my ears. I moved out of my seat abruptly, trying to create distance between us. Maybe I could diminish this before anything could get awkward? But Ethan began speaking before I could move any further.

"Who are you?" he asked with slight annoyance.

It only took a few strides for Levi to reach me, placing his front behind mine, his hands latching onto my waist like he was about to pick me up at any moment and run. I swear stars blurred in the corners of my eyes at the feeling of his thumbs pressing into my hips. Similar to the way ex-boyfriends had held onto them when—

"Levi, Daniella's boyfriend." I could hear the tight smile in his tone. The sound of my name, his warm breath on the back of my head, and his hips against mine made me dizzy. Almost making me miss the fact that he referred to himself as *my boyfriend*.

We were pretending. This was pretending. He was pretending.

Ethan glanced at me with raised eyebrows, finally pushing himself off the desk to shake Levi's hand. I didn't miss how his hand made Ethan's look small in their combined grip.

Ethan smiled his casual smile when returning his hand to his pockets, standing like the cool jock rather than the esteemed advisor. "Boyfriend?" he asked, looking at me. "You never mentioned a boyfriend, Dani."

His grip on my hips flinched for a moment. "I didn't think it was appropriate," I said with my best attempt to be casual. But honestly, I was shaking with anticipation, nervous that Ethan was going to bring up the dinner conversation again. If he did, Levi was going to say something—I'd bet every vintage purse in my closet on it.

When the silence lingered, I spoke up. "Okay, well, we've got to go now …"

I scrambled to come up with an excuse.

"… and let Levi's cat out …"

I began moving backwards towards the door, forcing Levi with me. I tried to ignore the feeling of my body against his front as I pushed him. "She's on this really weird medication right now, so if we don't hurry, his apartment will be a total wreck." When my foot hit the threshold, I threw up my hand to wave. "Bye Ethan, see you tomorrow!"

Wooo. I exhaled, rushing us down the stairs and out of the building.

"Do I have a Schizophrenic cat?" Levi asked.

"I panicked!" I threw my hands in the air.

"Why were you panicked, though?" God, I hated this man for knowing me so well. He knew something was going on before he walked in but he wanted to hear me say it.

My mouth went dry. There was no way I was going to explain the conversation Ethan and I had, especially not after Levi and I just got through an argument over this. I didn't need him to have another excuse to treat me like a younger sister and—

"Oh, I almost forgot!" I shouted, my mouth cutting off my

train of thought. I ran back into the building and came out with Levi's freshly altered suit for the wedding. I handed him the garment bag like I was carrying a sleeping Snow White. "I wanted to steam it first with the fancy steamers in the building."

"Fancy steamers?" he raised an eyebrow, mimicking my humor and taking the garment bag.

"*Very* fancy." I smiled at his ability to match my energy. But as I looked up at him from the dark sidewalk, I realized that we never had plans to hang out tonight. "Why are you here?"

His posture straightened. "I told you, I didn't want you walking back to the train by yourself anymore." I opened my mouth to speak, but those weren't the words I was expecting to respond to. I didn't think he was serious, let alone that he would remember my meeting with Ethan tonight.

My thoughts came to an abrupt halt when he opened his mouth to speak again.

"Someone needs to make sure that your shoes are tied before getting on the train. Wouldn't want you to experience death by shoelace-stuck-in-moving-train." He finished with a closed smile and bright eyes, trying to suppress a giggle at his ridiculous joke.

We stood under the lamp light in the dark, crouched over in laughter and in silent agreement to not discuss why he was really here and how I wanted him here.

He just wants to make sure you're okay; friends do that, I told myself. Because that's what Levi and I were truly becoming again—friends. We were slowly falling back into our old rhythm.

Phone calls in between sewing binges; jokes about each other's appearances that became equivalent to hugs; visits from him at the flower shop that were no longer surprises but rather expected.

It was like the four years of distance between us were lessening by the day. All except this unspoken list of conversation topics that we'd been avoiding.

As we walked towards the train station, he turned to me. "How much do I owe you?" he asked, referring to the altered suit in his arms.

"Nothing," I shook my head briefly.

"Then I'll drop off an exuberant amount of money in your mailbox."

"Then I'll sing to the birds from my window like Cinderella and tell them to peck you when you arrive."

He returned the favor with a similar, unphased look. "Then I'll mail it to you," he said, narrowing his eyes in a competitive manner.

"I—"

"Say another word and it will all be sent in quarters."

Quarters? That made me giggle. He briefly glanced at me in surprise at my laughter, and I responded with a small smile. "You're funny."

"*You're* funny."

"But I don't want your money."

He rolled his eyes. "Now tell me what happened with Edgar."

"*Ethan*," I corrected him. Levi didn't give up, ugh. Instead of telling him everything that happened, I'd only shared how it started.

"He managed to tell me that the paper was horrible without explicitly saying the word horrible. So I'm back to square one with only three days left until the Lazaro application is due."

We stepped down the stairs of the subway in unison and

walked onto the train. He guided me in front of him, a hand on my arm as we got through the closing doors. I instinctively grabbed one of the subway poles with my inside elbow, but he ushered me to an empty seat, and stood in front of me, grabbing onto a handle above.

"Hmm," he hummed in thought. "This is going to sound cliché, but what you write should come from the heart. It should come easily so that the administrators can feel who you are through your words. You shouldn't write what you think they'll want, but what you know and feel."

"You should really think about teaching," I said inquisitively to the education major.

He laughed. "I'm flattered."

"Thank you for the advice, really. I'll try that this weekend."

He glanced at the ground, his soft lips forming a small pout that only appeared when he was nervous. It made the muscles in my hands ache with the struggle to keep them in my lap and not reach out to his. "Are you still around for this weekend?"

"This weekend?" I started filing through our conversations in my head. Did we have something this weekend?

"The ball?" he asked, hoping to prompt my recollection.

The ball, the ball, the ball … Oh. *Oh*. Oh no, for the engagement. And I never got a dress.

I know this is going to sound unbelievable as a designer in the making, but my options were slim. I didn't make my dresses with myself in mind. Those were often more revealing and made for people seven inches taller than me. Borrowing something of my mom's would probably be my most ideal option but it would also be my own worst nightmare. That woman *breathed* bodycon and

Liana Cincotti

boobs.

"Oh, yes, yes! Sorry, sorry, sorry. Of course, I'm still available." I smiled.

"You're sure?"

"Positive. We're getting you this job, Levi."

He nodded, his teeth puncturing his lip momentarily in lost thought. It made me wonder what he was keeping bottled up and whether it would spill out before this charade came to an end.

20

I've never heard anything more
terrifying

"I just want to wear my overalls," I huffed, landing on my bed, falling backwards into the pile of clothes I had tried on and ripped off.

"Why can't you wear one of those dresses?" Jia asked with confusion, referencing the few dresses on my bed that were handsewn before I entered college and actually fit me, which was codeword for: outdated and horrendous seam lines. And the nicer clothes I had worn to fashion shows and events weren't formal enough.

"I feel like Levi has this new image of me compared to High School Dani. High School Dani wore oversized clothes covered in fabric paint, and jeans that didn't fit her. College Dani is supposed to be sophisticated and feminine."

"What *is* femininity really?" Jia pondered—unhelpfully.

"You realize College Dani still dresses like High School Dani, right?" Gabe asked—also unhelpfully.

"I just want to look nice," I sighed, feeling incredibly defeated over my lack of effort to push myself out of my comfort zone since entering college. It'd just always been easier to design and dress others, than trying to do it for myself. I was the designer, the person behind the camera, not the model.

But since seeing Levi, and how he'd grown and the steps he'd taken towards his career, it made me feel like I'd been too comfortable. I hadn't *challenged* myself. I needed to challenge myself.

Pulling myself out of my pile of clothes, I stood up and exhaled a breath of new air. I was going to try something new. Turning to Gabe and Jia, I announced, "I'm asking my mom."

The two gasped and immediately sat up. "Linda?"

Jia shot up from the ground. "I'm coming for this, let's go."

We moved down the stairs and towards my mother in the kitchen. She was seated at the island with a coffee in her hand and a magazine in front of her, dressed in satin pajamas and slippers. When she turned to see us, her calm demeanor shifted to surprise. I opened my mouth to ask—

"Can we use your closet, Linda?" Jia looked at my mom with a pleading smile.

My mom looked between the three of us in suspicion before landing on me to ask, "Is this for Sarah's ball?"

I nodded my head.

All it took was one, "Of course," from my mother for Gabe and Jia to shoot back upstairs into her closet. I remained where I was to explain, but she brushed it off.

"Thank you, Mom." I moved around her coffee to hug her and was greeted by the softness of her pajamas, and the smell of her fruity perfume.

"Of course, sweetie." A kiss landed on the top of my head. "You had some mail come for you yesterday by the way."

She slid the pile of mail across the counter. Rummaging through them, my eye caught on one: *ESMOD Paris, France*. I held the envelope up for her to read.

"Open it!" she shouted impatiently.

"I'm getting there!" This wasn't a master's program on the top of my list, let alone on the list at all. I'd applied strictly because Ethan and my mom said it could be a great opportunity. But now that I was holding the envelope in my hands, trying to get it open … I think I wanted it to say *accepted*, and I had no idea why.

Tearing the top off and pulling the contents out, I rushed to find the answer.

Dear Ms. Maria, we are happy to congratulate you on your acceptance …

I whipped my head up and looked at my anxious mother across from me. "I got in."

"You got in?" She jumped forward, wrapping me in a hug, but quickly reared back. "Wait, are we happy we got in?"

"Yes, yes, of course! This… I–I just wasn't expecting this. I didn't know going to Paris would be an option."

"Well, it is now." She beamed with a large smile on her face.

"But this wasn't the plan," I responded, thinking out loud. This could change everything.

Her hand came up to hold my shoulder. "You can have new dreams, sweetheart. Plans change."

"Lazaro is still my dream."

She nodded, understanding. "Okay, let's wait on Lazaro's response then. But don't rule out this opportunity yet, promise me?"

I thought her question over. I said I wanted to challenge

Liana Cincotti

myself, and going to Paris would definitely achieve that. Let alone the fashion opportunities and inspiration that laid there.

"Alright," I promised.

"Go tell your friends and finish getting ready. I've heard quite a bit of buzz about tonight."

21

There was no such thing as a crowded room
where you stood

Jia and Gabe had a field day going through my mom's closet because she had a variety of clothes, accessories, and shoes from various designers over the past three decades of her career. Despite designing wedding dresses for a living, she was invited and dressed for numerous fashion shows and red carpets.

When I arrived upstairs, Jia and Gabe were arguing over whose choices were better. Until I directed them to her second … and third closet … In which they actually picked the same dress, shoved it into my arms, and forced me to try it on.

It was a simple, silk silhouette, in a rich blue that almost looked black, but was too deep to be called cobalt. It was floor length, fitted from chest to torso to hips, and unfortunately, hugged all areas of my butt as well. The low scoop neck made my eyes jump to my boobs, especially since it was held up by incredibly delicate, thin straps. My dark, short hair complimented the back of the dress—Jia's words, not mine—because it was completely backless.

I desperately wished my hair was long.

My arms were exposed, my neck was bare, my back was

naked. My bust, waist, and butt felt just as exposed because the thin fabric revealed every curve and angle of my body. The only reason I was in it right now, getting out of my cab, was because it was A-line, so the fabric loosened in a short train around my legs.

Stepping out of the cab, I placed one foot down onto the curb, determined not to fall. I was in five-inch stilettos that perfectly matched the dark blue of the dress.

Don't ask me how many times I'd considered how much closer in height I'd be to Levi in these. How much easier it would be to memorize every curve of his face and crease of his smile.

My wrists, fingers, and neck were draped in delicate silver jewelry that Mom wore to all her favorite red carpet events.

I questioned everything that Jia and Gabe dressed me in, but when I looked in the mirror before leaving, I felt quite lovely. My ears sparkled when I turned, and my short hair looked chic rather than messy. It was really … *exhilarating*.

The sun was just setting, and the city lights were slowly blinking on, mimicking the color of the sun. New York City was something I had only imagined living in in the romance films. And standing in front of the large venue, watching crowds of luxuriously dressed people walk in with dates, felt like one of those movie moments. Diamonds, silk, velvet, and cashmere swayed in an ocean of formal attire, up the stairs, and into the grand stone building.

I hadn't realized just how famous of a politician and businessman that Sarah's soon-to-be father-in-law was. But apparently, he was famous and rich enough to afford this venue and know this many well-dressed people.

There was an ample crowd in the lobby formed around the

back wall. Just enough people moved apart for me to see Jeff, Sarah, and an older gentleman that must've been Jeff's dad (they had the same nose and stance) who was responsible for this event. They were faced with journalists and photographers, presumably asking questions about the wedding.

My hand shot in the air to wave at Sarah like she was a celebrity. She looked like one, dressed in what appeared to be a white dress covered in diamonds. *How did you make a wedding dress top that?*

She spotted my hand, responding with one as equally frantic. It made me laugh.

I ran a bejeweled hand over my hair, making sure there were no pieces astray before heading for the stairs, following everyone else. I told Levi I would meet him here, because I honestly had no idea how long it would take me to get ready. Between Jia picking out my accessories, Gabe straightening my hair, and me trying to dust eyeshadow and lip gloss on—it was a process.

But I started to regret it because as I made it to the entrance, handing a tall man my invitation to be ushered in, I felt lost. The floor in front of me looked like glass and sparkled with the reflection of women's shoes and champagne. I refrained from accepting any alcohol, knowing how poorly that went senior year of high school.

The more I glanced around, the more I recognized faces: editors, photographers, designers, bloggers, online personalities. They all had something to do with the fashion or wedding industry. I understood now why my mom knew of the event— everyone in her industry that meant something was here.

My dress started to feel too tight and the air in the room began

Liana Cincotti

to feel too heavy. Pulling my phone from my purse, I reread Levi's message: *Bring your invitation, hand it to the man at the entrance, and then go up the stairs to the right. I'll be right there waiting for you.*

I made my way to the marble stairs, clutching onto the thick railing in order to keep from falling.

Every step I took, the thoughts in my mind multiplied. What if I ran into someone from Lazaro? What if Bella was at the top of the stairs talking to Levi? Would he even notice me when I got there?

Twelve steps left.

I wanted to imagine his jaw dropping, him stopping mid-conversation and walking in long strides towards me, grabbing the sides of my face and kissing me like he had dreamed of it since high school too. But that wasn't going to happen because that wasn't my story. I wasn't the one he fell in love with.

Nine steps.

The groups of people on the stairs became denser; the second floor was crowded. People turned as I tried to get by but followed my figure like there was something to be stared at longer. Did they see something on me that I didn't catch in the mirror?

Breathe, breathe. Two steps. But then I hit the top step—

"*Daisy.*" The slip of nostalgia from his voice jolted my head upward, where I found him across the room, wearing a dark black suit that made his hazel eyes sing and his brown hair burn with attraction. His lips parted as if he had more to say but had forgotten. My name wasn't loud when it left his lips; it was simply all I could hear because his voice was so in tune with my sleepless mind.

And he *saw me*; drank in every ounce of my essence and

presence, and it felt like I could breathe again.

It felt like the air he was breathing was mine, and him and I were one—the only ones in the room. He was several footsteps away, but there was an understanding in his stance. That despite our distance, he had been waiting for me the entire time, not wanting to miss me. And now that he had caught me, he wouldn't let his eyes leave me. I didn't want to get my hopes up, but it seemed as if awe was written in his eyes, with the way his head had this small tilt, and his tan skin held a blush.

I smiled with pure joy, and it seemed to wake him up. A surprised smile lifted on his face, and he waved this little flustered wave with his hand. Mid-wave, he stopped to run it through his thick hair, laughing at himself. It made me laugh with him. *Was he nervous?* He turned to the people beside him, whispered something short, in which they spared me a long glance, and he began walking over in strides.

I watched as he moved towards—

"Did you come alone?" Surprised, I found a man with a trimmed beard and suede suit in front of me. My disbelief must have been evident, because he laughed. "I'd love to buy you a—"

"She's with me," Levi interjected. Suddenly, a hand was on my exposed back, and I was being guided by Levi through the crowd. His breath hovered over my ear as he said, "I'm not with you for one second and men are already throwing themselves at you."

Goosebumps riddled my spine at the warmth of his breath and tone of his voice. My knees felt weak. With every person that we moved around through the crowd, his hand would grasp firmer onto the muscles of my back. His fingertips seemed to spill across my waist, just above where the curve of my underwear ran.

"You clean up nice," I said with a wink, making him laugh.

"You're not too bad yourself," he replied with a smirk. Though it was in a joking manner, it still warmed my heart.

"You definitely had a glow-up since Junior Prom."

"You're never going to let me live that down," he laughed, shaking his head.

I pinched his arm lightly and said, "Never." I cleared my throat for a moment, realizing that we were supposed to be a couple tonight and instead I was acting like a teenage friend. "You always look handsome, though, especially tonight."

He looked at me in surprise, caught off guard. It made me wonder if all the compliments I'd given him were only in my head.

"Thank you. But it's not anywhere close to how beautiful you are." I opened my mouth to argue but closed it at the sight of the ballroom.

The area looked like a greenhouse with its ceilings and walls made of windows. The darkness of the city swept into the room, the only source of light being a single chandelier. It was a dim and romantic space where you would take a mistress and twirl her around. That's what was happening now: twirling and dancing.

His hand left my back to take my hand and bring me into the room. The skin on my lower back felt more naked than before. I was one step from entering before someone else approached me, stopping Levi and I from moving any further.

"Dani!" I was encapsulated in a hug before I could see who was hugging me, but I knew that voice.

"Sandra! What are you doing here?" I asked, pulling away to look at my classmate and take in her glowing appearance.

"I'm interning as an editorial assistant for a wedding magazine now!" she shrieked.

"That's amazing, congratulations!"

"I know, thank you! It helps distract from those grad school jitters. Have you gotten any responses yet from your applications?"

I wanted to share the news of Paris but the reason for my appearance tonight stopped me. The entire point of our plan was so that Bella and her mom believed Levi wouldn't be up and leaving the city. If they found out his "girlfriend" had the option to move to Paris, they would never believe he'd stay here.

"No," I shook my head. "Not yet." I'd let her know another time.

"Umm, is that *the* Levi that showed up at class with your bag the other day?"

I smiled and turned my head to introduce Levi but found him talking to someone else.

My heart sank. She was gorgeous. Dark skin, curly hair, and a smile that would shine on cameras. My eyes were glued to them as they spoke. She brushed his arm, and he watched her every word. It was so completely Levi: to watch every word that left someone's mouth with complete intent. To pay attention to their emotions and the shape of their lips. It was just who he was.

But that didn't mean it didn't hurt to watch.

I exhaled in hopes to lessen the grip choking my heart as I refocused on Sandra. "Uh—yes, yes, it is. I think I just saw someone walk in. It was lovely seeing you." My feet had never moved faster in heels, pattering against the marble like a tap dancer, until—

"Daniella." The sound of my full name caught me off guard. I spun and saw Ethan.

22

How could you provide me air and suffocate me
at the same time?

"*Ethan*—hi," I replied, retaining my shock. He looked so sophisticated. His usual Californian beach look was cleaned up. His dirty blonde hair looked darker under the crystal lights, while his skin appeared sun kissed by freckles more than usual. I always imagined him in a suit like this; he had the face of a persuasive businessman that went out for drinks every night and signed contracts. Not the look of someone who wore designer T-shirts and taught students draping techniques.

"I think you're the most attractive girl here, it was impossible to miss you." He said it with complete confidence. Blood immediately rushed to my cheeks. His words were kind, but all I could think of were Levi's words in the back of my head: *It's not his job to be friendly.*

I brushed them away. He was just trying to be nice. "I didn't expect you to be here."

He hesitated momentarily before responding. "I was invited by a friend."

"Oh, where is she?" I forgot that staff members had dating

lives.

"It's not like that, just a work thing," he smiled. "Also, I was notified by ESMOD of your acceptance, that's incredible."

Oh. I forgot he would be notified about the status of my applications. "Thank you, it was a complete surprise."

"We should celebrate, not many people get to say they got into such a competitive program. It's impressive." He looked almost … impressed with me. He finished by clicking his tongue.

A small laugh rested on my tongue. Something about Ethan made me feel uneasy. I wasn't sure if it was his confidence (and lack thereof of mine) or his overwhelming experience in the industry (and lack thereof of mine). He made me feel young in a way that made me feel like I knew nothing, despite us only being a few years apart in age. My insecurities often did that on their own, so it was difficult to have them heightened around him.

"Thank you, Ethan, I really appreciate it. Maybe we can—"

"Hey, I couldn't find you." I jumped in surprise at the sound of Levi's voice and touch on my bare back. I watched as he registered who I was talking to, and then in seconds, witnessed as a silent fury swept over his face. *Holy shit.* This made it two times now that Levi had caught me and Ethan in close conversation.

The other half of me was frustrated, though. Why should I care if Levi saw us talking? Nothing was happening between us— me and Ethan, *or* me and Levi! Levi was busy talking to someone else anyways.

"Levi, right?" Ethan asked.

Levi nodded, rolling his tongue under his cheek, and tightening his jaw. Masculinity rolled off of him in the way he stood, sizing up Ethan. All areas of Ethan that were light, Levi's were dark. Dark suit, dark hair, dark gaze.

"Evan, right?" he asked with no shame. I almost choked. *What was he doing? This was a new level of the Worried Older Brother Look.*

Ethan looked bothered, scratching his chin in quick thought. "Ethan."

Without an apology, Levi said, "I need to steal my date away." And with that, he began walking away with my hand in his.

When we were far enough away from Ethan that he wouldn't hear my fuming tone, I stopped short. "Levi, *what* was that?" Tugging him back so that he'd stop moving.

"Exactly—what was that? Is this man following you?"

My jaw went slack. *He* was frustrated? "That's ridiculous, do you hear yourself? He works in this industry, of course he would be invited here."

"I just don't think he has good intentions."

"I don't care what you think, Vi! That's my advisor. I see him every single day, do you know how awkward that's going to be now? You don't get to be mad when you were busy talking to some other girl anyways." My shoulders were rising with every breath and my face felt hot with frustration and my hands were curling and uncurling into fists, itching to pull at the fabric on my dress.

I had no right to be upset at him for talking to someone. He was single. We weren't together. And even if we were, he could still *talk* to people. I didn't know why I was overreacting.

That was a lie. Of course, I knew why I was overreacting. Because tonight I was putting myself out there by showing up alone, wearing a dress that was as revealing as the things I wore as a toddler, just so that he would notice me.

But he had no right to be upset at me for being around

another man either.

I avoided his eyes, not wanting to overanalyze every one of his emotions. I started searching the room for a reason to leave the conversation.

It must've shown because his voice softened. "Daisy, wait—"

"Oh great. I see Bella." *Time to pretend*, I whispered under my breath. I immediately began walking away, expecting him to follow.

Frustration or confidence; it could've been a tad of both that raised the hair on my arms. I was moving with intention, and I was not about to question it because the look of surprise that spread over his face as I moved to the center of the room was priceless. Taking charge was at the bottom of my vocabulary, but I could pretend. I could use this frustration as feigned confidence for a moment.

Dancing scared the shit out of me. I loved to go dancing with friends after our club meetings, but that was different. That wasn't dancing in a gown with someone you used to be in love with while people watched.

But the high of my frustration hadn't worn off just yet, so I led him by the tips of my fingers to dance.

I had seen *Pride & Prejudice* enough times to know the hand placements.

Taking his hands, I placed one on my back and the other in my right palm. A shift in his gaze took place; his eyes were no longer wide with surprise but were resigned. He seemed stiff, almost.

Until he began to lead.

He pulled me in close, his right hand holding onto my lower

back with determination. Our conjoined hands remained close to our bodies as he moved us back and forth. His jaw rested above my own, his cheek against mine. There was no space between us with my chest pressed against his, and my legs finding a space between his.

I couldn't focus on any of the footwork because we were *touching*. Our chests were pressed together like two books pushed by bookends. Our faces were only inches away, similar to the way children exchanged whispered secrets behind school. His hand was firm enough on my back that his two rings were etching their shape into my skin.

I never tried drama or theater in school, but I didn't need to fool anyone with my performance because this simply wasn't a performance. Every touch, every breath, every look he gave me made my heart slam against my rib cage. The way his thumb roamed my back with just short movements made my eyes roll back. It felt scandalous to do something so intimate in front of so many people.

There was no way he couldn't feel the tremor of my heartbeat against his chest.

"I was talking about you," he whispered suddenly.

"What?" I whispered, rearing my head back to look at him.

"The girl I was talking to earlier—while you were with Sandra and then Ethan. I was talking about you. She was a student in one of the classes I TA'ed. Apparently, she switched majors to study fashion. I was telling her about you."

My heart was pounding against the rock of reality I kept over it. Embarrassed was the best way to describe how I felt. Flattered was the second-best way to describe how I felt. And yet all I could suffice was an, "Oh."

He had been talking about me, and I had made an assumption and then *yelled at him* the way my eighth grade English teacher would. How was I supposed to form an apology that would be appropriate enough to encapsulate how much I messed up?

"I'm sorry." It wasn't me that apologized, though, it was Levi. I looked up at him in surprise as he continued to speak. "I didn't mean to abandon you like that. You were talking to a friend, and the student had just seen me and said hi and then I mentioned you and ... I got carried away."

From the curve of his lips to the pocket of stress between his brows, he looked wholeheartedly apologetic and genuine. As if *I*, of all people, was not going to accept his apology. I didn't even want to be mad at him for the way he spoke to Ethan, but he had crossed a line.

But trying to be upset at him as his hands remained on exposed areas of my body was impossible.

He looked conflicted as he glanced down at me.

In moments, he was releasing me to spin me, and then just as quickly, he was bringing me back in, pressing my back against his front. The way his hand tightened on the edges of my hips, and how easily they found a home on my waist; all other thoughts became lull in my mind because all I could think about were those hands.

I'd tried to never let my mind go there—to think about what Levi's hands could do below my waist. I wouldn't be able to function appropriately around him if I did. And the more I heard his shuddering breaths in my ear and felt his dominating grasp on my waist like he owned it—*it* was all I could think about.

"I think they're watching," I whispered, not feeling confident enough to speak at full volume, fearful that I'd possibly lost my voice from all this thought.

And, God, his response could have undone me right there.

"Let them watch," he whispered back.

I itched to turn my head just enough to see his face. I needed to know if this was having even a fraction of an effect on him that it was having on me.

Our feet followed each other slowly to the music. Every step we made together, I felt more confident in my next. I moved my hand up his shoulder to the collar of his jacket, and then to the back of his neck. I could only imagine all of the women that had put their hands there. I was getting a glimpse into something that wasn't mine.

"You look beautiful, Daniella." I almost tripped. Anytime I heard my full name from him, I knew he was serious. While he used *Dani* for every day, casual purposes, and then *Daisy* for … Well, the use of my middle name only appeared in rare moments now.

But it was all for show. The truths I thought I used to know were tearing at the seams.

"You don't need to say that. Bella can't hear you."

He stopped instantly, confusion and frustration passing over his face. "I—*No*." His eyes narrowed, aghast. "I would never say something like that to you for," he stumbled to find his words with such surprise, "for some performance. I mean it, you are beautiful. You always were."

My bones were humming with energy. "I'm sorry."

He shook his head and scoffed. "You need to stop apologizing for what you say." He took a breath. The only reason I was still standing was his hand on my back and his feet in between mine, grounding me. "I wanted to tell you that you looked beautiful because you are. I knew I wouldn't miss you when you walked in tonight because you're *you*. You're so physically enthralling, let alone when you speak. And when you speak, all of the light in the room comes from you. You're absolute sunshine and spring. I could watch you speak—"

"I need some air," I said tightly with the last stable breath I had before moving out of his grasp and away from the ballroom.

23

Intimacy was to be seen by you; free falling was to be touched by you

I wish I could've had those words etched into my heart and every pillow I owned. Painted them onto ceramic vases, sewed them into corset tops, frosted them onto blueberry cakes, and cut them out of chartreuse construction paper and glued them into my scrapbook.

I wish I could've.

If he were another person, maybe. Not someone who wasn't in love with me.

I couldn't listen to another charming, romantic word that came out of his mouth, and still remember the fact that he didn't love me. He found me beautiful and enthralling, but he didn't *love me*. That was why I'd left in the first place, senior year. I couldn't go through this friendship happy, only to be reminded that I wasn't beautiful *enough* to be loved by him.

The grip I had on the skirt of my dress was quivering as I exited the ballroom and moved down the stairs that I'd only walked up an hour or so ago.

What was I thinking coming here? What was I thinking doing

any of this? Jia was right; I was an idiot to believe something could come from pretending to be with Levi.

I shoved the front door open and inhaled the cool, spring air. Goosebumps formed on my bare arms and back, but it was a needed distraction from the filing cabinet of thoughts and insecurities moving through my mind.

Create a plan, make a next step in order to avoid a full wave of tears. "Taxi, call Jia and Gabe, order a pizza," I listed out loud to myself in hushed tone, like an athlete tired from a run.

Walking down the steps, a valet approached me, asking if I needed a taxi. I replied and smiled as he moved towards the street to get one's attention. One quickly pulled up to the sidewalk. The valet held the door open for me as I collected my dress and—

My next step was broken off by a familiar sound shouting behind me.

Levi.

I quickly stepped out of the cab, apologizing to the driver and the valet, meeting Levi halfway up the stairs.

He had these eyes that were so bright, a complete juxtaposition of his dark eyelashes; it was criminal. It made you want to confess all of your sins because his look was so angelic. Maybe he would grant you one glance if you told him your secrets.

He skipped the formalities and urgently asked, "What did I do? Was it something I said? Tell me, and I'll fix it." His eyes were urgent in his plea, but I felt defeated.

"There's nothing you can do. It's me," I exhaled. "It's me." I turned my head down, needing to look anywhere but his face. But looking down seemed to bring all of my stored away tears to the brims of my eyes.

When did I get so dramatic? It made me feel like I was fifteen all over again. All these emotions I didn't know existed were bubbling to the surface and fighting for my attention and my only outlet was the tears in my eyes.

When he placed a palm on my jaw, and lifted my face up, it brought me back to prom night. Where I was drunkenly sobbing in the hallway over not being able to find my date or my phone that had my romantic confession. Levi had come jogging down the hallway, crouching in front of me, tilting my head up, saying:

"Hey, hey, hey, no, no, no, don't cry. What'd I miss? What's wrong?"

Both of his large hands encapsulated the sides of my face now, catching thin tears.

I couldn't tell him I loved him, I couldn't. But he could identify my lies the way I could identify grief in a person. So, I sufficed for a pocketed truth that haunted me every day. That even haunted me tonight when I dressed in the most beautiful of dresses, but still couldn't help comparing myself to all the beautiful women around us.

"I'm not beautiful, Vi." My voice cracked, causing another tear to fall. It was the first time I had said that aloud in years. I had thought if I stopped saying it, then it would become less true. But all it did was make me lonelier in my insecurities.

His face fell, a storm of emotions passing in his eyes. He looked *broken*. "You don't think you're beautiful?" he asked honestly.

I imagined someone from afar painting a picture of this bittersweet moment for a sad, romance film poster. They'd paint roses around us on the border, but my ankles and knees would be pricked by thorns while he remained in the bed of the flowers. *The*

Lover and the Archer, they'd call it. The girl who kept falling in love, and the boy who could receive love from whomever he aimed his heart at.

I shrugged my shoulders. "I'm a little funny and have a few good sewing skills, but that's all," I tried to joke. But the tears and clotted weight in my voice remained gloomy.

"Are you insane?" he asked, his eyes darting around the spaces of my face for any mistruth.

"Mostly on Sundays but I try to keep it to a minimum during the work week."

He ignored my humor. "Everywhere we go, people are infatuated by you, looking at you and yearning to talk to you. I …" He paused for a long moment. "I am infatuated by you."

I craved to tell him that it was because of my flaws that people stared. I shook my head at his nonsense. His thumb wiped a tear from under my eye before it could fall any further.

I couldn't believe I was letting him see me like this.

He continued. "Every time I see you, I think about …"

I searched his face in wonder. I so badly wanted to peak into his mind.

When his eyes caught mine in what appeared to be clarity, my breath stopped in my throat, and then he … he pressed his lips against mine.

The city was a dark blanket around us, but right then, it felt like the whole world lit up.

I let myself melt against him, the way wine slid against a bottle, or how a burning candle's wax ran along its side. *That's* what it was, that's what it felt like—a candle softening from the heat of its flame.

His lips were softer, fuller than I had ever imagined. The way they took in my bottom lip as his hands moved from the sides of my face to the back of my head, touching every wave of my hair. It was slow and steady. *Was I dreaming?*

His thumb traced a path under my jaw in a commanding way, nudging my head up higher to kiss me deeper. I gasped, unsure how to process all of these feelings at once. *His lips, his hands, his chest against mine.* My lips and hands were slow to catch up to reality, but then our heads slightly shifted, and I was kissing him back, tasting him, allowing myself to divulge.

Pushing my hands into his soft hair, I pulled and wrapped my fingers around the curls I had dreamed of. I silently thanked my heels for being so high because I *needed* to be eye level with him for this. Needed to have full access to what his body had to offer at this height.

"*Daisy,*" he moaned in between our lips.

And then it hit me like a train, right then I realized, I was madly, deeply, *undeniably* in love with him. I loved him so much that my heart was pounding against my chest, trying to reach his to tell him.

Instead, I traced the outline of his body feeling desperate, *hungry* to touch every muscle under his suit. I tried to memorize every place his tongue brushed on my lip and the precise softness of them, but it felt like my feet were falling through the ground and my hands were holding onto him for dear life as if this moment was going to disappear.

Romantic playlists burned into CDs. Hearts embroidered into scarves. Soft kisses on foreheads. Dark theaters on rainy Friday nights. Dainty gold jewelry against soft skin. French poems written while drunk. Protective hands against your hips guiding you through crowds.

I felt all of it at once.

Every ounce of it was Levi consuming my attention and consciousness with his presence.

His skin was warmer than I had realized, while his lips were poetic as they left mine to make their way around my jaw. I think he may have actually been speaking in sonnets from the feeling of his lips against my collarbones. It gave me a second to breathe and think.

What did this kiss mean to him? I asked myself.

He cradled the back of my head while his other hand gripped my waist, his lips capturing all perimeters of my jaw. *Oh, god.* My train of thought was becoming alphabet soup; words and sentences falling apart to letters that were jumbled up in my head.

I was breathing so fast that I clung to his biceps to keep from falling under my weak knees.

"You intoxicate me, Daisy. The scent of flowers lingers on you everywhere you go, and I always want to follow," he murmured against my neck. *That.* I wanted to hear that every morning, day, night, daydream, and nightmare. I wanted him to say it to me in *French*.

That had to mean something. This had to mean something. I should tell him then, right? Tell him how I feel because he must feel the same way?

My thoughts became blurry as his lips came back to mine. I must have groaned because he laughed lightly. His young, childish laugh that made me physically giddy.

Mustering up every ounce of self-control, I pulled away. The man that looked back at me had red wine cheeks, full lips, tousled hair, and eyes brighter than the moon at midnight. He looked at me with concern, as if *I* was about to turn him down.

I placed my hands on his chest in reassurance. Pressing my eyes shut, I tried not to think about the last time I did this and how epically it'd failed. "I–I need to tell you something—"

"Dani!" I was cut off by Sandra running down the front stairs of the venue with a smile. She wrapped me in a hug the moment we were close enough. "Congratulations on ESMOD!"

Oh.

"Gabe just texted me; I can't believe you didn't tell me! Flippin' Paris, babe!" She pulled back from our hug, clutching my biceps in joy. "When will you leave?"

"Oh, I, I haven't made a decision yet on ESMOD."

"What? It's the Harvard of fashion! There's no other choice to make—crap, that's my boss calling, we'll talk later!" She smacked a kiss on my cheek, and finished descending the stairs, leaving me and Levi.

"You're moving to Paris?" he asked, shock seemed to etch itself into his forehead.

"I only found out about it today. It's not my top pick, though." He wasn't supposed to find out this way, no one was. I hadn't made a decision yet; I wasn't ready to make a decision yet.

He picked up one of my hands, running his fingers over my rings. His eyes were distant and reserved. "Well, that's amazing, congratulations." He gave me a small smile. "You should've told me sooner. Are you—" He stopped mid-sentence; his gaze now snagged on something behind me.

I turned instinctively to find … Bella. She stood far away,

watching us like a mourning ghost. She looked sad. But all I had room for in my heart right now was my own sadness.

She had been watching.

She watched Levi console me, tell me nice things, and then kiss me. Kiss my neck, touch my back, run his tongue across my bottom lip. Things a couple would do.

Pretending. He was pretending.

I was a pity to him. He felt bad for me. I was the stained, old dress that couldn't be rewashed any longer and got lost under the bed. She was silk, she was clean, she was summer—she was beautiful. I was tattered. I *am* tattered. I'd never be as beautiful.

My next movements became slow and robotic.

Leaning on the balls of my feet, I kissed him on the cheek.

"Good night."

Pulled my hand out of his grasp.

Walked down the stairs. Grabbed a taxi.

Held in the tears. Got out of the car.

Walked up my front steps. Sat down.

Cried. Called Gabe and Jia.

"It happened again."

24

My heart sagging like the stems of uncut

My prom dress, the color of green tea, was in a puddle around my feet in the Senior Prom venue corridor. Students I grew up with for four years were down the hall dancing, taking photos, and probably doing incredulous things that would remain forever engrained in this night. While mine would forever be pitiful.

"Hey, hey, hey, what's wrong, Daisy?"

My eyes opened as if on command at the sound of Levi's voice, watching him crouch down on the floor in front of me. His hands immediately cupped my face, tilting it up, forcing me to meet his eyes, where I found that his own face looked distressed. My heart pounded harder in my chest causing my face to heat up.

Could he see how my love for him was painted across my face, in the way that I looked at him? Could he tell from the way I shuddered when he touched me, that every fiber of my being was made to be touched by him?

Tears refused to reel themselves in. But when I registered the absolute devastation in his face, my heart refilled with the hope that he could feel the same way.

His hands refused to leave my face until I gave him an answer.

But the alcohol in my stomach was affecting every word that left my mouth and raced through my mind. I couldn't form a full sentence without hiccupping.

"Jeremiah." *Hiccup.* "I need him." Levi looked taken aback.

"Oh, okay, I can find him." He brushed one more of my tears away before standing up.

Another sob left my throat that immediately brought him back down to his knees in front of me. He brought my head to his shoulder and wrapped his arms around my trembling body. "Shh, shh, I'll get him, I'll be right back."

"He's not here." *Hiccup.* "A girl came up to me and said he left early." *With my phone and its entire romantic confessional contents.*

He pulled back. "He left you? He left you *at prom?*" He looked furious. The same fury I saw wash over him when Sarah, Claire, or Rhea returned home from school with tears in their eyes and a story about a boy. I didn't know how to explain that it wasn't like that without giving away my feelings for him. I didn't care that Jeremiah left early; I cared that he took my phone with him.

"I just really need him right now." When I looked up at him and saw sorrow in his eyes, the tears came again. The weight of my desire for him was pressing down on my clavicle, and it got heavier as I realized that it was getting less likely that Levi cared for me in a romantic way. But I couldn't endure the weight of my secret any longer.

I love him, I love him, I love him. "I love him," I voiced my inner monologue. I cried into his shoulder, too insecure to tell him to his face.

The hand that ran up and down my back paused.

Why wasn't he responding? Did he not hear me? I sighed.

My energy was running low from the vodka and crying. I just wanted to crawl into bed and email Dad. "I'm in love with you. I've always loved you." *Why wasn't he responding?* "I need Jere." I sobbed and hiccupped. He had my words, the words I wrote for Levi, to explain.

That's when the night became a crooked, silent film. Words were rushing out my mouth as quickly as my tears.

His body froze around my weak one. "We need to get you home. I'll run outside and pull up the car." He picked me up like a porcelain doll to stand up.

Did he not hear me? I loved him, *I'm in love with him.* And he had nothing to say? No response or explanation? My first reaction was to be angry and push back. To tell him that he couldn't just walk away from our conversation. But my habit was to sink into my insecurities. They pulled me back like puppet strings, telling me that I was wrong all along. He would never return these feelings. He came with another date for a reason. And now he was ignoring my comment so I could retain some sort of dignity by pretending it never happened.

But the part of me that was drunk was still cross.

"No," I reacted. "I don't want you to take me home." His eyes widened and he retreated just a step backwards like I had slapped him. I had created a line between the two of us that told him I wanted nothing to do with him. Maybe he thought it was because I was drunk. But he must've known deep down *why*.

He nodded, resigning. "I'll see if Nora can, then."

I crossed my arms, tears now dry. "No, I'll call Jeremiah. Go have a fun night." He knew I didn't have my phone to make a call. But he also knew that I was too stubborn to argue with.

"Fine. Text me when you make it home." And with that, he walked away, turning back to glance at me from down the hall. But I kept my head down.

I walked through the crowd like I imagined spirits did: unsteady and empty. I found Nora and asked to borrow her phone to make a call. I called my mom, of course, not Jeremiah. That would be a problem for tomorrow. She said she'd be there in five minutes at the front of the venue.

I returned Nora's phone with a brief thanks and made my way to the front of the building.

"*Levi.*"

My heart stopped. I whipped my head around, walking a few steps back to an adjacent hallway. Where I found Cora Messing kissing Levi. She moved her hands across every space of his skin, whispering his name, and touching every dark curl and wave of hair on his head. Levi's hands remained unmoving, stagnant on her hips.

When Audrey Hepburn said, "He doesn't even know I exist. I might as well be reaching for the moon," in *Sabrina,* I had never understood more until that moment. My throat tightened and opened just enough for me to breathe.

She was his date, after all, of course they could kiss. But this soon? This fast? After what I had confessed? I couldn't do this anymore. I couldn't hold onto the slow bleed of my heart or calm the tremor in my hands when he looked at me, knowing it meant everything to me and nothing to him.

There would be no *I'm home* text or call tomorrow. There would be no apology letter in the mail. There would be no more morning drives together or movie nights with the girls or trips to the thrift store or baking strawberry shortcakes or beach days or baseball games or, or, or … *any of it. I couldn't do any of it anymore.*

Losing our friendship meant losing a fraction of my heart that had been filled when Dad died. A piece that had been restored by him and his family. I didn't want to lose any of it, I never did. But I couldn't remain if it meant being on the sideline of his love life for the rest of mine. I was too much of a hopeless romantic for that. I'd rather be unhappy with a chance at love, than no chance at all.

But no one tells you how much love feels like grief until you have your heart broken and realize you can't take any of it back.

25

'Moving on' was a broken record that I never had the strength to lift the needle off of

I cried so many tears that I could've filled enough champagne bottles to serve to every man that ever made me feel insecure. Tears for my broken heart, for putting myself out there, for the constant rejections I'd been enduring in my career, and plentiful for Dad. I missed him so much. Nights like these, I forgot for a split moment that when I ran home, sadness weighing me down, that he wouldn't be on the other side of the door to hug me. I wouldn't be able to wrap my arms around his old flannel and breathe in the smell of the cologne my mom bought him since the day they started dating.

Gabe and Jia found me on my doorstep in my mother's designer dress. They cradled me like a child before guiding me inside and onto the couch. Fortunately, my mom and Mandy were out tonight so I could be spared with relaying this story more times than I wanted to recall.

I kicked my heels off, blew my nose, and pulled the skirts up onto the couch with me. Gabe and Jia ran around the first floor like fairy godmothers, grabbing me various things: tissues, makeup wipes, and pizza. The gratitude I felt to have them in my life was so overwhelming during moments like these that I almost began crying again. They were there for every instance where Dad would've been. The crying, the ranting, the complaining, the congratulations, the laughter. They became my family when I moved away from home.

"This doesn't make sense, Dani. Something needed to have triggered this. There's no way the man would've kissed you and then decided suddenly he didn't want to," Gabe explained with frustration.

"She said Bella was standing right there," Jia argued. "There's your trigger! This is all for her, remember!" *Ouch*, that hurt.

"I don't think it's that simple." Gabe shook his head. "Does he have any qualms with the French?"

Jia and I gave him a questionable look.

Gabe huffed and explained, "It didn't sound like he was happy about the Paris situation."

I shook my head in disagreement. "Levi's dreamed of going to Paris for years. He speaks French fluently." The blue silk of the dress folded up around my knees like waves. I brushed them down in thought.

I needed to be honest with myself. "The kiss was a mistake. I let my feelings take over and—"

"But Dani, he kissed *you*," Gabe urged with exasperation.

"It was in the heat of the moment. We were dressed up and we had been dancing. It happened whether or not he had planned it, and now it's over. Tomorrow, things will go back to normal as if it had never happened." I needed comfort in the fact that I knew what to do next.

Gabe and Jia exchanged looks but I didn't have the energy to explain more. I rubbed my eyes and began to speak thoughtlessly.

"I almost told him I love him."

"Oh no, this is too early in the romance movie plot for you to be confessing your love to him. That's not supposed to happen until at least the last thirty minutes of the movie," Gabe commented.

"If I'm part of a romance movie plot, then Levi and Bella are the stars. Jia said it herself when I agreed to all of this." I sighed. "I thought your twenties were supposed to be about finding yourself and traveling and making these big career moves—not missing a guy, eating pizza on the couch, and still crying over insecurities from high school."

"Did you not watch *Sex and the City*? That shit keeps going until you're forty," Gabe replied. I groaned in response.

There was a lull in the conversation where no one knew what to say next. Until Jia cleared her throat and looked at me with a face that told me she was serious.

"My father always says this Korean proverb when me or my brothers have a problem." She thought for a moment and then spoke slowly in Korean. "It translates to English as *at the end of hardship comes happiness.*"

I leaned over and squeezed her hand for her comfort and whispered, "I love you."

I just didn't know how to tell her that it felt as if the hardships weren't nearing an end.

I sat down at my desk in an old T-shirt and pajama pants after Gabe and Jia left, opening my laptop to start typing. Not an email to Dad though.

The Lazaro application glowed on my screen, blank, waiting for an essay to be filled in. I could've painted this screen on a canvas because of how often I stared at it.

Write about a pivotal time in your life that sparked growth and why.

But I didn't feel annoyance looking at it this time. Instead, I thought on what Levi said about making my essay unique to me. So, I thought of the one thing that always made me stick out: my insecurities, imperfections, and failures. I wrote about every failure I experienced.

The time Jack Huntington made fun of my clothes, so I went home, watched *Breakfast at Tiffany's*, and then created a (very rough) replica of the classic, black Givenchy dress Audrey Hepburn wore.

The instance in which I didn't get into a design summer program and spent the warm months drawing up twenty-nine dresses that I would later create for girls for prom.

I wrote about when Dad was first diagnosed and we watched every episode of *Project Runway* at the hospital together when I visited, learning sewing techniques and working with models and makeup artists.

When I saw Levi kissing someone and my heart broke. So I cut out hearts from crimson red satin and sewed them into a gown with delicately embroidered cursive sonnets, which I ended up submitting as my final piece for my college applications.

I wrote about every instance in which I experienced loss, and how I came back from it.

I didn't email it to Ethan for approval or consideration. I pressed submit, attempting to have a little faith in myself.

26

I tried to stop loving you, but along the way, you found your way into the sound of my laugh, the style of my writing, and the threads of my clothes

My body was riding on this high since submitting my last application last night. It was finally *done*. I wasn't even phased by the horrifying ladybug that flew into my window when I was getting ready this morning.

Well, I was partially phased. Meaning I didn't scream. Hopefully it'll be gone by the time I get home tonight.

Wanting to take advantage of this energy, I got ready for the day: I showered, sweeping my hair back with a silk scarf (one with blueberries that matched my earrings), and threw on linen pants and a tee.

Pulling my things together, I ran out the door into the warm air where trees brushed brownstones and mothered daffodils.

The wedding was two weekends away, and my capstone was due in one, along with the end-of-the-year runway show where they would be presented, which was days after the wedding. I didn't have a dress for either, but hopefully I'd solve half of that problem today.

There was a small fabric store not too far down the street from where I bought my bagels from Marty. It differed from the larger stores in the city because it only sold thrifted fabric; no two fabrics would be the same. It often wasn't my first choice since I required enough material to fix my mistakes, and there almost was never full rolls of fabric available. But I hadn't found what I needed in the city.

Walking into the store, the small space was suffocated by fabric. Every surface on the walls was covered in scrap pieces that had no home because they weren't enough to make a dress or maybe even a hair bow.

I headed to the back of the store where they kept their larger rolls, hoping to find what I had carefully created in my mind. It was so specifically imagined that I avoided asking anyone for help because it'd require a ridiculously long, complex answer, along with a look at my Pinterest board.

A fabric that resembled sunlight and ruffled like sand dunes when draped. The painting Levi had shown me the day at The Met, "Love Letters" by Jean Honoré Fragonard, had this warmth to it that I hadn't stopped thinking about since I saw it. I already had the silhouette in mind; something I had sketched the day we were there together. It would be perfect to tie together the last of my pieces for class.

Running my hands over the rolls of fabric, differing textures and patterns that could've been from curtains or couches, were all too dark. Floral patterns that were too similar to my first dress, and colors that were too neon to blend in, were all I found.

"Ugh," I sighed. I dropped my bag on the ground to free my hands and began tugging the rolls away from the wall. There had to be *something* here.

I piled them all into my hands: forest green, crimson red, black and white chevron, grey swallows—*orange*. I jerked the roll out in excitement. It was a crinkle fabric; light and soft, making it perfect to blend in with the other soft patterns and draping techniques I was using. The color wasn't an orange you'd imagine on a rainbow, but rather a shade deeper that would appear in the curvatures of the sun. It would complement my first gown, which was made of a watercolor fabric that I had custom made, with whites, yellows, and oranges, inspired by lantana flowers.

This last dress, though, would be simple. Nothing as complex or time consuming. But its simplicity would be its beauty— hopefully.

There wasn't much fabric left on the roll, so I hauled my bag over my shoulder and carried the roll to the register. Placing it carefully on the counter, I felt more excited and confident about a design than I had in months.

"I'll take all of it," I said with a smile.

I didn't know what had gotten into me—the new fabric shoved in my bag probably—but I texted Levi while pulling together a flower arrangement for a birthday bouquet in Daisy's. Blue and purple hydrangeas (a favorite) with white baby's-breath.

And he just texted me back.

Dani: Dinner tonight?

Levi: Always—am I picking you up at Daisy's?

He had responded within seconds, not keeping me waiting. I felt relieved at his casual response. *Phew.* Maybe I was right, maybe we could just pretend like nothing happened. It was an act anyways, of course it wouldn't be worth mentioning. However, I'd be lying if I didn't admit that I wanted him to be acting a little weird as proof that last night had an effect on him too.

Dani: I'll take a cab, don't worry :)

The last thing I needed was to be alone in a car with him when last night was all I could think about.

My phone buzzed again. I finished tying twine around the flowers and placed them in a ceramic vase.

Levi: I'm not letting you pay for a cab, that's ridiculous.

Dammit, Levi.

Dani: Maybe I have a sugar daddy that pays for my cab rides.

Levi: Does this sugar daddy go by the name of Mandy or Linda?

Dani: *gasp* how dare you name them!

Levi: I'm picking you up at 5.

Dani: I'll already be in the cab by then.

Levi: Dammit, Daniella. I'm sending you money then.

I texted, I don't want your blood money at the same time that he texted, I swear to God if you call it blood money.

I laughed, causing one of the people in the store to turn and give me an odd look. I covered my mouth to stifle my laugh.

Dani: Making money off the backs of students could be considered blood money…

Levi: They torment me!

Dani: See you at 5 ;)

The cab didn't cost much since it was only a fifteen-minute drive. I wouldn't have minded walking if it weren't for the fact that I

Liana Cincotti

closed the store later than expected. Levi also ended up sending me money with a message that said: *The blood money you requested <3.* Hopefully, the IRS wouldn't flag that …

I knocked on the door with a bouquet of pink tulips—mine and Sarah's favorite—when the person who opened the door wasn't a Coldwell, but Bella.

"Oh, hi," I said.

She looked surprised to see me. Her strawberry blonde hair was wrapped in a perfect bun, while mine was messy, hiding under a silk scarf. She had a pretty cotton dress on that emphasized her hips. She looked effortlessly perfect. I struggled to not look down at my linen pants and old shirt. At least I had lip gloss on.

"Hi," she said back in a rather uncomfortable fashion. She reached forward to take the flowers out of my hands. I didn't have time to think over how to react, so I let her take them. "These for Levi?"

"Um—no, no. They're for Sarah, actually."

"Oh, that was nice." She looked at me as if she was surprised. The way a person looked when they learned a new morsel of gossip.

"It's not much." I shook my head. I would ask her how she was if it didn't involve me standing on the doorstep any longer or having to relive her watching Levi and I kiss last night in my mind.

Before our conversation could continue though, Sarah shouted, "Is that Dani?"

Bella turned. "Yes. She brought you flowers." She opened the door for me and walked away. I chose to ignore the odd interaction because there were numerous other things to be focused on. Like seeing Levi and acting like we didn't just kiss last night—and that it was the best kiss I've ever had. Romance-movie-level kissing. Heartbeat-pounding-in-my-ears-when-he-leaned-into-me type of kissing. The type of kissing that would make you reconsider your marital choices ten years down the road like he was the one that got away.

I stepped through the warm threshold and was met with an instant hug from Sarah clutching her pink tulips. They matched the consistent rosiness of her cheeks. I hugged her back in joy, laughing. Levi and I were older than her by a year, but she always felt older. Her confidence in herself and her decisions made me feel younger.

"They're just flowers, Sarah!" I laughed as she squeezed me. It was easier to say that than to explain the symbolism of the type of flower you gave. Tulips symbolized perfection and love; two things that Sarah exuded.

She pulled away from me in haste. "They're not *just* flowers. They're my *favorite* flowers. If I weren't getting married, I'd steal you away from my brother! *Did you hear that, Levi!*"

"Yes, Sarah!" Levi shouted back from another room. My legs immediately tensed up with nervousness. Why hadn't he opened the door if he was down here?

"You *have* to see the photos from last night!" The way Sarah always emphasized one word in her sentences made me laugh. A smile that made my cheeks hurt was glued to my face anytime I was around her. She oozed positivity and excitement that was contagious.

The dining room table was covered in printed photos of Sarah in her a beautiful white dress from last night, sparkling in diamonds. Black and white and low exposure photos of her alone, and then her and Jeff dancing in the crowd. Most of the pictures focused on her dress, which made me laugh, because the point of the event was to focus on Jeff's family. But Sarah was meant to be photographed; she glowed.

"Dani!" I turned and found Trish approaching me for a hug.

"Hi, Mrs. Coldwell," I said warmly.

"If I hear you call me Mrs. Coldwell one more time." The fake threat was accompanied by a motherly gaze.

"How are you, *Trish?*" I corrected myself, and she laughed. I always called her Trish growing up, but it felt inappropriate to continue that after so many years of separation. I appreciated her constant effort to make me feel comfortable.

"Horrendous at the moment. My children are causing chaos in the kitchen. They thought it would be a fun idea to make a cake for us for dessert tonight," she groaned. *Us* seemed to only be Sarah's bridesmaids tonight, no extended family.

Which is why I felt comfortable saying, "Let me help."

"I can't let you do that—"

"I want to. I love baking, and I love the girls. It would make my night."

She looked at me for a moment. Her small smile appeared both somber and content; an expression she wore like lipstick that hung on her face in an exhausted state. She nodded her head. "That would be wonderful, Dani, thank you."

"No thank you necessary. Especially since there's no cake yet," I laughed, making my way into the kitchen. It was unfortunate that their kitchen was so spacious, because the girls managed to cover every surface in flour. Including their clothes, of course.

They turned in unison as I walked in, their hands in the air like caught culprits. But when they registered that it was me (definitely not an authoritative figure) they smiled and shouted, "Daisy!"

"Girls!" I crouched down and opened my arms. They ran at me with flour and giggles. "I heard we're baking a cake?"

"You want to help us?" Claire asked eagerly.

"Of course! What type of cake are we baking?" I asked.

"Strawberry shortcake," Rhea said.

"You like strawberry shortcake?" I asked with skepticism.

"No, it's gross. No one should put fruit in dessert," Rhea stated.

I smacked my hand against my forehead. "Why are you making it then?" I laughed.

"Levi tried making one earlier but failed *epically*," Claire said, sounding like her older sister.

"Levi hates strawberry shortcake," I said with confusion.

"*You* like it though," Claire said.

Liana Cincotti

27

I wish I felt the confidence to tell you the truth, as strongly as
I felt stubborn to hide it

The girls and I finished gathering and mixing the ingredients together, putting the cake in the oven before they could consume anymore batter, and then started on clean up. Claire was spraying the counter down while I washed dishes and Rhea dried them off. I did my best not to ask the girls more about Levi and his cake fiasco. If I went back to thinking about him possibly making me a cake, I'd melt away like the ingredients in the oven.

Fortunately, Claire had her own concerns that she wanted to discuss.

"Claire, Tyler's gross. He picks his nose!" Rhea flung her arms up in the air, causing soapy water to fling off the plate and onto me.

"No, he doesn't!" Claire shrieked back, which resulted in some cleaning spray ending up on my clothes.

"I've seen him do it!"

"Well, I don't care, I love him."

Rhea rolled her eyes. "No, you don't. You don't even know what love is. You're nine."

"You're nine too!"

"Daisy, how do you know when you're in love?" Claire asked me with an innocent and curious look, in need of saving.

I'd never spoken to the girls like they were kids, they deserved to be spoken to like humans, so I took their questions seriously.

"You'll know you're in love when being around them never feels long enough. Everything you learn about them will be beautiful pockets of information, no matter how flawed. Your hands will be clammy, and you'll trip over your words when you're around them. But if they love you back, they'll only think that it makes you lovelier."

"Wow." Claire looked up at me with wonder in her wide eyes. "I don't think I love Tyler." She said it with such a straight face that it made me laugh. Her face changed into a childish grin where I could see that she had lost a tooth.

"Is that how you knew you loved Levi?" Rhea asked from my left. I almost dropped the dish at her question, remembering that she didn't know the truth of our relationship.

In truth, Levi was the king of my heart. He'd had my heart in high school, and he'd been borrowing it all these years since. I didn't want to believe that I still loved him, but there was a reason every relationship or intimate moment I'd had since felt like a disappointment.

It was him. I always wanted him.

"Actually, it was the moment I watched him stuff seven donut holes in his mouth." The girls giggled at my response; it made me smile.

"Levi talks about you a lot," Rhea mentioned as if it wasn't something I'd replay in my mind for months—*who was I kidding?*

More like years.

"Does he?" I asked as calmy as possible, rinsing off another dish, passing it to her to dry.

"All the time. He says that you smell like flowers," Claire giggled.

You intoxicate me, Daisy. The scent of flowers lingers on you everywhere you go, and I always want to follow. The memory sizzled at the bottom of my stomach like a recalled sex dream.

"He never goes out, he's so boring," Rhea complained, sounding like a housewife.

Claire gasped. "You should come over next weekend for movie night!"

"Movie night?" I asked with surprise. They still did movie nights?

"We can watch any movie you want, please!" Rhea shouted.

"Please, please, pleasepleaseplease!" Claire yelled. They began jumping up and down; Claire wobbling back and forth on the stool and Rhea splashing the sink water everywhere.

"Okay! Okay! I'll come! Just stop spraying me with water!" I laughed as the girls calmed down. "I'm going to go dry off, so I'm trusting you to make sure the kitchen is spotless when I come back, and then we can decorate the cake!" They cheered as I left the kitchen.

Walking down the hallway and into the bathroom, I tried to not think of how the last time I was in here, Levi was pulling his shirt off. *Breathe, Dani. You're friends and nothing more.*

The linen closet was filled with towels. I pulled out a face cloth and lifted up my shirt to wipe the water from my stomach that had soaked through the fabric. Dabbing the front of my shirt, I—

"That was quite some show last night." *Bella.*

Levi sighed. "What show?"

I froze behind the bathroom door. *I should not be listening to this, it's an invasion of privacy.* I should exit the bathroom and go back to the kitchen. I should definitely not move closer to the door and listen.

"You and Dani. You were quite the romantics last night."

Well … this sounds like my business now too so I may as well stay. I kept my ear against the door.

"I have to say, I never thought I'd see *the* Levi Coldwell in love. I know my mother was definitely impressed, especially on top of your interview this week."

"Good to hear," he said. He didn't sound happy, though, but rather sullen. I moved to the crack between the door and wall, trying to catch a glimpse of what was going on, but could only spot Bella.

"She told me that you practically have the job," she said. If he "practically" had this job, was I needed anymore then?

Bella sounded different from the person I'd greeted at the door. Less robotic and more sultry. Particularly as she reached her hand out and ran it across his forearm. It was such a small movement, but it appeared so intimate. Like how she looked at him from under her lashes as her hair just perfectly laid behind her back.

He pulled his arm away. "Isabella, I'm so tired of this. You know I'm with Dani. I'm not doing this with you. I don't care if it jeopardizes the job or not."

My heart began beating faster than the trains that flew through the subway. Had Bella been hitting on him this entire time that we'd been "together"? Had he been returning her feelings?

Did he just say he doesn't care if the job was jeopardized?

"Fine. I'll see you in the dining room." I watched as Bella walked away and as Levi walked towards—*shit, shit, shit.*

"Dani?" Levi asked, taken aback. Seeing him for the first time since we'd kissed was more conflicting than I had expected. Looking at his lips and knowing what they felt like against mine was a new form of torture to endure. I only wondered if it had crossed his mind.

His words in between our kisses were lust and desire, that was all. But why did those kisses have to be so hard to forget?

"Hi sorry, I didn't—I wasn't—" Snooping? *Well, that would be a lie, because yes you were,* a voice said in the back of my head. I gave up trying to come up with an explanation and said, "The girls and I were baking, so we were washing dishes and then they were asking me questions and I wasn't answering quick enough so they—it doesn't matter. My shirt got wet, so I came to dry it off."

He looked down at my shirt. "I can get you a new one—"

"No, no, no, I'm fine, it's fine." The last thing I needed was a shirt that smelled like his cologne.

A blush slowly appeared on his cheekbones. He scratched the back of his neck and asked, "Can we talk?"

"Yeah, of course," I responded. This was what I got for snooping on a private conversation

"I wanted to talk about last night." Oh, *no.* I assumed that our texts from earlier were an unspoken agreement to pretend like last night didn't happen. "About what happened when we—"

"Oh, *oh*, don't worry." No, this wasn't happening. I couldn't have him telling me that last night was a mistake. Those were words I wouldn't come back from.

Confusion clouded his face. "Don't worry?"

I couldn't let him think last night meant something to me when it evidently didn't mean anything to him. He had to think this was mutual. I formulated the quickest lie I could think of.

"Yeah, it was no big deal. You just caught me off guard. I hadn't kissed anyone in a while." *Why did I just admit that?* "We were just pretending, I know." I shrugged with a smile. But I felt like I was crumbling away on the inside, my stomach clenching at the lie and a forced forged smile on my face. The same smile I wore when Ethan told me my papers were poor and when guys on dates told me that I wasn't usually their type. Those rejections hurt, but to be rejected by him again? To have him tell me that last night's kiss meant nothing?

"Pretending," he repeated stoically.

"Did you think I would be upset?"

"I just wasn't aware that it was ..." He stared at me for a moment with confusion, but then laughed quietly to himself. "I'm an idiot, sorry, ignore me. Let's go have dinner."

Dinner was on the table, with two seats left for us, the girls sandwiching us in. Sarah and her bridesmaids all discussed the wedding; from seating arrangements to dresses to how the weather would be since the wedding would be on the beach.

He was silent for the entirety of the conversation, only lifting his head when Rhea spoke. He was sitting beside me, but his mind was somewhere else.

"Dani, are you driving with us?" Sarah asked, catching me off guard. I must not have been listening to their conversation enough.

"I'm sorry, I missed that. Driving with you ... where?" I asked.

"To the beach house!"

I looked at her with a tilted head.

"Where the wedding is happening! The wedding party is going up the day before. I know that you're not a bridesmaid but you're family and I want you there, and I know Levi wants you there too."

As fun as a weekend wedding in the Hamptons sounded, all I could think about was how staying the night would go. Who would I talk to when Levi wasn't in the room? Where would I sleep? How many showers were there? What would be acceptable to wear to bed that would look cool but not overdressed?

My worry must've been obvious to at least him because he intervened.

"There's no pressure. I could easily run back to the city and grab you in the morning before the wedding." That lost mask of thought no longer appeared on his face.

"The Hamptons are at least a two-hour drive from the city, I'm not letting you do that," I said firmly. But there was also no way I could leave the city—neither Mandy nor my mom kept a car. Mandy worked down the street and my mom travelled too much to bother buying a car. Paying for a cab to take me two hours out of the city was out of the question. The most logical solution would be to drive up with Levi the Saturday before the wedding with everyone else.

"I'd love to come if there's room for me, thank you, Sarah." I smiled.

"Perfect!" she cheered.

Something bumped my knee. I glanced down to find Levi's knee against mine under the table. The pressure felt similar to standing in front of a fireplace.

Are you sure? he mouthed, craning his head towards mine. It felt intimate, the way his eyes searched my face, pausing on my lips.

It's just lust, I told myself. But I still desperately yearned for it.

I nodded my head, unable to speak, thinking too much about how his face looked up close. The soft curve of his nose and the warmth of his hazel eyes. I wanted to lean in and remind myself of what his lips tasted like. And I could almost swear from the look in his eyes that he was thinking something similar.

A whisper in the back of my mind wondered that while he loved Bella, maybe part of him wanted me too.

"So, Wednesday is my last dress fitting. Levi, can you come? I really need your opinion, especially since none of the girls can come," Sarah said, referencing her bridesmaids.

"I teach until six, but can come right after," he said, the romantic gaze on his face gone now.

"Bring Dani with you too, I'd *love* your expertise. I want this dress to be perfect," she said, lines on her forehead forming with determination.

He started, "Oh, Sarah—"

I knew that he was going to tell me I didn't have to go, but I had worries of my own. "I really don't have much expertise," I shook my head.

"Oh stop, Levi told me all about where you go to school and your portfolio." My *portfolio?* I hadn't updated that website in years, I didn't even want to know what he had seen on there.

Liana Cincotti

"Give yourself some credit—I need you there. I promise it won't take long!"

Sarah was impossible to say no to. I also loved wedding dresses ever since I saw Mom design one from sketch to finish. I grew up attending wedding dress exhibits, runway shows, and magazine shoots with her, watching women glow in white gowns holding colorful bouquets. I never dreamed of a wedding, but I dreamed about the dresses and their unique designs. Which is why I had to say: "I'll be there." I smiled. "What time?"

"I can pick you up," Levi answered instead.

"You said you're teaching though."

"It's not a problem for me to get you."

"Why don't I just meet you at your class, so when you're done teaching, we can go together."

"You're sure?"

"Yes, now stop worrying," I told him. But I was incredibly worried. Seeing him teach? This was going to be the death of me.

28

Glances, gazes, eyes following places they
shouldn't have seen

For the first Monday in months, I was dreading going to class to see my friends. I thought seeing Marty at the bagel shop as I picked up six bagels and cream cheese (plus a dairy-free one they just got in for Sandra) would've helped, but it only made me more nauseous.

Every instinct in my body told me that Sandra would want to talk about Levi. And to be reminded of what happened Saturday night between us was the last thing I wanted to talk about.

The only thing keeping me walking in the right direction to the school was the new fabric I had picked up yesterday. I was cutting it close by only leaving myself a week to make this dress before we had to fit them to the models next week.

I wasn't the only procrastinator in the class, but I was the only one with a whole piece missing from their collection. Everyone else was working on smaller things, like sleeves, trims, and beading. Don't get me wrong, nothing about putting together a collection of haute couture was small or easy. But I wished I only had the details left.

My own fault, of course.

That stress was accompanied by the stress of my Lazaro application too. I knew that it was unreasonable to think I'd hear back two days after submitting my application. But my ability to operate had been thwarted by my application status. If I didn't get in, would that be a sign that Paris was meant to be? I wanted to start challenging myself, but moving across the world for a year was more than just challenging myself.

Swiping my student ID, I pushed open the door to the design building, and walked up the stairs. It was more so a dash than a walk because I was paranoid about running into Ethan.

How did one react when being called Evan and cut off mid-conversation by a student's boyfriend? No idea, and I was anxious to find out.

"Bagels!" the girls cheered as I entered the room. Their pieces were all out early, along with their pincushions on their wrists. By the end of class, we'd look like we were working in a sweatshop.

Removing pins from mouths and pin cushions from wrists, they came and got their bagels, thanking me with kisses on the cheek and arm squeezes.

"I got dairy-free cream cheese too, Sandra!" I said cheerfully.

Camille, Vera, Daya, and Lexi laughed, while Sandra gasped in shock. "This may be the best day of my life," she said, clutching onto the cream cheese like it was gold.

Everyone gathered around a table at the front of the room. We discussed what we had left for our pieces and the vision we had for hair and makeup.

"I want the models to have this neon eyeshadow and overly fake nails," both Lexi and Daya said, while Vera wanted, "tight buns and gelled back hair."

Camille and I had similar style, so I wasn't surprised to hear that she wanted, "loose ponytails and natural makeup." I would most likely pick a similar style when speaking with the hair and makeup students next week.

"What about you, Dani?" Daya asked. Camille was who I went to most for advice because she knew my vision as well as I did, so the rest of the girls didn't know much of what I was doing. Most of my work was done in the middle of the night or after breakdowns, as you could tell.

I had four dresses, and one suit, with the colors of spring flowers, and fabric that mimicked the airiness of clouds.

"Something similar to Camille," I said, taking another bite of my bagel. I hadn't thought once about hair and makeup, but it was usually an afterthought. Making sure my pieces were complete was my main focus.

"You guys are asking the wrong questions," Vera spoke up, sweeping her ink black hair up. "I want to hear about Dani's *boyfriend*," she cooed, wiggling her eyebrows.

I groaned. "You told them!" I accused Sandra.

She gasped. "I did no such thing! I only told Vera."

"Told Vera what? I want to know!" Lexi yelped.

As much as I hated talking about this and enduring this pretending through my social life, I loved them. To have people that cared about me enough to ask about my weekend and my relationship, despite it being fake, was a reassuring feeling as an insecure friend.

Sandra gave me a look as if to say, *Can I tell them?*

I rolled my eyes before nodding. Then she was off to describe how Levi and I looked this weekend.

"This man was the hottest human in the building—*no*, the *city*. He had this black suit on that complemented his dark hair, which had this perfect curl above his eyebrow," Sandra explained with a dreamy look in her eye.

Is this what my train of thought sounded like?

"Sandra, this is Dani's boyfriend!" Daya intervened in horror, but it wasn't enough to disguise the ghost of a smile on her face.

"I'm just appreciating what she has!"

"Did he wear those glasses again?" Vera asked with total seriousness.

"I wasn't done yet!" Sandra responded. "No, no glasses. But it would've hid his gorgeous eyes." I snorted, regardless of the fact that I agreed. "And he had his hand on Dani's back the entire time."

The girls awed. The blood rushed to my cheeks. I was so focused on Bella seeing me and Levi, that I hadn't thought of how we'd appear to my friends.

As Sandra continued to describe our closeness, I grew more hopeful that Levi was attracted to me. My optimistic heart wanted to believe those words. But habitual whispers returned. *He loves to flirt. Most of all, he loves Bella. He's acting.*

"I didn't get to meet him because he was talking to someone else. But he kept glancing back at her, like he couldn't believe she existed, like she was the only one in the room," Sandra explained in a dreamy state. We all waited for her to continue, wanting to hear more of this fairytale, but she had finished.

"It was probably the way her butt looked in that dress," Lexi commented, making us all laugh.

"Is he coming to the show?" Daya asked.

The exhibit was after the wedding. Bella said Levi practically had the job, and Sarah's wedding would only confirm that he was committed. I didn't know what would become of us then. But there would be no point in our ruse lasting to that point.

"I'm not sure," I said. And it was the closest thing to the truth I had said this month.

29

To be close to you was to be haunted by
what I couldn't have and to be reminded of how much I truly wanted you

I think if Vera were here right now, she'd physically combust. Because when I decided earlier today to go to Levi's class early, I hadn't expected to find him at the front of the lecture hall in his glasses.

Levi had mentioned that the professor he TA'ed for offered him a lot of freedom in the class to teach. But I hadn't expected to find him standing at the front of the class completely alone, teaching like a dark academia dream.

He had on a brown sweater that matched the color of his hair, the same shade of a wooden, walnut-stained bookcase you'd find in the corners of a smalltown bookstore. His hands anxiously adjusted the bridge of his glasses as he spoke, returning back to the safety of his trouser pockets to keep from fidgeting. Despite the nervous ticks, he looked in his element standing at the front of the room. A room completely filled with women, and only one guy at the front.

I had been looking forward to this moment all week, because experiencing him teach firsthand during high school when he got me through writing persuasive essays was one thing. But to see him teach a classroom full of college students was like witnessing an athlete make it to the Olympics.

I stood outside the open door, listening to him discuss the agenda for the next class as a girl in the back of the lecture hall spoke up.

"Mr. Coldwell, could you say that in French this time?"

All of the girls began giggling. My hand flew to my face to stifle a laugh. *Mr. Coldwell* was the hottest thing I'd ever heard, and I'm a diehard historical romance film watcher, so that says a lot.

Levi laughed. It sounded like his embarrassed laugh when a blush hit his cheekbones, and the sound came from his throat rather than his stomach. He ran a flustered hand through his hair, relaxing his tall stature against the surface of the desk behind him.

"If this was a French class, I would, but last time I checked, this was Austen Literature. Also, I said this before, you can just call me Levi," he responded rather professionally. For someone who did quite a bit of flirting in high school, he had a difficult time receiving it without blushing. These girls were more forward than Bella.

"*Levi,*" the girl replied with a smirk on her face, "don't you think it would enhance the romantic literature experience if you said it in French though?"

The image that formed in my mind of Levi speaking in French caused my bags to practically leap out of my hands in surprise. *Dammit.* I jolted forward in front of the doorway to grab them, bringing everyone's attention to … me.

"Dani?" he asked in surprise, obviously unaware that I had been hiding behind the doorway watching.

Liana Cincotti

Shit.

Brushing my hair out of my face, now crouched on the ground trying to collect my things, I replied, "*Hey.*" Very nonchalant of me.

Levi looked up at the auditorium of seats where everyone was staring at us, registering the attention I had gathered. "Class is over," he replied, permitting everyone to gather their things and leave early.

Rushing over to me, he nudged his pant leg up, getting down on one knee to help collect my things. The only thing that could have made this more mortifying was if my heart rolled out of the bag with his name written across it, along with my dignity.

I began to apologize for the interruption but the sole male student I noticed earlier joined us on the ground to help me gather my things.

"Hey, thanks, man," Levi said in a more casual tone that I had expected, sweeping the last of my things into my bag and standing up.

"It's not a problem, you looked like you needed the help back there anyways," the guy said with a laugh, referencing all the girls giggling at Levi.

"With no help from you! I swear you enjoy witnessing my embarrassment." They both laughed. "Oliver this is Daisy— Dani, I mean," Levi said in a stumbled manner. "Oliver's one of my roommates."

Oh! I had yet to see Levi's apartment, but I knew that he shared it with three roommates. Oliver was cute but didn't come off as the type to take a literature class, let alone an Austen literature class, with his football hoodie and chestnut slippers. It left me to assume that he took it to see Levi.

"*Daisy*?" Oliver said in surprise, like he was putting together pieces of a puzzle where one had been missing. He turned to Levi with a narrowed gaze before asking me, "Have you read Levi's book?"

"I haven't," I said with confusion. "I asked a couple times, but the response was an immediate no." I rolled my eyes at Levi, knowing that he had said no because he was embarrassed, even though there was no reason for him to be.

"Well, I'd keep pushing. You'd learn quite a few things," Oliver said, nudging Levi with his elbow. I wasn't sure what that was supposed to mean, but Levi looked uncomfortable.

"See you later, Levi." They exchanged a casual half-hug, half-handshake. "It was nice finally meeting you, Dani," he said with a wave and then walked out.

"What was—"

"You're here early," Levi said with confusion, phrasing it like a question.

"I got out of class early. I thought I could walk over and watch you teach a bit. I didn't mean to interrupt, I'm sorry." I winced, wanting to press my fingers into the corners of my eyes and erase the moment. Luckily all of the students had left, so hopefully I wouldn't have to relive that moment ever again.

He turned toward the front desk, shuffling some papers together and moving them into his bag. His hair fell forward over the tops of his ears and forehead, shielding the look in his eyes.

"I should be apologizing to you. Out of all the classes you overheard, it was me being tantalized," he said, shaking his head with embarrassment.

I wasn't used to this blushing, flustered Levi. He had never been like this in high school. Confidence, decisiveness, and cool, *yes*. But this? I wasn't used to this.

"Tantalized? Levi they were flirting with you!"

Levi scoffed in disbelief as if he has no idea what I was talking about. He shook his head, locking the drawers to the desk hastily. *Oh, he had no idea what I was talking about.* "They think my French accent is funny, that's all."

"Oh my gosh, you're an idiot," I said in a deadpan tone, stunned by his ignorance. For once in my life, I knew something Levi Coldwell didn't.

That caused Levi's head to whip up, a crooked smile on his face that was as sweet as limoncello. "You punk," he said with a smirk. It would've made me giggle if I wasn't so determined.

I continued with urgency, determined to wipe that gorgeous, idiotic smile off his face. "They're into you! Speaking French is one of the most romantic things on the planet that a man can do." He raised his eyebrows in disbelief. Did he not notice how attractive he was? "Huge turn on," I emphasized.

"You think it's a turn on?" Levi asked, cocking an eyebrow, and leaning back onto the desk, crossing his arms.

"Well, yes—and every other breathing woman," I responded with exasperation.

"I didn't ask about every other woman; I was asking about you." There was a look on his face that I couldn't determine. Not shy but not flirty. Almost a euphoric curiosity that existed on scientists and attractive, mysterious male leads from 90s romances.

I stood there frozen. Unsure of this territory we were moving into by having this conversation. Clearing my throat, and adjusting my shirt, I said, "Yes."

He pulled at the tie around his neck with one hand. "Yes, what?"

My eyes skipped from the hand that was gripping his tie to the way he licked his lips. What if I just loosened the tie for him? Wrapped my hand around his, moved it out of the way, and grabbed onto the neck of the tie and pulled him forward. I'd bring his lips to mine, taste the espresso on his tongue that he drank this morning, and tug every curl of hair on his head. I'd kiss him until every ounce of my heart was full and had to burst. I'd—

"Yes. I find men that speak French attractive."

His eyes widened with a sort of surprise I haven't seen before. "I—"

An unfamiliar voice sounded behind us. "And if you come this way ..."

"Shit." He swore with horror, grabbing my hand and pulling me into a—*closet?*

"The admin can't know the professor left a TA alone to teach," he rushed, shuffling us into the closet and shutting the door behind us, leaving us in darkness with just a sliver of light under the door.

He pushed himself against the wall, giving me space—as in one footstep between our bodies. I could only see an outline of the right side of his face from the light outside the door. But it was enough to suffocate my focus.

I imagine I looked alarmed; he must have thought I looked like a character in a horror film who was running from the masked killer because my mind was processing the precise distance

Liana Cincotti

between us and how similar it was to Saturday night on those steps before we kissed. My hands shook, moving away from my sides in the darkness, hoping—*wanting* to feel his. Wondering how close they were.

Stop. Stop looking. I reared my gaze up hastily from the distance between us and found Levi looking at me. And for a split second, I swore he wanted to kiss me, but—

"This is where I take lit."

His shoulders slumped with relief. "*It's just a student,*" Levi whispered. I gave a look that said, *ohhhh.*

His arm moved past my waist towards the—

I latched onto his forearm. "*What* are you doing?" I whispered.

"Leaving, it's just a student," he whispered in confusion.

"We can't leave now; you'll look like the crazy TA that spends his afterhours in the lecture hall closet with women."

"We can't just wait in here."

"Just give it a minute."

The two of us leaned into the door trying to listen.

"It's my last class of the day so I must've left it in here," a girl said.

"*See,* she must've just forgotten something, it'll be quick," I said in a hushed tone.

"The rom-com class," a guy corrected her.

"It's on Jane Austen, not rom-coms," she responded with impatience.

"Yeah, yeah," the guy brushed her off.

"Oh stop, you're just jealous because Mr. Coldwell is hot," the girl scoffed.

I swear my smile could've glowed in that dark closet because of how satisfied I was. "I told you!" I whispered in victory. He brought his hand to his face, silently laughing.

Shaking his head with a smile, he said, "I can't believe this has been my reputation."

The two students spent a few more minutes arguing while chairs scraped against the tile, obviously still looking for something.

I took that moment to tell him about the girls. "Claire and Rhea invited me over for movie night," I said in a less hushed tone because of the amount of noise the two students were making.

He groaned. "You must think I'm the most boring man—still doing movie nights."

I knew he was teasing because he took pride in his family. He loved them and wasn't ashamed to choose them over nights out. But part of me thought he looked sad when he said it. So, I hope it helped when I said, "I think that makes you the most compassionate man on the planet."

The hairs on my arms rose at the unexpected contact between our fingers. Just the tops of our knuckles touching. A silent thank you.

"I actually had a girl once call me lame because I stayed home with them." An empty laugh fell from his lips. He sounded somber in a way that I hadn't heard since high school when mornings felt like midnights because insecure and grieving thoughts stirred. There wasn't a moment we hesitated to call each other about it.

"Levi, I'm so sorry." I didn't know what to say. I was so angry with this girl I'd never met before for saying something he'd never forget.

His Worried Older Brother Look fell into place. "They're my entire life. If they need me, I want them to know that I'll always be there for them. I don't want them to ever feel like they have less of a family because they don't have a dad."

His voice cracked and my heart crumbled. "I don't regret it. I don't regret not having a social life. But what if it has made me lame? It's like I've forgotten what I want out of life because I'm so worried about them every second of the day. I'm so worried something's going to happen to them." *Like it did to my dad* were the words left unsaid. That's what grief did to you, right? It never let you live in peace.

I pressed my hand firmer against his. "They love you to pieces, but you also need to take care of yourself, Vi. You can't give them a happy life if you're not happy."

"How were you always so wise?" he asked.

I laughed. "I'm going to remember that the next time I'm in the driver's seat," I said, poking his shoulder. He smiled. Good. "So, what should I bring to movie night?"

30

Am I a ghost in your story?

It took only a few more minutes until the student found whatever she was looking for and left. Levi and I were then free to exit the closet and go to Sarah's last fitting. We only arrived five minutes late since he had ended his lecture early.

Sarah looked beautiful in her dress; it had these grand Juliet sleeves that had the volume of freshly baked cream puffs. She sparkled, and it wasn't just because the dress was covered in crystals.

She asked for my input numerous times; if the length should be shorter, if the sleeves were too much, if her boobs looked smooshed—her words, not mine. It felt nice to have my opinion matter so much, but my answer was no to all of her questions because the dress was perfect. I also didn't want to explain that she didn't need my opinion because one, I wasn't a professional and two, a professional seamstress had altered the dress already.

Levi was there to reassure her when more doubts arrived, ultimately leading her to conclude that nothing was wrong. She was allowed to take her dress home tonight.

After pointless arguing, he drove me home, despite it being

in the opposite direction of his apartment.

"It'll only take a quick second," is what he tried telling me.

"Quick second my ass," is what I said back. He laughed, tugging on a strand of my hair like a kid. It was a small moment, but it warmed an empty place in my heart. *Maybe we can go back to how we were in high school.*

Not after that kiss, a dark whisper alerted me.

"Are you teaching tomorrow?" I asked, brushing away my worried thoughts. The sun was only just beginning to set despite how long the day had felt. It was my favorite part about May in New York. The sun tried to stay up late with you at night, whereas it was too tired to even try during the winter.

"No, thank god. I need some time to process my new fame as *Hot Mr. Coldwell*," he said with sarcasm, laughing.

"I've ruined you!" I shouted back in sarcastic agony, laughing. "Oliver seemed nice though. He must *really love* Jane Austen."

He laughed, knowing what I meant. "He signed up for the class the day I told him I would be TA'ing. Thought he could get by with automatic extra help—which he has because I have a hard time saying no. But he didn't expect all the women, which lets you know that he's never heard of Jane Austen."

"Well hopefully that doesn't make him a bad roommate. I would subtract points though, personally."

"Points have been subtracted," he confirmed. "And he's a pretty great roommate."

I wasn't sure if he was finished but we pulled up to the townhouse, ending our conversation.

"Thank you for driving me, *again.*" I rolled my eyes in a joking manner. For a man who had trouble saying no, he was a hard person to say no to.

"You're welcome," he said, returning my eyeroll.

In high school, I would've reached my hand over and squeezed his palm as a thank you, but that felt too intimate after this weekend. Too soon. So I reached for the door and pushed—

"Wait." He stopped me. I turned back around. He was reaching into the backseat into his bag, pulling out a book.

"I owe you this," he said, handing me the book, *his book*. I had never seen it, but the French on the cover was enough of a hint.

I didn't know what to say. So I sufficed for, "Thank you. I'll see you this weekend." I tried to smile, but I had too many questions elapsing. "Good night."

Closing the car door behind me, I ran up the steps and into the house without turning around. I stashed the book away into my bag like a poor report card and got ready for bed.

Its presence followed me like a camera as I left the room and returned, watching my moves as I unfolded the bed sheets and tugged them over my body. It's as if it knew how badly I wanted to read it.

But you know that part in the romance movies when the main character does something that they obviously shouldn't have done, and the audience is practically screaming at them not to do it, and then they go and do it anyways? This felt like one of those moments. But I was trying to do the *right thing*.

I knew he gave me the book. I was well aware. But it felt like his hand had been forced because Oliver had said something— didn't it?

If he truly wanted to give it to me, wouldn't he have done it sooner? I didn't want to read something he hadn't originally

Liana Cincotti

shared with me, despite how desperately I wanted to read it. But my fingers and focus were itching to open it. I had practically seared a hole into the cover from staring at it so hard.

Opening that book would be opening a can of worms. I didn't know what Oliver meant when he said I could learn a few things from it, but I'm not sure I wanted to know, because my mind was going to worse-case scenarios. *All Levi's Past Flings* was a billboard appearing in my head with blinding lights. The poems were all in French, even the title. And weren't the French all about romantic rendezvous? It would make perfect sense for this to be a book about Levi's relationships.

I was saving myself more heartbreak by avoiding this entire situation.

I let the shape of the book from my bag sketch a tattoo in my brain as I fell asleep.

I wouldn't succumb to the bad decisions of a romance lead and open that book because that would be the lit match that set fire to the idle gasoline in my heart.

And I refused to burn again.

31

I feel lucky to have had you, but dismayed to know what life is like
without you

Yet again, another argument had broken out during our club meeting. To say I wasn't enjoying it though would be a lie because it was *hilarious*.

Jia stood in front of Daya and I, where we both sat off to the side, gesturing to her celebrity look on the projector. It was an actress in an off-duty look wearing a matching red track suit, the zip-up open to showcase a white bralette, matching the white of her underwear pulled above her hips. Apparently, someone didn't love the visible underwear look—

"Watch your mouth, freshy," Jia sneered at … I followed her gaze to where Amelia, a freshman (*the* freshy), was leaning forward in her seat arguing with Jia.

Despite Amelia being a freshman, she definitely had the same level of outwardness as Jia. Which made for a great show, but it also made me happy to see that she was so comfortable around us. It wasn't too long ago that she was the quietest in the club, often sitting and watching silently because she hadn't known anyone before joining. But now she was as involved as the rest of us.

Looking around the room, watching our group smile and laugh, it broke my heart to accept that this was the last time I would be part of it. Next week the seniors would be preparing garments for the runway exhibit and then graduating.

Daya stood up abruptly beside me, whistling to grab everyone's attention.

"I think we're all a little stressed about projects being due next week, so I'll let that one slide Jia," Daya said, while Jia rolled her eyes. "It's time we vote anyways." Daya listed off the names of those who presented, asking people to raise their hands for their vote. I kept count as she went. At the end, she looked at me for the answer.

"And our winner is …" I tried to stifle my laugh before saying, "Amelia!" Amelia then stuck her tongue out at Jia. I stood up with Daya at the front of the room. "Amelia's look is this week's Look of the Week, closing out our semester. I just want to thank everyone for not only a great semester, but an amazing couple of years. If I could come back here every Thursday night, I would. I am going to miss all of you so much." I finished with tears building up in my throat.

It must have been obvious because everyone *awed* and joined in on a group hug. I squeezed their shoulders and rubbed the backs of whomever was closest to me. This was one of the reasons the idea of moving to Paris seemed so difficult; I wouldn't have them for a year.

"Okay, ladies, suck up the tears. We're still seeing each other next week," one of the other seniors grumbled, making us laugh. We pulled apart and everyone returned to their seats to collect their things.

Daya and I shut off the projector and grabbed our things as—

"Since when do you speak French?" she asked.

"What?" I replied off guard.

"That book in your bag, the title's in French," she commented. I looked down at my bag sitting on the chair where it laid wide open. Levi's book right on top.

"Oh… it's not mine."

"Are you asking me?" She quirked an eyebrow.

"No, no, it's not mine. It's Levi's," I explained quickly. Why was I flustered? "He speaks French."

She picked the book up examining it. "It has his name on in it…" She gave me a look that said, *What aren't you telling me?* "Did he write it?"

Well, I couldn't say no. "Yes."

"Levi, your boyfriend, *wrote a book?*" Daya was amazed. Amazed enough that those who we were going to dinner with— Sandra, Gabe, Vera, Jia—overheard her.

"Yes… a poetry book," I clarified. Gabe and Jia were fully aware that Levi wrote a book, but I hadn't gotten the chance to mention that he gave it to me last night.

"Can this man get any more attractive?" Sandra shouted in disbelief.

"Men can write?" Vera joked, earning a slap on the shoulder from Gabe.

"The last guy I went on a date with said he'd never read a book in his life, and you're telling me your boyfriend"—it was incredibly difficult to not wince when hearing *your boyfriend* every time—"is writing French poetry," Sandra repeated.

"Have you read it yet?" Gabe asked. But he had no idea that

Liana Cincotti

was the exact thing I was avoiding.

"I haven't." I smiled, as if I was looking forward to it.

"Do you need me to translate?" Daya asked kindly, opening the book like an accordion.

"*No,*" I urged. "No, no thank you." I smiled. Daya gave me a confused glance but returned the book to my bag without question.

I almost outwardly sighed with relief. Jia intervened before anyone could ask any more questions. "Can we please go eat now? I'm starving!"

Sandra cheered, "Tacos!" as Vera shouted, "Wine!" We left the class and practically raced down the stairs with excitement for tacos (and wine) down the street.

The sun was a fire atop of Central Park's trees as it set. The temperature was picnic perfect; no breeze, no hot sun, and warm enough to go without a jacket. Jia had in a fitted, black mini dress that she said Adelaide Adorno had been spotted wearing a few months ago in France. "If she's wearing it, I'm buying it," Jia had said. I got a closer look at it now as she walked alongside me.

"Ouch, why'd you pinch me?" I asked, pulling my arm away from her reach.

"What was that back there?" she asked, slowing us down from the rest of the group.

"I don't want to know what's in that book," I stated.

"That makes no sense. You haven't read any of it?"

"He only gave it to me yesterday, so it hasn't been long, but no, I don't want to read any of it. Levi felt forced to give it to me, that's the only reason why I have it now."

Jia thought over my response for a moment. "And let me

guess, you feel bad."

I hated it when she was right. "Of course I feel bad! If he actually wanted me to read it, he would've given it to me sooner. Reading this would be an intrusion of privacy, the same way looking at one of my unfinished garments would be."

"That was *one time*."

"And you wore it out to a fashion show!"

"Water under the bridge," she said, waving her hand around as if to shoo away the problem. "You need to read it."

"I'm not reading it." And that was that. I'd made up my mind. I wasn't going to touch the book again, let alone look at it, for the sake of Levi's privacy.

But then Jia asked, "What if one of the poems in there is about you?"

It was the one shameful thing that had been running through my mind since the book landed in my hand: what if something in there *was* about me? To think that he could've written something about me felt arrogant. But I had several stress-made dresses sitting in the back of my closet because of Levi.

Warning signs flashed in my head with the words: Levi loves Bella. He was still in love with her. I saw the way he held her in that bar and the way he looked at her after we kissed. Our relationship was exclusively transactional and *fake*.

"No. None of those poems would ever be about me."

Even Sandra hitting on the waiter wasn't enough to get my mind off my conversation with Jia, but it was great entertainment. (And Sandra did leave the restaurant with a new number in her phone.)

Going home was an excuse to distract myself. There were flowers spread across the first floor of the apartment, meaning that Mandy was in the middle of switching out all the flowers in the apartment and most likely ran back to Daisy's to grab more.

I exhaled; it was my first quiet minute of the day. Thank you, flower gods.

Dropping my bag on the stairs, I cleared the island counter and began pulling out the ingredients for blondies. Butter, eggs, brown sugar, eggs, salt, flour, vanilla extract, baking powder, and white chocolate chips (optional and controversial, but mandatory in this house). The ingredients were burned into my brain since the day I'd accidentally used baking *soda* instead of baking *powder*. Apparently, those are very different... But the measurements always slipped my mind.

Searching for the recipe book, I found it squished between Mandy's florist books. I lacked any patience to find a stepstool to reach the top shelf of the cabinet and began stretching every muscle in my legs to reach but—*crap*.

Padded footsteps rushed down the stairs. "What happened?" my mom asked as if she were prepared to be told there was an earthquake. In New York. Meaning I woke her up.

She was wearing silk pajama pants and slippers, but on top she wore a blouse and all of her jewelry.

"I dropped some of Mandy's books, I didn't realize you were asleep already." It was only 8 p.m.

She groaned. "It's still," she checked her watch, "one in the morning in the UK. I must've fallen asleep answering emails." She pinched the bridge of her nose. "I'm struggling to shake this jetlag."

She'd been going back and forth between the city and London for a few months; working on a collaboration with a designer there and working with celebrities here. I had no idea how she did it.

"I'm making blondies," I replied with a smile, collecting Mandy's books, and laying them on the counter.

She groaned again. "I shouldn't."

"But you should. You probably haven't eaten anything since you fell asleep."

She took a seat on the barstool of the island while I measured ingredients. This was a silent yes from her.

"The sugar will be good for your lack of energy."

She laughed. "It sounds like you're also convincing yourself. Is there a reason you need more energy right now?"

I blew a strand of hair out of my face because my hands were covered in flour. "I may or may not need to start on my last dress for my senior project."

"*You haven't even started it?*" My mother had always been a Type-A, two weeks ahead of the due date, planner. Other than our love for design (and sugar), my mother and I were very unlike. The shape of our noses and color of our eyes, yes, they were the same. But I did not have any of her strength, decisiveness, or confidence. She took her decisions in sprints and didn't second guess them. Whereas mine were in strides; second guessing every stitch.

"I have the sketch down!" I said in defense. "I'm just nervous it's not high-class enough." I continued to whisk until the ingredients were mixed thoroughly enough to be poured into the pan.

"Why do you say that?" she asked.

"I'm a haute couture design major, my pieces should be

grandiose and avant-garde, not simple," I emphasized with my hands.

"What makes it simple?"

"It doesn't have a lot going on. There's nothing groundbreaking about it or special."

"Do you like it though?"

"Well, yes but—"

"Daisy, if designers only made garments that they thought fit some sort of criteria, then there would be no such thing as haute couture to begin with. You should be designing from the heart; something that you love and care about. Or then, what's the point of designing at all?"

I could continue to feel as unsure as I wanted, but she was right. "Thank you," I said wholeheartedly.

"Your mother doesn't design dresses for celebrities for a living for nothing," she joked with a wink, making me laugh.

There was a pause as I started the timer on the oven and tucked the pan away into the heat. The kitchen was already beginning to smell like melted brown sugar and chocolate.

"Have you given Paris anymore thought?"

My muscles tensed up. I was trying to avoid checking my emails for a response from Lazaro, but it was on my mind all day, along with Levi's book.

"I have … but I'm still waiting to hear from Lazaro."

"I'm surprised you wouldn't be more excited about this opportunity with ESMOD. It's in *Paris*, the city of love and fashion. It's made for you."

"I don't know, Mom, it's just a big change: leaving New York for a year."

She exhaled, leaning her chin on her fist, mulling her thoughts over before speaking. "When you were younger, you dreamed of going to Paris. You used to go through all of my pictures and scrapbooks of my trips to southern France and Paris fashion weeks. You said that you were going to make your own scrapbooks one day and that they'd be filled with photos of the Eiffel Tower and the Louvre. But when your father died, it's like all the excitement and light had disappeared in your eyes. I felt the same way for a long time."

She paused.

"I'll have a crack in my heart until the day I die; he was my *best friend*. But to see you never speak of traveling again, to only watch Paris through a lens in your Hepburn movies ... I've always worried. You stopped taking chances. I remember when you applied to a summer fashion program in high school and didn't get in, and then you never applied again because you thought it meant you didn't deserve it."

Tears were finding a home in my eyes; I pinched my hands together to keep them from escaping. I was so tired of taking things personally, so I tried to keep my thoughts on the side as she spoke.

"And then Levi came into your life, and it's as if he gave you inspiration again. Your father inspired so much of my work too. He pushed me to follow my dreams, no matter how much physical distance it created between the two of us at times. So I know he wouldn't want to be the reason you're not challenging yourself. I just, what I was trying to say is that he would be, *he is*, happy for you and everything you've accomplished. He wouldn't want you holding yourself back because of what ifs. You have to do the scary stuff to get to the good stuff, remember?"

32

Burden me with your secrets

Sitting on my left was Jia, eating the blondies I'd made last night. While on my right, Josh was hogging the container.

"Josh, *give them back*," Jia whispered with rage.

"You already had four!" Josh whispered back. Well, I don't know if you could really call it whispering but—

"Because they were made for me!" Jia looked at me for back up.

"I can make you your own batch next week," I said decisively to Josh. He rolled his eyes at Jia, who looked satisfied with her victory, sliding the container back over.

Usually, Josh would be seating guests or taking orders tonight, but the restaurant was so dead that he had the time to sit with us while we watched Gabe on his date. Rather than watching intently though, I was busy refreshing my emails.

Six days and no response from Lazaro about my application, not even a confirmation that they got my submission. It made me think more and more if Paris was the right option then. I had been accepted by the other grad schools I applied to, some only a train ride away. But all I could recall was last night's conversation.

Paris was my dream for a long time, a dream that I hadn't revisited because it reminded me of what life was like with Dad. And being reminded of that meant being reminded of what life was without him. Those were two different lives, two different versions of myself. The Paris dream died when my life with Dad died.

"How many dates do you people go on?" Josh asked, looking at Gabe and his date.

"As many as it takes until I have a boyfriend," Jia scowled.

"I haven't seen Dani go on one of these dates in a while though," Josh commented with speculation.

"Um, I—" I was saved by the buzzing of my phone ringing with Levi's name on the screen.

"Hello?"

"Daisy!" Rhea shouted through the phone.

I laughed. "Rhea, does your brother know you're on his phone?"

"Well … no. But he wouldn't call you and ask for help, so *I had to*. I really had no choice."

"Help with what exactly?"

"Bella can't come to dance class tonight so now Levi doesn't have a dance partner! Sarah is acting like a crazy person now, it's scary. She said Bella always pulls this shit—"

"Whoa, whoa, whoa," I said in a rush before the nine-year-old could swear anymore. "So you need me to be Levi's dance partner?"

"Yes!" Rhea shouted. But then I heard a voice in the background of the call. "Rhea is that my phone?" Levi asked. "Who are you talking to?"

Jia stifled a laugh at his confusion.

"Hello?" Levi's voice came to the surface.

"It's awfully rude to interrupt a phone call."

"Dani?" he questioned. "I'm sorry, I didn't realize she had my phone."

"She's more fun to talk to than most people, don't apologize. Rhea said that you're out a partner for dance class?"

He groaned. "Yeah, Sarah's not happy about it. It's the last dance rehearsal before the wedding next week so you can imagine how panicked she is."

"I'm around …"

"Oh, *oh*, leave it to Rhea to fix a problem. I'm not going to bother you and involve you in more family drama—"

"Levi, I offered, so you're not bothering me."

"The girls are already dragging you over tomorrow. I'm not taking up any more of your time."

"I want to come. It's nice being around a big family. I miss it." I used to tell him that all the time when we were kids. I didn't have any grandparents or cousins growing up. It was always just me, Dad, Mom, and Mandy. Going to his house felt like I was entering a family sitcom from the 90s. There was so much laughter and yelling and arguing in the best way. And after Dad passed, I craved anything but the silence of my empty house.

A pause. "I just … I don't want to be a burden."

"Never. What time is the class?" I asked.

Another pause. "Thirty minutes, I'll pick you—"

"Levi, is your girlfriend coming? Rhea said she's coming!" Levi's grandma cut him off, making me laugh.

"*Oh Jesus*," he muttered. "Yes, Grandma, she's coming! I'm

going to pick her up now!" he shouted to her. It both warmed and stung my heart to hear Grandma Coldwell refer to me as his girlfriend, and then to hear his response. It was a painful reminder that we'd have to tell them at some point that we'd "broken up" and then, well, I didn't know what would come after.

"Wait!" Jia interjected. "You can't wear that, Dani." She pointed at my overalls and canvas shoes.

"What, why?"

"One, you're going to need heels. When my brother got married last year, we did dance classes, and all the women wore the heels they'd wear to the wedding. Two, you also can't be wearing that." She waved her finger up and down my outfit. "You're not going to be able to move in a pair of jeans, let alone overalls."

I scowled at her; my overalls were not something Jia and I agreed on. It wasn't that she had an agenda against overalls or anything, but she said I should be styling my clothes to the shape of my body, not using them to hide it.

I disagreed.

"What am I supposed to wear then? I'm not exactly carrying outfits around!" Something said by no fashion major ever.

"Ask him if he can stop by your house," she explained.

"Can you do me a huge favor?"

"Anything," he said. "You're the one doing me a huge favor."

"I need clothes. I'm currently wearing overalls."

"I love your overalls," he said, confused.

Jia must've heard because she took the phone from my hand. "Hi, Lover Boy, she can't dance in sneakers and denim, so I'm going to need you to grab a skirt and a pair of heels from her closet, preferably ones that match."

She paused, obviously listening to Levi's response. "Too many questions, just get a skirt that won't scar your grandmother and a pair of heels that won't make her look like a hooker." My face went crimson, and Josh was laughing as result. Gabe's date was officially on the backburner.

"We're at our usual restaurant, so bring them here when you're done." And she hung up.

33

So I can carry the weight you're so fearful
of letting go

Fifteen minutes later, the most striking man I'd ever laid my eyes on walked through the door. Even Gabe's date stared at Levi as he entered the restaurant with his well-tailored dress pants, dress shoes, and a short sleeve button down that had just enough buttons unbuttoned to look handsome. In his left hand was a folded garment and a pair of heels hanging from his two fingers. Along with—

"Did he buy you flowers?" Josh asked with a surprised look on his face.

Daisies actually. He was carrying a bouquet of daisies.

I couldn't remember the last time anyone had bought me flowers.

He spotted Gabe and his date before seeing us in the back. And then, just like that, I caught his gaze, and his face shifted from this look of quick surprise to wonderous bliss, as if he had found his friend amongst a room of strangers.

He walked towards us with a slight blush and the most

beautiful, quiet smile; his brunette curls bouncing above his ears.

When he reached the table, he timidly held the bouquet out like an unaccepted invitation, and immediately began apologizing, "I know it's not much—"

I wrapped my arms behind his neck and hugged him with the joy I felt on the first day of spring, muffling his unfinished apology in my neck. His occupied hands didn't hesitate to hold my torso.

"What did I do to deserve this?" he whispered into the crook of my shoulder. The warmth of his breath and the proximity of his lips to my neck, flooded my body with heat.

"You bought me flowers," I said pulling away. "Thank you."

"I'll buy you flowers every day for the rest of my life if it makes you this happy." The tone of his voice and the look in his eyes: it all appeared sincere, unlike a joke or the line of a fake boyfriend, which was not what my heart needed right now when it craved him constantly.

"Thank you for bringing me clothes, I'll be quick," I said with a smile, taking the clothes from him.

Josh let me use the employee bathroom so I could avoid changing in a stall. I hung the skirt on the hook of the back of the door as I unbuttoned my overalls. I stepped into the skirt and zippered it up. It fit well because it was something I made for myself, but it hadn't hugged my hips *like this* before. The feeling of fabric hugging my hips wasn't a sensation I was familiar with, but looking in the mirror, it actually looked … nice.

"What are you possibly doing in there!" Jia shouted through the door.

"Questioning my life!" I shouted back.

The floral of the silk skirt hit my knees, a length I preferred because it reminded me of how Europeans dressed during the summertime.

I definitely looked like I was about to go out dancing. I didn't know where to focus: the petite heels, the knee length skirt that hugged my butt, or the top that was so tight that you could see the shape of my chest and every freckle on my back.

Opening the bathroom—

"Holy shit, I forgot what your hips looked like," Jia said.

I smacked my hand against her shoulder. "Very funny, I get it."

"No, I'm being serious. James Dean out there is going to start drooling when he sees you."

I rolled my eyes. She returned it with a glare.

"This is a no though," she said waving a hand at my hair. Without my response, she tugged the hair clip out of my hair and ran her fingers through it, bringing over my shoulders. Working her "stylist magic" as she liked to say, she rushed me back in front of the mirror to look. And, well, I—I think it worked. "You design beautiful clothes, Dani, it's time you start wearing them."

I usually brushed those responses off but looking at myself in the mirror now without immediately critiquing myself, I said, "Maybe."

"It's okay to say you're pretty, you know that right? It's more than okay actually, because you look amazing," Jia said earnestly, that caring look in her face that made her look like her mother.

I touched her shoulder. "I know," I said. But the more I thought about it as I walked outside to meet Levi, I didn't know. I never thought about saying something like that out loud to myself.

But I felt good, like there was an extra muscle in my back fixing my posture.

Walking out the door, with a confused look from Josh on the way out, I found Levi leaning against his car, looking down at his phone.

"Hey, sorry about that." My voice startled him, driving his gaze up, and watched as his lips parted. He was either realizing how inappropriate my clothes looked because of how tight they were and what Grandma Coldwell would think. Or he was thinking what Jia had assumed; the tightness of the fabric around my hips and waist and how they would feel under his—

No. No, no, no. We were friends, and nothing more. Hormones were what carried his eyes over my clothes, not love.

I wasn't looking for some *She's All That* moment. "I know, I know. I never dress like this so I swear to God if you ever bring it up, I will personally add laxatives to the next thing I bake for you." His mouth immediately closed, and he cleared his throat. I rocked back and forth on the balls of my feet, the heels already bothering them. "Ready to see me bust out some horrible dance moves?"

He laughed. Any inclination of conflict in his face before had disappeared as he opened up the car door for me. "Just you wait until you see Sarah try to dance."

On the ride there, I hugged the bouquet of daisies to my chest as we talked. Every few moments, he would glance over at the flowers and suppress a smile. Flowers weren't meant to stay out of soil or water, so leaving the bouquet in the car as we entered the dance center *pained me.*

"We can bring the daisies inside if you want?" he asked me with a laugh as he opened the passenger door.

"No, that's alright. They should be okay." I winced internally. As you could see, I radiated this concern.

"I will buy you more if they get ruined." The gesture was really kind, but I didn't have much time to mull it over because I was busy getting out of the car without tripping. Nothing like moving around in a skirt and trying not to flash anyone.

"Quick question: how many of these classes have you done?"

"About enough that I should look like I know what I'm doing, but not enough to do any *Dirty Dancing* moves."

I groaned. "So I'm like really *really* behind compared to everyone else?" I may not be a perfect student, but that didn't mean I was okay with being the one who had to play catch up.

"I saw you dance last week, it's just like that." He held the door open for me where we walked up a set of stairs to find a room full or mirrors and several of the Coldwell's, the bridesmaids, and the groomsmen. Rhea and Claire were sitting off to the side with Grandma Coldwell, while everyone else chatted and changed into heels and removed jackets. I couldn't have been more thankful for Jia forcing me to wear heels. However, I still couldn't help but pinch at the tight fabric around my torso and hips.

There were so many people there, about fifteen, all who are about to see me step on Levi's feet and not to mention, had already watched me chuck a softball at Bella's head a few weeks ago. I wasn't great at making group impressions apparently. At least Bella wasn't there.

Sarah rushed towards us in the doorway and crushed me in a hug. "I cannot thank you enough for being here. My wedding would be plagued by Levi's horrible footwork if you hadn't come." I'm pretty sure Jeff and Levi were rolling their eyes.

"Well, you haven't seen me dance, so I wouldn't thank me just yet."

She laughed. But little did she know, I was completely serious.

The instructor insisted we all grab our partners and get into position. This involved me standing in front of Levi with an incredibly anxious face (that made him laugh) because I had no idea what they'd been learning the past few weeks.

"It's just like last weekend," he repeated, but last weekend was the *last thing* I wanted to be reminded of. "You're going to place your hand here," he said, taking my left hand and placing it on his shoulder.

"And then I'm going to place my hand here," he said, his voice sounding rougher than before, placing his right hand on my hip where the fabric of my shirt and the silk of my skirt met, leaving an area of my torso exposed to his hand. "And we're going to hold hands here, just like last time. The only difference is to raise your elbows."

"Alright class, you know the drill, begin dancing and I will come around!" the instructor shouted. Levi began leading us and I attempted to follow his steps. We were basically creating the shape of a square with our feet, was how he explained it.

"She's scary," I said with a horrified look on my face, while staring at the ground. If I stopped staring at our feet, then I was going to step on him.

"Oh definitely. She hit me off the head with a heel the first class. I'm slightly traumatized."

I laughed; he made it easy. He smiled back.

"Is that a bird glued to her headband?" I said looking up. "Shit—sorry, sorry," I said in a rush for stepping on his foot.

"Dani, you're fine, don't worry. Our only real audience right now is Rhea and Claire."

I looked over at them and they had huge smiles on their faces, giggling at us. He was right, no one else was paying us any attention. They were busy not stepping on each other's toes.

Levi was pulling my attention back to him though as he tugged on a piece of my hair.

"You used to always do that when you were uncomfortable," he commented.

"What?"

"Pick at your clothes."

"I'm not picking at my clothes."

He rolled his eyes. "You are. Now tell me what's wrong because I know something's wrong."

"Closer together! There's too much room between you two. What is this, church? This is the tango, move closer!" the instructor shouted at us.

As embarrassed as I felt to be shouted at as an adult, it took every muscle in my face not to laugh. Levi was bursting at the seams with giggles.

But when we moved closer together, our bodies only inches apart, the laughter died.

"Dani." I followed his footwork.

"Hm."

"What's wrong? I'll take care of it." I tried not to tighten my grip on his shoulder as I almost tripped forward.

What wasn't wrong? One, I was so close to him that all I could think about were his hands, two, I wished my fake boyfriend was my real boyfriend and three, Lazaro hadn't called, or emailed, or

Liana Cincotti

mailed, or anything.

"I haven't heard from Lazaro."

"You submitted the application? You finished the essay?" I stepped backwards and then to the left.

"I did, over the weekend actually, I forgot to tell you. And now it's been six days and nothing, no response. They're ghosting me."

Levi laughed at my attempt to humor the situation. "They're not ghosting you. These things just take time." Forward and to the right.

"Hmm," I muttered. But I could already imagine the rejection letter in my head. I could've written it for Lazaro at this point.

We are sorry to tell you that you have not been picked for our program. Your designs are basic and lack personality, and you'd be better off never designing a piece of clothing again—

"Hey," he interjected, forcing my attention away from our feet and to his face with the movement of his thumb on my back. Goosebumps made a home of my spine.

His eyes appeared so brown then, so dark. Like the sand of a beach after it rained or the color of coffee after it was brewed. A shade that mimicked the darkness of his hair.

"I can see what's happening in that head of yours. I know we haven't seen each other in a long time, but I haven't forgotten, and I won't let you think another cruel thing about yourself. You are *incredible*. They would be absolutely senseless not to want you."

A silence passed between us.

"Dani, say it."

"Say what?"

"Say you're incredible."

I laughed with a sound that came all the way from my belly.

"Pfft, not happening."

"Say it or I'll do something that'll make the bird instructor come over and embarrass us."

"*You wouldn't.*"

"*Try me.*"

I groaned.

"… I'm incredible." I said it in a monotone voice, obviously.

"That was pathetic."

"Thank you very much, I accept tips in the form of bread and flowers."

"Again."

I rolled my eyes. "I get to pick the movie tomorrow night," I tried bargaining with him.

"That's a battle you'll have to fight with Rhea over there."

"Well, I need some incentive here."

"You know, the instructor is getting pretty close to us, maybe I should ask her about the bird—"

"Fine, *fine*. I am … incredible. God, that was painful."

"Such a punk."

The class was unsettling until suddenly, it was fun. Levi and I were laughing, Rhea and the Claire would blow kisses at us whenever Levi twirled me, and we were all making fun of Sarah and Jeff's first dance because Jeff would move too quickly, causing Sarah to topple forward.

Even Rhea and Claire joined in at the end, fighting over who got to dance with their big brother. Levi, of course, made it a priority to give each girl their turn, picking them up, holding them close, and spinning them around to the music. The girls giggled and shouted with joy to not be put back down because they were having so much fun.

He had this smile on his face that could've powered the sun. The corners of his eyes crinkled with laughter; the way dough of croissants creased in the oven. His brown curls bounced with the balls of his feet, and I stared in awe.

Setting aside my feelings that were bursting from the seams of my heart, I thought over how I wouldn't get to see this or be a part of this for a year if I chose to go to Paris. If that was a decision I made, I'd only hope that this friendship wouldn't come to a complete halt again. Maybe I'd send postcards and they'd call. Maybe.

Levi and I followed Jeff, Sarah, the girls, and Grandma Coldwell out of the studio to the parking lot. Levi knelt down and picked up Rhea, putting her in her booster seat, and then did the same for Claire, planting a kiss on each of their heads.

"I'll see you tomorrow night, alright?"

They nodded and shouted, "Love you!" through the car windows as we walked away.

"Bye guys, be careful," he said to Sarah and Jeff, giving Jeff a death glare in the driver's seat that was evidently a *drive careful or else* look.

"Ready to go?" Levi asked me. I nodded.

We got in the car (daisies droopy but not dead on the console) and Levi snagged my attention from his seat.

"What?" I asked curiously.

"Thank you, again, for coming. It's been a long time since I had fun like that. I'm always worrying about everything going on that I forget to have any type of fun, even with the girls."

I reached my hand over and rubbed the back of his hand in a

friendly, caring gesture. "Thank you for letting me be a part of it." Things felt normal, nice.

Until I saw Bella's name appear on his phone; a cruel reminder after the fun we'd had tonight. Dancing and laughing together while also being intimate, only to realize that he'd been doing that with Bella for the past four weeks. My hand behind his shoulder, *her* hand behind his shoulder. His hand on my waist, his hand on *her* waist.

I'm so over being the side character.

I clutched the bouquet of daisies to my chest for the rest of the ride home.

34

If hearts were meant to love, then why did mine
feel so empty?

It was statistically proven that if you didn't tell the person you were in love with that you loved them, then it'd be written across your face at all times. That was completely factual. And I had the evidence, because it was how I looked at the moment, walking into Levi's mother's home to find him chasing Rhea.

Normal, I know. But Claire had opened the door for me and told me that Levi had only just gotten out of the shower, so he'd be a second. But then Rhea seemed to have stolen something from him, because he was in the hallway with soaked hair, no shirt, and just a towel ...

"Rhea, give me the clothes *now* or——"

"Hi, Daisy!" Rhea stopped mid-run and shouted.

His head snapped up to spot my presence at the front door. His cheeks went crimson, and his hand tightened on the towel around his waist. The towel was catching the droplets of water that fell from his hair at the nape of his neck and traveled down the muscles in his chest and abdomen—I was going to pass out.

I threw my purse in front of my face. "Sorry, sorry! Claire said you were still in the shower, I didn't realize—"

He grabbed the clothes from Rhea's hand and placed them in front of his— "No, no it's fine. This is what I get for showering here after work. My mom had to go to a real-estate class, so I came early. I'll be quick, I just need to get dressed." And then I heard the bathroom door shut.

I didn't think I'd ever get that image out of my head. Levi must've been equally scarred because he took more than a moment to get changed.

Fortunately, I had Rhea and Claire as buffers to distract me from this situation. They pulled me into the kitchen to show me all the snacks they prepared: bowls of popcorn, chocolate, chips, and—

"Is that strawberry shortcake?" I asked in surprise from the kitchen threshold. Two tiers of vanilla cake with white frosting and cut strawberries wedged in between and on top. It was the kind of cake you wanted to make a home out of and live in because it was so pretty.

"We made it for you." I turned and found Levi in the hallway, dressed this time, looking at me with a shy smile. I'd be lying if I said it wasn't difficult to ignore what'd just happened and how he looked under his shirt.

"For me?" I asked incredulously, pressing my finger to my chest. He was talking about me?

"Who else?" he asked. And suddenly, I felt naked in my linen pants and T-shirt. The way he was looking at me felt too vulnerable. He rendered me speechless … I–I didn't even know what to say. "Do you want some?" he asked.

I laughed at myself, thankful for him filling in my blanks.

"That would be amazing."

The last time I watched Levi cut into a strawberry shortcake was when I turned eighteen. He made me one for every birthday I had in high school. It was like déjà vu watching him now. Only this time he was taller and the muscles in his arms under his T-shirt were toned.

The girls gathered chocolate and popcorn for themselves while Levi handed me a (huge) piece of cake. It only took seconds for me to eat it all.

"That was *incredible*. I can die happy now."

Claire giggled at my comment.

"Rhea, what movie are we watching tonight?"

"I don't know, Levi picks the movies. He has to make sure they're appropriate first," she responded.

Slowly, I turned to Levi and threw a strawberry at him. "You liar!"

He laughed, catching the strawberry before it could hit him. "What! I take movie night very seriously!"

"It sounds like you're questioning my taste in movies."

"I definitely am."

"Jerk," I said with a laugh.

Moving into the living room, I panicked when realizing I hadn't planned for this: seating arrangements. This was a moment I didn't know I needed to be concerned about until it arrived. Should I be sitting close to him? Would the girls think it was weird if I wasn't since they think we're dating?

I sat down on the couch before he could—I shouldn't have been allowed to make this decision. But it seemed like he didn't have a chance to either because Claire sat on my left and Rhea sat on my right, both of them clutching numerous toys and candy.

"Guys, can we let Dani breathe a bit?" he asked when he walked in and found them both beside me.

They responded to him with pouty lips. "Give her a little bit of room at least," he said. The girls each moved about an inch away from me.

I laughed. "It's alright, don't worry."

He sighed and sat down on the other side of Claire, and rifled through the movies, listing off ones they could pick from that were appropriate. *The Princess Diaries* won. And when it ended, they begged him to play the second. He gave me an unsure look, so I clicked play on the second.

Thirty minutes in and Rhea's head felt heavier under my arm and Claire's posture became slouched, slowly falling into Levi's lap. The scene where Mia and Nicholas were in front of the fountain began—

"Hey!" I angrily whispered at him for pausing the movie.

"What?" he whispered back.

"This is my favorite part. You can turn it off after." I took the remote and resumed it.

Mia and Nicholas were fighting and then suddenly, they stopped talking for just a moment, and Nicholas pulled Mia forward with his hand behind her head and kissed her. *Really* kissed her.

Every fiber of his being was being put in this kiss. My shoulders sagged with relief and I could feel the blood from my heart traveling through my body. His arms around her, her hair in his face; her leg popped up, right before she pulled away and they tripped backwards into the fountain.

I·clicked the TV off and look at Levi as I said, "Now wasn't that worth it?" But he was already turning away from me, lifting Claire into his arms. She was wrapping her delicate arms around his neck and her legs around him like a koala bear.

"I'll come back for her in a second," he said, walking away.

I looked down at Rhea. Her small lips were parted, releasing tiny snores. Her bangs were all over the place and popcorn was in both of our laps. The various toys filling the space on the couch were laughable. Picking the pieces of popcorn off us and dropping them into the bowl, I lifted her up into my arms, careful not to wake her.

I went up the stairs to where he had gone and found him in the room furthest down the hall, tucking Claire into bed. His head turned swiftly, like any movement around them had to be accounted for.

"Thank you," he whispered, taking Rhea out of my arms. She immediately clung to him, like she could recognize the sound of his voice even when asleep.

I watched as he tucked her into the bed across from Claire, and led us out of the room, leaving the door open a crack. Levi looked tired; his shoulders were rolled forward, and his eyes were half closed as we walked down the stairs and into the living room.

He fell onto the couch with a groan. I fell beside him. His face was clouded with worry but also with sleepiness as he stared up at the ceiling like it was singing him lullabies. How often was he here taking care of the girls after work? How often were there messes being made that had to be cleaned?

We were surrounded by toys. I began tossing them into the basket across the room, the sound jolting him. He sat up and watched me.

"You're pretty good," he said.

"It's those softball skills," I responded with a wink hoping to make him laugh. He did. It made me smile.

He grabbed a stuffed bear and tossed it.

"Oh my gosh, you suck." I laughed.

"It was one bad shot!"

"I bet you the next one will still be bad."

"What do I get if you're wrong?"

"Hmm. Flowers?"

"I'll buy you flowers anyways. What about … a question?"

"A question?" I asked, trying to act as if the first part of what he said hadn't made my heartbeat speed up.

"If I win, I get to ask you anything." His eyes flickered to me quickly before looking back at the basket. The air in the room was thick.

"Fine. The same goes for every one I get in too."

We began throwing the girls' toys into the basket from the couch. Levi landed one in seconds.

"Oh my gosh, you punk, you were bad on purpose!" I said in shock.

"Not true! You just doubted my abilities, and now you must answer a question." He thought for a moment. "Are you still a bad driver?"

"Oh my—" And I chucked a (soft) toy at his head.

"I'm kidding, I'm kidding! I'll be serious now. Do you …" He hesitated. I still struggled to place this Levi in my head. This nervous, blushing, second-guessing man had never existed in the catalog of actions I had created in my mind. "Do you still bake when you're stressed?"

"How do you remember that?"

"How could I forget?" A beat between us went by where neither of knew what to say. But: "What do you bake now?"

"Blondies," I said, still surprised. I threw a toy in and landed it. "My turn."

"Ask away."

I laughed when I figured out my question. "Has a girl in your class ever hit on you?"

He groaned. "You are determined to embarrass me, I swear." As he spoke, it was difficult not to look at the shape of his jaw and the muscles in his arms. We were both so drunk on drowsiness that this line we had drawn ages ago was becoming blurry. There were so many things I'd wanted to ask him and apparently, he'd felt the same, so I was taking my chance. Maybe he was tired enough that he wouldn't remember the details tomorrow morning.

"Yes."

"I need specifics here, Coldwell. How many?" He tipped his head back on the couch with a laugh. His Adam's apple bobbed and his lips—*stop*. I needed to separate myself from his body and scoot over; it'd only be torture to smell him on my clothes later.

"Six girls."

"*Six*? Six girls have hit on you?" That was a third of the class.

He nodded his head, pressing his eyes closed with embarrassment.

"Why are you embarrassed?" I asked in alarm.

"I'm supposed to be an academic in training. They're not supposed to be interested in me, it's not appropriate. And the last thing I'd want is to make anyone uncomfortable—"

"Vi, *you're hot.*"

He turned his head, his eyebrows raised. "You think I'm hot?"

"Well, everyone does."

He nodded, closing his mouth and bit down on the inside of his cheek. Sitting back up, he threw another toy. He missed. I missed. And then he got one.

"Why did your last relationship end?"

I forgot that I had told him about the TA I'd dated for a bit. I just, I hadn't expected him to remember. "It wasn't really a relationship; it only lasted a month. The guy was cute but, I don't know, it felt average. I'd rather live through romance movies and be single than have a bunch of average dates." I shrugged my shoulders. He nodded but looked as if he wanted to ask more.

I missed. He missed. Then I got one.

If we were talking about relationships, then it seemed okay for me to ask the question I hadn't stopped think about since seeing him in that bar.

"Do you still love Bella?"

His jaw twitched and his gaze was far away. Maybe the line wasn't as blurry as I had thought.

But then he started speaking. "She pushed me to challenge myself, but at a pace I wasn't ready for. She cared for me, and I cared for her. But she said things about Rhea and Claire I'll never forget. She treated me in a way that made me seem like I wasn't enough because I was so focused on them—which I understand. But it also meant she didn't understand our situation as a family or understood them."

He exhaled. "It's bittersweet. She also didn't appreciate how much the girls talked about you. Or how much I talked about you." His eyes flickered to me before looking away again. "I don't know why I said all of that, I'm sorry."

Those words poked at a never healing bruise of what I imagined his relationship with Bella to be like. It took everything in me to hold in my surprise because the last thing I expected was for him to have been unhappy with her. The idea of her treating him less than for how much he cared about his family and what she possibly said about the girls … It made my spine tighten with anger and my mind whirl with questions.

But I already got to ask my question. It was his turn.

"If you could have anything in the world, what would it be?"

He looked at me like he truly wanted to know, like my answer would mean something. There was always this sense of comforting safety in his voice. It was safe to tell the truth. So I did, even if it felt like telling your enemy where you hid your knives.

"Love," I exhaled; that answer had been as easy as drinking water. It existed in all of my daydreams. "I want an all-consuming love. Not one that suffocates, but one that makes me so thankful that my chest feels physically overwhelmed with emotion. To have this silent, unspoken communication with a person through touch and gazes."

I let out a tired breath. "I want to be noticed in a crowded room. I want to be the *only person* in a crowded room. I want to be wanted, truly *wanted*, and desired. I want to laugh and to sing and to dance with someone and not feel self-conscious over it because I love them and I'm confident that they love me. I want to be touched and kissed and held because I've forgotten what it feels like … and yet, I think I deserve it."

By the time I had finished, my face had flushed, and Levi was watching me. Lips parted, eyes curious, and neck taut. His head was only inches away from mine in the dark living room. I so badly wanted to lean forward and show him how I wanted to be kissed. But it wouldn't have even mattered because he already knew. He knew exactly how to kiss me.

I thought wanting him was enough, but now that I've kissed him, tasted him, nothing would ever be enough.

"Are you in love now?" he asked. My heart tripped over itself and hit the bottom of my stomach. That was a secret I wouldn't even give up in my dreams, no matter how tired.

"You only won one question."

He looked down, but there was nothing left to be cleaned.

"Did you ever read the book?" he asked. The book? I gave him a confused look before I realized—

"I, no, I haven't," I stumbled.

"Oh, okay." He sounded disappointed. The quick nod of his head and indirect eye contact. I thought I was doing the right thing by protecting this private thing he hadn't shared with me the past four weeks. But maybe I was wrong, maybe he had changed his mind.

"I just haven't gotten the chance—"

"No, no, it's okay, there's no obligation for you to read it or anything. I was just wondering."

I nodded. "I should probably go." Getting a cab at this time of the night was going to suck. Cabs weren't exactly in the masses in the Village on a Saturday night.

"Stay," he said. "Sleep in my old room, I'll take the couch."

"Levi—"

35

Maybe you weren't mine to love

He cut me off. "I don't want you going out this late at night by yourself, it's not safe." I knew he wanted to take me home. It was a comforting thought. But we both knew someone had to be home with the girls.

"Levi—"

"Dani, you will give me a heart attack if I have to think about you going home by yourself. My mind will wreak havoc on me, and I will think of the absolute worst that could happen, so I beg you to please save me some sanity and just stay the night."

"I was going to say okay," I said with a smile.

He groaned in embarrassment and hid his face before laughing. "Why don't I ever just shut up?"

I laughed. "I'll take the couch, there's no reason for you to sleep down here."

"I'm going to make sure there's sheets on the bed," he said, ignoring my argument and walking straight up to his room.

After a moment, I walked upstairs to his room, finding him folding over a comforter on the bed. The room was clean and plain, with two bookcases on either side of the window where moonlight poured in, and a small wooden desk that sat beside closet doors. The headboard of the bed was pressed against the furthest wall with a nightstand beside it.

His room was full of greens and greys, and he had random photographs and papers peppering the walls and surfaces.

Next to his bookcase were numerous photos framed on the wall of him and his family when they were younger, along with images of friends and places he must've taken.

Among them all was one picture of us in high school that stood out. It was a photo strip from a concert we went to for Levi's seventeenth birthday. I could remember it like it was yesterday. I forced him into that photobooth—he *hated* taking pictures. But we had no other photos from that day, and I knew it deserved some physical memento. It was his birthday! I had slipped the photo strip into his wallet, but I never knew he would've kept it after high school graduation.

We were smiling in the first picture, sticking our tongues out in the second, laughing at each other in the third, and I was hugging him in the fourth. It was before I realized how far my feelings went for him.

Levi cleared his throat from where he now stood leaning against his desk. "I took out some old pajama pants and a T-shirt if you want to change?"

"Thank you." When I offered to take the couch, it was an immediate reaction. But now that I stood in front of his bed ... I should've argued more. I couldn't help but think of all the girls he'd loved before. The ones who've sat on this bed with him and had been in this room. Not only would I have to sleep in his bed where the sheets smelt like his cologne, but I'd have to put on his shirt and his pants and they'd— "That's okay. I can sleep in these." My linen pants were comfortable enough.

He began fidgeting with his watch. Undoing it and tightening it again. He had said something else to say, I could tell. I carefully sat on his bed and watched him from across the room, waiting.

"Can I ask you something?" he prompted.

"Of course."

"Why did you say yes? To this, to helping me and agreeing to come to the wedding." He brushed a hand through his thick hair and crossed his arms. Not in an intimidating, questioning way, but in a handsome, nervous way. He gnawed on his lip.

I thought of how he asked me to stay only ten minutes ago, and how honest he was. I don't know if it was the effect the exhaustion had on my brain, or the desperation I had to feel confident for once in my life. But I said earnestly, "I missed you."

Part of me felt satisfied with his surprised look. Surprise grew in his eyes, and then warm relief bloomed in his cheeks. His shoulders went slack as if he had come in from the cold and sat in front of a fire.

"I missed you," he said.

My chest ached. "Why did you ask me?"

He didn't hesitate. "Because I needed an excuse to see you again."

The surprise was blatant on my face. "Why?"

He laughed quietly. "I could write a book on why."

If I'd learned anything about unrequited love, it was to stop asking questions. The more I dug for answers, the more it hurt, and I only discovered the same results: we were friends.

He missed our friendship, I did too. But I couldn't deny that when I looked at his dark hair, I thought of how it was to run my hands through it when we kissed. And I couldn't deny that when I watched him move, I watched the way his hands flexed and thought of how they felt on my back and behind my neck. And when I watched him speak, all I could focus on was the movement of his lips and how they whispered *Daisy*.

"I'll um, I'll let you go to bed." He left the room and shut the door behind him.

I exhaled and tried to not think too much about what he'd said. Looking down at my top, I sighed. It was fitted around my chest and tight under my arms. I couldn't sleep in this. I gave Levi's folded T-shirt another glance before tugging mine off and pulling his on. It reached the middle of my thighs and smelled like a mix of fresh laundry and sandalwood.

I refused to change my pants.

Picking my jewelry off like flower petals, I left my rings and earrings on his nightstand. Reaching behind my neck, I toyed with the clasp of my necklace with my short nails. *Ugh, not working.*

I stood up from the bed with an awoken frustration and padded down the stairs in my socks.

Levi was sitting back on the couch reading. He heard me before he saw me, asking, "Hey, what's—" He paused when he saw me, his eyes glued to my—his—shirt.

"Would you mind taking off my necklace? It's stuck."

He ran his hand up and down the back of his neck. "Of course. Sit." The couch was fairly spacious, so it didn't feel weird to sit in front of him, in between his extended legs.

He made an unidentifiable sound before moving my hair over

Liana Cincotti

my shoulder. He laughed.

"I'll just hold it." I laughed, knowing that it was too short to stay.

I collected my hair as his hand brushed the back of my neck. His forehead tapped the back of my head as he focused on the clasp, and I felt myself wanting to lean backwards into his chest. To let his head fall between the crook of my neck and my shoulder.

I didn't know what he was thinking, but I did know that he paused for a moment after undoing the fixture. The air felt too warm, and we were incredibly aware of how much space was left between us.

"Dieu, aide-moi," he sighed.

I turned my head in surprise. I hadn't heard that phrase in French before. "What does that mean?"

He cleared his throat. "Here's your necklace."

I took that as my cue to leave, but as I moved to get up, he brushed my wrist. "Dani."

"Yes?"

"You do deserve it, to be loved. You deserve it more than anyone."

It was unexpected to hear him bring up our conversation from earlier. There was too much that had happened today for me to try to dissect that. Looking at him from over my shoulder, I pressed my eyes shut. "Goodnight, Levi."

I didn't know which was harder: to be told you deserved love from someone who wasn't in love with you, or to pretend like they'd never said it at all.

36

And suddenly, I fell

When I went to bed last night, I almost crawled across the comforter and dug through my bag for Levi's book in desire for some type of answer to our weirdness. He had given me the approval to read it last night. But I knew if I started it, I wouldn't have stopped, and I needed sleep. I hadn't even heard Trish come in last night from her class.

I was on my way to campus now to finish my last dress. Sounds productive, but I desperately needed a distraction because I hadn't stopped refreshing my inbox all morning. I knew Levi understood, so he didn't try to hold me up. He did say he'd pick me up tonight for Sunday dinner.

"If you're around tonight," he said quickly.

I laughed and hit his arm and said, "Of course."

The classroom full of sewing machines, sewing patterns, and dress forms was empty. I went to the corner of the class where I left my cut fabric and began pinning the matching pieces in order to stitch them together. Sewing together the structure would be the longest step. Making sure that the seams were clean and that the dress lay comfortably would be the most difficult part, and

Liana Cincotti

then working on the details, like adding pearl accents, and doing alterations would be the exciting part, like decorating a cake.

Hours of sewing flew by before the structure was done, and I was ready to be done for the night. Levi would probably be here in twenty minutes. I opened my emails and scrolled until—

Lazaro finally emailed. I jumped out of my seat and did a lap around the room before finally finding the strength to sit still.

We appreciate your time and interest in Lazaro's Master's Program. The Admissions Committee has received a record-breaking number of applications this semester. Therefore, we regret to inform you that we are unable to ...

The rest of the email was a mystery because the tears in my eyes made the words blurry. *I didn't get in. I didn't get in. I wasn't good enough, again.*

Tears were clogging my eyes and my throat and my chest, and my hands were shaking, and my face hurt from the headache that the tears were causing. What now? What do I do now?

Instinctively, I picked my phone back up to call Levi, only to realize that he'd be here soon and that it was possible Ethan actually may be here. I quickly collected my bag and rushed down the hallway to Ethan's office, where fortunately, he was.

I held up my phone where the email sat and said, "Did you hear?" knowing that he as my advisor would get the same notices.

He gave me a sad look and said, "Yes."

I sat down in the chair in front of his desk. He stood in front of me, leaning against his desk. I'm surprised he wasn't more horrified by my red-rimmed eyes and the tear stains on my cheeks.

I fought to stable my shaking hands; I–I just needed someone to talk to. "This was my dream, Ethan, this was the goal. And I ... I thought I actually had a chance."

He sighed. "This is why you applied to other places though, you have backups."

I knew I had backups, but they were backups for a reason. "I know," was all I said.

"You knew how difficult this program was to get into. Many students from here don't get in." His response only made me feel worse. *You're just like everyone else*, is what that sounded like. I nodded my head. When you faced rejection in your life so often, how were you supposed to think otherwise?

He sighed again, sounding exasperated. "You could have your mother make a call."

My spine went rigid, and my headache immediately cleared. There wasn't a corner of my mind that was clouded now. "I would never do that." Not only had I explained to him numerous times that I didn't want her involved, but I also would never take away someone else's place at Lazaro because of it.

"Daniella, if you want things in life, you need to take the extra help. That's how this industry works: fighting tooth and nail and cutting some corners when necessary." I sat there horrified. He was an esteemed designer, a training academic, and now he was talking about cheating?

He pushed off his desk and leaned over me. My body immediately reacted like a tide in a storm, pushing away. My back collided with the cushion of the chair as his hands gripped the armrests, caging me in. Air stopped traveling through my lungs. His face was only inches away from mine, and I could smell the gum he was chewing; it made me nauseous. I clamped my mouth shut.

He cocked an eyebrow. "Well, if you're not going to ask her, you could always ask me …"

Who was this person? I refused to look into his eyes. His hand moved from the armrest onto my knee as my heart sped up and my mind reeled. *How did I misjudge him? I thought he was trying to help me.*

He kept talking. I squeezed my eyes shut as his face came closer. "We both know you need the help. Your designs are fine, nothing special. You don't even make any of the designs for yourself." I cringed and he laughed. "You think I didn't notice? I know you better than you think. Not using your mother's name because you don't want to be compared to her; the constant need for approval; never designing clothes that fit you because you don't think your body is good enough."

My throat was closing in on itself and my eyes burned from closeted tears. The muscles and bones in my body were fusing together, too scared to move an inch. I was paralyzed.

"I doubt I'm the only who's noticed, but I am the only one who is willing to help you."

"Please stop," I whispered.

He laughed quietly before his lips reached the crest of my ear. "Maybe break up with that boyfriend and I can make my own call to Lazaro for you." *Levi.* I was this close to him last night, but it felt nothing like this. He should be on his way.

But he wasn't here right now.

Ethan moved his hand further up my leg, and I reacted with a jolt, like a torch was tapped against my leg, burning my skin through my denim. I lifted my knee up with as much adrenaline as I could. He grunted and fell forward. I shoved him off of me and ran out the door. *Breathe, breathe, breathe.* Breathing was too difficult, between processing what just happened and running out the door and sobbing at the same time. *Levi, Levi, Levi*, was all I could think, all I could *hope*.

I ran down the stairs of the building and through the exit and—

I ran straight into Levi's chest. His smile quickly fell and turned into a worried look. His hands latched onto both sides of my jaw, cradling my face upward. "Daisy, baby, what's wrong?"

But I couldn't answer because tears were clogging my throat. I was gasping for air in between sobs. He pulled me into his chest, and I held onto him like he was keeping me above water. I cried, and I cried, and I cried, soaking his shirt. He brushed my hair with his hand trying to calm me down and pressed his lips to the crown of my head. Slowly pulling away, he held my face in his hands, my heart in his hands as he looked at me.

He wiped away my tears as they fell. "Baby, I need you to breathe, okay? We're going to take a deep breath in, just like that, and exhale. Good, give me one more."

I obeyed, trying to slow down my heartbeat.

"Now tell me what's wrong, I'll fix it." His voice was so sincere, so quiet, so worried. Wrinkled skin between brows and a sloped frown.

My voice was trembling like I was a frail shed made of straw about to blow away. "We need to leave, now, right now." I was so terrified that Ethan was going to come running through the door.

His face was a storm of emotions, shifting from sweet concern to quiet rage. He stilled and I watched the gears turning in his head. He spoke with an even, assertive tone. "Daisy, what's wrong?"

"He–I–Ethan," I stuttered, I couldn't say it, I couldn't say it, or it'd be real and then I wouldn't be able to pretend like it never happened.

Levi looked as if I slapped him. "*Ethan?* What did he—" He exhaled, trying to collect himself. I'd never seen him so angry. "What did he do?"

"He … he tried to"—*sniff*—"he tried to touch me." My eyes were filling like wells again.

Whatever internal battle Levi was fighting in order to stay calm, he had just lost. He looked *ruined*. Ruined, and vengeful, and sick.

His lips were pressed in a tight line as he uttered, "I will *kill him.*"

He dropped his hands from my face and moved to walk back into the building. "*No*, Levi, no, please, please don't leave," I begged.

He stopped. His face went slack, looking at me with sadness and conflict. He wanted to go back in and do something. He glanced at the building one more time before looking at me and bringing me into his arms.

"I am going to take care of this," he insisted as I clutched onto him. The tears kept coming.

It was the end of an era of my life. I was rejected, again, by something I loved. Lazaro didn't want me. And someone who I thought I could trust had thought nothing of me.

Levi continued to run his hand over my head and through my hair, whispering to me, trying to soothe me. "You don't deserve this, I'm so sorry, I'm so sorry. You're spring, baby. You're more radiant than flowers and the sun and no one can take that away from you."

He was peppering the top of my head with kisses as he held onto me like he was the one who needed to be reassured. The second that thought appeared in my head, I noticed how he was shaking.

I pulled away and looked up to find him teary-eyed. It punctured a hole in my heart that I didn't know I had any spaces left for. Every inch of my heart had been for him though. It had always been punctured and repaired by him.

When his eyes met mine, my hands started moving before I could think the movements through. My thumb was brushing his tears away, and now it was moving to the side of his head where I touched his hair, and then I was reaching for the nape of his neck. The instant my hand was on the back of his neck, it was pulling him towards me, closing the space between our lips.

When his lips met mine, my shoulder deflated, and I tasted our salty tears as he groaned at the contact. He was surprised, hesitating. But it was only a moment before he realized what I had started. And when he reacted, my body relaxed and woke up simultaneously.

I had only kissed him once before, but it was enough to know I never wanted to kiss another man again. No one else had compared.

I had gone further with other men, and it had never caused my legs to go weak and for my eyes to roll back like the way they did when Levi kissed me.

His lips were soft, and they were intentional in how they pressed against mine. It became a desperate mixture of excess tears and grabbing and kissing. It was as if I took in enough of his air, he could be mine. My hands tugging at his short curls and my nose brushing the side of his nose as I enveloped my lips in the softness of his. Then his hands were on my hips, gripping my waist, claiming my body and pulling it closer.

I was pulling at his shirt, somehow trying to pull him closer when there was no more space left between us. Two flowers intertwined because they had grown alongside each other for so long. His hands were drawing maps across my body, wiping any evidence that Ethan had ever touched me.

Ethan.

Lazaro.

I pulled away.

"I'm going to accept the spot in Paris," I blurted out.

He looked at me in shock. "You're what?" His lips were maroon, and his cheeks were flushed. His hair was tousled in spots where my fingers had been.

"I didn't get into Lazaro. I'm going to go to Paris. I'm going to take a chance." It was as if I was watching myself from afar. Making this wild decision based on one moment. Paris wasn't the only option, but it felt like it now.

I was so tired of being scared. I was exhausted of thinking I wasn't good enough. *Your designs are fine, nothing special*, Ethan's voice haunted me. If ESMOD thought I was good enough, then I needed to go to Paris and prove I was. Prove it to myself.

"You're going to leave?" His voice broke. "When?"

Why was I telling him like this? Why was I hurting him when he was already hurt. I wanted to shake myself, but I felt frozen, and I felt numb.

"It wouldn't be until August."

"For how long?"

"A year, and then I'd return to New York."

He looked away, stuffing his hands into his pockets. "A lot of things can happen in a year."

Tell him you love him, Daniella, tell him before it's too late. Tell him that you love him and that you want him to come with you. Tell him how you want to kiss him every day and you want him to twirl the ends of your hair like he did in high school. That you want him to come to Paris with you, and experience love the way the hopeless romantic tourists did.

But … I already knew the answer. He had obligations, responsibilities. He couldn't leave the girls. Wasn't that what made him so insecure? How Bella had hurt him for taking care of the girls? I couldn't ask him that.

Stop being so scar—

I simply nodded.

"I should get you home," he finished.

I didn't tell him I didn't want to be alone right now. Instead, I pushed him away and isolated myself just like I did last time.

37

Unkempt flowers because of the sunlight you held in your
faraway heart

Last night was long, to say the least. I skipped Sunday dinner with his family, which meant Levi drove me straight home. Despite our intense, and abrupt, conversation, he held my hand the whole way home. He offered to walk in with me, to help unpack everything to my mom. I said no. I didn't need Levi to see me cry again.

I did indeed cry again. Not only because of Ethan, but because of Paris, and how I'd kissed Levi and then hurt him. She was furious about Ethan, tearing up as I explained what happened in as minimal detail as possible. I could see how much it hurt her to know, and I didn't want this to be another thing that kept her awake at night stressed. But I also couldn't keep it from her.

"I'm so sorry, honey, I'm so sorry," she swore as tears rolled down my cheeks.

I shook my head. "It's not just that. I'm going to go to Paris, I'm going to leave. And then I told Levi, and I made it so much worse," I cried.

"Wait, slow down. You're going to go to ESMOD?"

I explained my on-the-whim decision, and then further explained the entire façade of my relationship with Levi. How it happened, why it happened, and what's happened since.

"It was really all pretend?" she asked in disbelief.

I nodded my head.

"I saw the daisies on your desk. Should I assume those were pretend then too?"

"He was just being nice." I shook my head.

"What about the day he called to ask me for my strawberry shortcake recipe?"

My head shot up. No, no, no. I could feel those holes in my hearts stitching themselves up with hope. *No.* I wouldn't mistake his care for romantic love again. "That's who he is, you know that. He always does for everyone else and never for himself. That has nothing to do with me."

She held up her hands in surrender giving up. A second later: "He wasn't happy about Paris?"

It was like recounting the plot of a film as I recited how he looked. "He was taken aback. It felt like I was dropping this huge decision on him, and he had no idea it was even an option. We didn't speak after that."

"It sounds like Levi doesn't want to see you go," she said slowly. "Maybe being together this past month has made him realize how much he misses you. And to hear that you'll be leaving again is probably not easy to process." She was right, of course she was right. But it also solidified my concern for what happened next.

But what scared me most was that "I love him," I told her, trying to hold the pieces of my heart together with the strength of my voice.

"Oh, Daisy. You've always loved him, there's nothing wrong with that."

"I don't think he loves me back, and even if he somehow did, I'm going to Paris now. I wouldn't see him for a year. So much can happen in a year," I said, echoing Levi's concern.

She mulled over my words and said that she wanted to make a phone call to the school first before it got too late. I listened to her shout at the first person who answered, but when she asked for another administrator's number, the man on the phone reassured her that a young man had already chewed his ear off about having Ethan reported and fired, interrupting him during a fundraising dinner.

"Who called?" my mom urged.

"He said his name was Mr. Coldwell."

My mom looked taken aback. I felt just as surprised when I heard it through the phone. She demanded the number anyways and said she'd be making another call in the morning, and then hung up.

"Doesn't love you, huh?" she said.

If classes weren't already over for the semester, I would've skipped today. However, I had spent the whole day finishing my last dress.

I thought it would've helped get the image of Levi's hurt face out of my head, along with the idea of moving to Paris. Instead, Ethan's voice lingered over and over in my head like a recording. *We both know you need the help. Your designs are fine, nothing special; not using your mother's name because you don't want to be compared to her; never designing clothes that fit you because you don't think your body is good enough.*

That last line was burning itself into my brain like a branding. Not only because it was so cruel that it gave me whiplash, but because it was true. I never created designs for myself, because I never envisioned myself as the one to be looked at. And it *was* because I didn't think my body was good enough. It hurt to know someone could see through me so easily.

When the dress was completed in the middle of the night, it felt like it was taunting me. So I chopped off five inches of the bottom of the dress and took in the bust so that it'd fit me.

Screw men.

I'd wear whatever I want.

Two more hours and it fit as good as a pair of skinny jeans from 2009. It rested at the middle of my calf and hugged my chest. The drop waist of the silhouette fell in exactly the right place, showcasing where my waist started and curved out to my hip. I also ripped the pearls off; they looked too preppy. And then I took a breath and titled my head back to shake my hair out of my face.

The daisies in my windowsill still stood tall in their vase. Flowers like that never lasted this long, especially after being in a stifling car. Was it a sign that everything was going to be fine? Or was I grabbing at strands to make myself feel better?

But then I thought of Levi as he walked into the restaurant and handed them to me like I deserved them.

I reached for my plethora of thread under my bed. White thread for the petals of the daisies, magnolia gold for the center, and an ivy green for the stems. I collected the coordinating beads too; beading was an excruciatingly long process because you had to thread individual beads onto string and then sew them into the right shape onto the dress.

But I wanted him in a part of my dress.

Both of my index fingers were bleeding by the time I finished, and all of my pink nail polish was chipped.

Right then was when I decided it'd also be a good idea to write one more letter to Levi. I'd be in Paris in three months; I had nothing to lose.

I wrote until my hand cramped up and I swore I was developing arthritis. Then I walked into the cold night air, caught a cab, and took it to Levi's apartment, telling the driver to wait; I just needed to drop something in the mailbox. And then I stared up at the apartment building that held a room of Levi's that was a mystery to me.

This was a horrible idea. Write eight years of emotions in a letter and drop it off like it wasn't a bomb? This was a horrible—

"Dani?"

I turned and found—

"Marty?"

"What are you doing out at this time? And in my neighborhood?" he asked.

"I was about to drop something off but, wait, this is your neighborhood?"

"I live in this building," he pointed up at the complex in front of us. "A friend of mine watches my cat during the day, I just went to pick her up after closing the bakery." He offered me a concerned look, still confused as to why I was here.

Marty had a cat and lived in the same building as Levi? Oh my gosh … Levi mentioned being attacked by a neighbor's cat, that neighbor being named Marty. Levi's Marty was *my* Marty? "I know this looks weird, but you actually may know my friend, Levi?"

A warm smile appeared on his face. "Levi's your friend? He's a great kid, what a small world! I can drop your mail outside his door if you'd like?"

"I …" I exhaled and handed him the letter before I could change my mind. "That would be great, thank you, Marty."

"I don't mind. He actually helped catch my cat once running out of the building, and let me tell you, that's no small feat. For that alone, I hope the kid goes famous one day for his writing."

I laughed. But I had to ask, "You've read his work?"

"Yes, his words are beautiful. That boy's been through quite some heartbreak in his life for such a young age though." He shook his head in sadness. "What's his book called again?"

"Oh, I'm actually not sure." I'd never translated the French title, no matter how long I stared at the book.

"Something wordy with a flower in it …"

"Well, I'm just going to go now. I'm happy you were able to pick—"

"That's it! That's it! *Picking Daisies on Sundays.*"

38

*My heart has been broken a million times by the same hand, yet I would let it
happen a million times again if it meant it was by you*

My heart stopped in my chest. It was frozen the whole ride home
and had yet to thaw while I was sleeping. The two halves of my
brain went back and forth with thoughts and responses, but all
roads led back to the same question: *what did this mean?*

I tore my room apart before going to bed last night, and again
when I woke up this morning, looking for this book. My options
were either: one, ask him why the name of his book included my
name—which was never happening—or two, find the book,
translate it word by word, and try to dissect its meaning like a new
Taylor Swift song.

But I couldn't find the damn book. My only guess was that it'd
slipped out of my bag before I rushed to Ethan's office. (Thinking
of his name gave me chills that made me nauseous, but you
deserved to know where this book could be hiding.)

It consumed so much space in my mind that I almost forgot
about the letter I left for Levi last night. I walked around the house
in this thick olive-green sweater that tickled my neck and had

sleeves that constantly rolled down as I was rolling dough.

Oh yes, I was making bread right now. Now that my last dress was finished and altered, I had nothing else to take my mind off of the whirlpool that was my mind. Ethan, Levi, Paris, my letter, *Picking Daisies on Sundays*. Ethan, Levi, Paris, my letter, *Picking Daisies on Sundays*. Over and over and over.

I kneaded the dough with the palm of my hand, over and over until my wrist was trembling and I had officially come to the conclusion that I wrote way too much in that letter. And while I was leaving in a few months, that didn't mean I wanted to live in total embarrassment for the rest of my life, even if I never saw Levi again! Imagine if I bumped into him at Marty's bakery in a year? He'd look at me like I was some lovesick stalker.

My written words replayed themselves in my head:

Hi Levi. I wanted to apologize. I wanted to apologize for throwing Paris on you like that, you didn't deserve that. I should've included your opinion in my decision because that's what a friend would do. But honestly, it wasn't a decision I thought I would agree to, it was spur of the moment. But that's not what this letter is about. What I really wanted to apologize for was lying to you this past month.

Being your friend has hurt as much as it did in high school, because friends aren't supposed to love each other romantically. And I do. I love you. I love the sound of your voice when you're worried. And I love the way your hair always looks so stupidly perfect, even when it's messy. And I love the way you make me feel; like my heart is about to take off down a runway before catching air. I love it all. But I know how you felt in high school, and I don't expect that to change.

So yes, I'm leaving again, and I'm sorry for not being strong enough in this friendship to suppress my feelings for you. But I can't look at you any other way. And I can't be there to watch you fall in love again, because it may just kill me.

I'm sorry. I'll send Sarah and Jeff a wedding gift and explain why I can't come.

Love, Daisy.

I spared him the details of seeing him kissing someone at Senior Prom and watching him gaze at Bella. He didn't need the details of my unrequited love. The kiss we shared when Bella wasn't there and the name of his book still left question marks floating in my head, but bread making was a phenomenal way to push those aside.

Mom was on her flight to London now while Mandy was out at the farmer's market picking up groceries. She said she'd be home soon, but I knew for a fact that the cucumber vendor would be there today, and Mandy liked to talk his ear off. Tonight, we were cooking rigatoni with this lemon sauce and—

Ding dong. "One second, Mandy!"

I rinsed the flour off my hands and jogged to the door.

"How was the—" I stopped short as I swung the door open and found Levi standing there. Standing on my doorstep. Disheveled brunette hair, black rimmed glasses, and a look on his face that could only be described as someone who had a lot to say but didn't know where to start.

"Oh, I thought you were Mandy," I said, like an idiot, because what else was I supposed to say? *Hi, did you get my ridiculous letter?*

He held his hand up, showing me a letter—my letter—and it looked as if it had been folded and unfolded numerous times.

"What is this?" he asked, his face indifferent as he waited for my response.

"An apology."

He exhaled in frustration. "One, I told you that you never owe me an apology. Two, I almost showed up at your house at 4 a.m. because I have read this over and over and over and it still doesn't make sense." He was fuming.

"Which part?"

"All of it! The part where you say you can't be around me; the part where you said you have to leave this friendship for the same reason four years ago; the part where you say you love me and *are going to leave*. As if I'd be alright with that!" His brows were shaped with concern and sadness and frustration, and his cheeks were flushed from shouting. His chest was filling and releasing with air, empty without the words that spilled out.

"Just forget it, forget that I wrote anything." I shook my head, flustered, walking back into the house. I didn't want to have this embarrassing conversation where we talked about my feelings. Levi followed, shutting the door.

"What is it then! Do you love me or not?" he asked with frustration.

"Don't." I spun around, equally as upset. Why was he making me relive this letter, this decision? "Don't make me say it again. I don't need a repeat of prom night."

Levi froze. "What are you talking about?"

I stopped on the other side of the living room. Now *I* was fuming. "Are you kidding? You don't remember? You don't remember when I told you I love you—"

"*What are you talking about!*"

"*I told you I loved you!* I told you I loved you and then you ignored me and went off and kissed some other girl!" I was so livid that I didn't even care if I sounded irrational. I had imagined this conversation in my head for years, and not a single instance included Levi not remembering.

He stared at me in shock. "I didn't know that you loved me."

I laughed at his response. "*You didn't know?* I spilled my whole heart out to you!"

Now he was upset. "You were *drunk*. You were on the floor crying so much that you didn't care that the dress you designed was getting dirty. You were covered in tears and couldn't stand when I lifted you up. You kept ranting to me about how Jeremiah left early and how badly you needed *Jeremiah*. I didn't forget a word you said to me that night. But when you told me that you loved me, I thought those words were for *him*, not for me. And then you got upset at me, wouldn't talk to me, and wouldn't let me drive you home. I assumed you hated me for being overbearing, so I gave you space. But then I spent weeks calling and texting and knocking on your door, and you refused to speak to me."

My insides were twisting and crumpling like pieces of thrown-out fabric. "But I saw you kissing Cora," I said with confusion.

"Because I had just listened to you cry over Jeremiah! I never thought you felt anything for me."

My lungs were filling and releasing air. I wasn't prepared for this conversation. These questions and responses weren't something I had already rehearsed. "What are you saying?"

"I'm saying that if I knew four years ago that you loved me, I would've never let you go."

No, that couldn't be true. That didn't match up with the nightmare I'd been replaying for years. Levi didn't love me; he didn't love girls like me.

"But what about Bella?" This whole thing started because he cared about her.

He rubbed his face with regret. "Whenever you mentioned my feelings towards her, I let you assume because I thought that made you more comfortable with being around me. That maybe you needed proof that I wouldn't try to take anything to an intimate level while we pretended to date. But then we kissed, and it stopped before it could've started when you mentioned Paris. I thought that was your way of telling me this couldn't lead anywhere. And even if you wanted to include me at the time, I… I couldn't leave my family."

The habitual parts of my brain that collected cobwebs from a lack of change refused to accept what he was saying.

His face twisted with realization. "You don't believe me?"

I felt lost. All I could picture was how beautiful Bella was, and how her and Levi looked together. Her full lips, sultry eyes, and shiny, commercial hair. That was a girl that was easy to fall in love with. She was gorgeous.

He pulled his bag off of his shoulder and took a book out, handing it over to me. The spine was cracked, and the pages must've all been dog-eared at one point. "Read it."

It was his book. White font, a pastel pink cover, a small table in the bottom corner with two chairs and a vase of daisies. But the front was ruined with marker. A translation: *Picking Daisies on Sundays*, just like Marty had said, written beside the printed French title. I flipped through the pages and found the same thing:

scribbled translations in dark marker on each page, beside the typed French poems.

I started on the first page and read.

My heart has been broken a million times by the same hand, yet I would let it happen a million times again if it meant it was by you

I was weaker than I thought / my heart sagging like the stems of uncut, unkempt flowers because of the sunlight you held in your faraway heart / Maybe you weren't mine to love / I think I'm falling

The wallpaper above her bed frame was glued in my brain the way it was glued against her walls / I got so close to running my fingers against it / I wish I felt the confidence to tell you the truth, as strongly as I felt stubborn to hide it

Do you hear that? That's my heart knocking against my chest at the sight of you / I've never heard anything more terrifying / how could you provide me air and suffocate me at the same time?

Blue hydrangeas, pink tulips, red bleeding hearts / it's all you ever loved, but never yourself / I never understood why anyone spoke poorly of the color brown, it was a dream on you

And that kiss ... I think about it all the time / was it wrong of me to think of you when you were never mine? / I feel lucky to have had you, but dismayed to know what life is like without you

Don't worry if the flowers pass, I'll be right there to plant you more / and when the soil grows old, I'll comfort it in the chaos of the storm

Am I a ghost in your story? / because you look at me with conviction when I don't even know the crime I committed

Burden me with your secrets / so I can carry the weight you're so fearful of letting go

To be close to you was to be haunted by what I couldn't have and to be reminded of how much I truly wanted you / and I'd be lying if I said I never thought about where my hands would take me across your body

Midnights and daydreaming hours of retracing steps to how we possibly got here / how did I ever let time pass this long without seeing you? / my heart was so full of our memories that painted my body like a scrapbook

I tried to stop loving you, but along the way, you found your way into the sound of my laugh, the style of my writing, and the threads of my clothes / I would've gone down on my knees just to hear you say yes

Neck stiff, legs weak, eyes set on what we could've looked like if you hadn't left / 'moving on' was a broken record that I never had the strength to lift the needle off of / If hearts were meant to love then why did mine feel so empty? / and suddenly, I fell

Glances, gazes, eyes following places they shouldn't have seen / intimacy was to be seen by you; free falling was to be touched by you / there was no such thing as a crowded room where you stood

She lives in between the pinks and yellows of the world / where a beautiful color is unknown to others / and when she speaks, I become a bee enthralled in a field of daisies

My eyes couldn't absorb the words quick enough, catching words and phrases, the poems just kept going. *Daisies, bleeding hearts, wallpaper above her bed frame.*

"I—I don't understand," I said. My hands were shaking

holding onto the book tight. His written words kept ringing in my ears. *Do you hear that? That's my heart knocking against my chest at the sight of you.*

"The whole book," he breathed. "Every poem in there is about you. Everything I wrote came back to you." *I tried to stop loving you, but along the way, you found your way into the sound of my laugh, the style of my writing, and the threads of my clothes.*

"I…" I didn't know what to say. This was about me? No, no, it couldn't be. But he'd just said… All the corners and nooks of my mind were trying to process it.

"This is about me?"

"Every. Single. Word." He breathed those words like they had been prepared for months.

But my brain immediately jumped to: "I thought you loved Bella." My voice cracked. *If hearts were meant to love then why did mine feel so empty?*

He looked at me in astonishment. There had never been a moment in my life where we doubted each other. But I … I just couldn't come to terms with this. Was it pity? Did he feel bad for me? Has he just convinced himself that he likes me because of my letter—*but the poetry book was written before all of this.*

He looked away, rolling his tongue under his cheek, and exhaled. Then he looked at me, and my heart took off down a runway.

"I'm so grateful for everything I have in life, I am. But when I see you, all I can think about is how much better life would be if you were mine. I'm so infatuated with everything you do, from the color of your lips to the way you slide your hips back and forth when you dance to the way you twist your earrings when you're upset or how you blush when I touch you and how you breathe when I say *Daisy*."

I was stunned.

He took a step closer, not an inkling of regret in his statement. *To be close to you was to be haunted by what I couldn't have and to be reminded of how much I truly wanted you.*

Another step closer, and I was backed into the wall. His hands held onto my jaw the way they always did when he was worried about me. My knees simply went weak as he spoke. Jesus, did he know what he was doing to me?

"Say something," he pleaded.

"But I'm moving to Paris." That thought hung on me like a rusty keychain that refused to come off.

There was an equal sadness in his eyes. "It's just for a year."

"A lot can happen in a year," I echoed his past statement.

He winced. "That's not fair. That was before I knew how you felt. Before I knew I could fly out to see you, and send you letters, and call you every day and tell you that I love you."

My heart whacked against my ribcage. *He loved me.* The book he wrote was about *me*. He didn't love Bella. He never rejected me that night of prom. He loved me. *He loves me.*

His thumb moved over my cheekbone. "Daisy?" he said, trying to get my attention. He was nervous again, that smile gone.

My throat tightened up. I was nervous to say the words that always played in my head like a soundtrack when Levi was around. But the gorgeous look in his eyes, it … it took a weight off my shoulders.

"You love me?" I whispered. His shoulders relaxed and his eyes went weak with desire.

"I love you more than my heart can physically handle."

He waited for my response, but I had no words left that could explain what I was feeling. So, I leaned in and reminded myself of what it was like to kiss him.

I felt his whole body shudder. His hands were still on my face as I pressed my lips against his and grabbed onto his shirt, pulling him closer. The sun lit in my heart, radiating my whole body with warmth at the touch of his lips. He pulled away for a quick moment, dragging his glasses off of his face, and diving back in. My stomach fluttered with a million frantic butterflies and my hands vibrated with desire to touch him.

I had never been so forward, but his urgency matched mine, kissing me back and releasing small breaths, like neither of us could get enough. He tasted sweet and his lips were soft. The fullness of his bottom lip and the smell of his cologne at the nape of his neck reminded me of angelic piano melodies that hypnotized you with their beauty.

I was running my hands through his hair, and my heart was beating at the same pace of rain when it hit the pavement on a hot summer night. His hair brushed my forehead while mine was twisted in his fingers.

I saw stars as he encased my jaw in his palm and kissed me deeper. His chest was against mine and it was like we were two halves of a broken heart friendship necklace. I didn't want to let go. I don't think he did either, and it made me smile into the kiss like an idiot.

He smiled back. "Say you love me," he murmured against my lips.

Without a second thought, I said, "I love you."

He pressed a smooth kiss to my surprised mouth.

"My favorite flowers were always daisies," he said in a dreamy state. I shielded my face in the crook of his neck. Flowers were growing in my heart and sprouting through my chest. *He loves me.*

"So you think my hair always looks stupidly perfect?" he asked.

I blushed before laughing.

"I hate you," I muttered.

"You love me," he argued.

"I do," I succumbed.

39

And when she speaks, I become a bee enthralled in
a field of daisies

When Audrey Hepburn questioned, "Am I so much in love with him that all others seem ridiculous?" in *War and Peace*, it was all I could think of as Levi and I drove down the highway towards Sarah's father-in-law's beach house in the Hamptons. Black sunglasses sat on the brim of his nose, and he wore a short-sleeve button down with a few buttons undone, the ocean wind coming in through the car windows rustling his collar. Like some male model shooting for a car or sunglasses campaign.

"*Lay all of your love on meeee!*" Levi sang ABBA at the loudest volume from the driver's seat. I was laughing like a kid in the passenger's seat to the point that I couldn't even get a breath in to sing the song myself—and I *loved* this song.

Our packed bags were in the backseat with two garment bags—one with his suit, the other with my dress—for the weekend. The warm air came in through the windows, and the sun was beating down on our shoulders through the windshield despite all the symmetrical green trees we were driving in between.

You could smell the salt water of the ocean nearby. *Summer.* It was so close I could taste it in the air.

He held my hand over the console with his left on the steering wheel. His fingers were interlaced with mine. I couldn't stop glancing back down at them and the way they squeezed mine. Every few minutes he would lift them to his lips and place a kiss on the back of my hand. It made me shiver. We hadn't stopped touching each other since he showed up at my house with my letter and his book. "Making up for lost time," is what he had said. What he had done after made me dizzy.

I tried to push away the reminder that all of this would be gone in a few months. I'd be in Paris and Levi would be here in New York. Seven hours and thirty-five minutes—that's how long the flight was. I kept telling myself that it could be worse. This could be a 1700s period drama and we'd have to travel via boat to see one another, which took about six weeks and a chance of being killed by pirates or scurvy. In other words, it could be much worse.

We already talked about flying back and forth every few months. It was just one year. Twelve months. That was nothing in the grand scheme of life. Levi and I had already been apart for four years; what was a few months in between visits? The sadistic part of my mind reminded me of all the women that hit on him during those four years. The girls that asked him for his number, that asked him to speak in French, that grazed his arm and probably tried leaning in to kiss—

"You okay?" Levi asked, cutting off my inner turmoil.

I smiled quickly. "Yeah."

"You can tell me if my singing is that bad, I won't be

offended," he said, poking my ribcage. He was trying to make me laugh.

I appreciated it, but I could only offer a small smile.

Being around Levi's family and the rest of the wedding party didn't feel as stiff now that he knew I loved him. No pressure to pretend that I wasn't really pretending.

He must've felt the same way because he didn't hesitate to hold my hand as we walked around the property, or to lift my chin up and plant a kiss on my lips in between Jeff and Sarah's random arguments. I even found him twirling strands of my hair around his fingers as we sat by the beach, watching the bride and groom rehearse their vows. The day goes by quick when you're part of a wedding party though.

By the time Levi and I finished with putting out the center pieces for the tables while everyone else worked on place sets, it was 8 p.m. and the sun was setting behind the ocean. The home we'd be staying in for the weekend was also the venue. It was also more than just a house; it was very much the epitome of luxury in the Hamptons.

Three floors, a long gravel driveway that secluded the house from the neighborhood, and a private beach for a backyard. Tall bushes hid the house from its neighbors, which I assumed were also some variations of white or sandy painted homes with numerous windows. It oozed *set for a Nancy Meyers film.*

"I'm going to see if Sarah needs anything else before calling it a night," Levi commented.

I nodded with a smile before he pressed a kiss to my head, and we moved in opposite directions. I aimed for the foyer where everyone left their bags. Hearts, hearts, hearts—there it was. My duffel bag covered in tiny pink hearts was lying behind Levi's black bag. Maybe I'd take his too—

"You're rooming with Aparna down the hall." My head snapped up and—oh.

"What?" I asked Bella. Maybe she wasn't talking to me.

"There's not enough room for everyone, and since we lost the softball game, the groomsmen get their own rooms. Remember?" Nope, she was talking to me, and I didn't remember that. I completely forgot about the softball game.

She looked at me like I was half listening. But I was fully listening, digesting every word actually. Especially the way she hadn't asked if I was staying with Levi.

"Oh, yeah, of course, I remember, yes," I said with a smile, trying my best to cover my lie.

"I heard you're going to Paris. Levi was just talking to Sarah about it. He seemed pretty happy." My heart dropped. He was *happy?* My mouth was dry. Shouldn't your boyfriend be somewhat sad when you're moving across the world? I tried my best to lift a smile and say, "Yeah, I'm excited." She nodded and then walked off.

I moved down the hall timidly, trying to find Aparna in one of these rooms. I could only deal with one stressful thing at a time. Instead, I found a large, quilted bag with her initials on it, and dropped mine beside hers.

Anxiety grew in the pit of my stomach. This was going to be like some sleepover from hell. I didn't even know where the bathroom was, let alone how we would decide who got to shower

Liana Cincotti

first—

Oof. "Sorry," I immediately muttered before looking up and seeing Levi.

He latched onto my arms to keep me from falling. "I was looking for you."

"I was just dropping my things off." I waved to my bag in the room behind me. I tried to not think about what he and Sarah could've been talking about.

"Oh. I thought, maybe you could stay with me." I must've looked panicked because he picked his sentence back up. "I can sleep on the floor—"

"I'm not letting you sleep on the floor."

"But if it would make you comfortable—"

"We can share a bed, it's not a big deal." His eyebrows shot up. Never in my life did I think I would say those words to a man before, let alone to Levi. "Bella just told me that I was rooming with Aparna, so I assumed your family wasn't comfortable with us sleeping in the same room."

"If it's not a big deal for you, then there's no problem," he said with a smirk. He was testing me; he knew that *I knew* it was a big deal. But I refused to be wrong. I may have told him I love him, but that didn't mean my competitiveness from our high school friendship had disappeared.

Two hours later though, I'd eat my words. It was most definitely a big deal. A big deal in the shape of Levi's shirtless torso getting into bed where I was expected to lie beside him without blushing.

"Can you like, scooch over?" I asked him, my arms crossed over my baggy T-shirt that read *Florals? For Spring? Groundbreaking* with Miranda Priestly's face underneath and a bunch of flowers doodled around her. She'd be horrified by my collection of garden-inspired dresses, let alone my ratty flannel pants.

Levi was in bed, shirtless, as I mentioned before, with a book on his lap and his glasses on his face. I was flushed head to toe seeing him in this state—glasses, abs, book, messy hair. A woman's dream. I imagined the equivalent for men would be a woman in one of those racy magazines you could only buy by asking the man behind the counter for them.

I startled Levi with my request. He was sitting in the middle of the bed indulged in a book, not second guessing this arrangement at all. I couldn't make it any more obvious that I was nervous.

He looked up at me in surprise and moved over without a second thought. "I really don't mind sleeping on the floor, it's carpeted."

"I'm not letting you sleep on the floor." I pulled back the covers and slid in, careful not to touch him. Why was I being weird, you may ask. Well, the short answer was I'd never been this close to a man that was this attractive.

Sleeping in the same bed as him felt as if I was setting myself up for failure.

What if I snored? What if I was one of those people who stole the blankets in the middle of the night or had a little bit of drool on the side of their faces when they woke up? *Oh my gosh, he'd smell my breath in the morning.* What were the chances I could sneak out of bed in the morning before he woke up to brush my teeth?

"Daisy," he said, catching my attention. He closed the book over his thumb, his focus on me now.

"Vi," I replied, fixing my shirt.

"What's wrong?" he asked, his eyes soft.

There was no sense in lying to him, he'd be able to tell from a mile away. "I'm nervous." I pursed my lips.

"What for?"

"What if I snore?" I asked, almost sounding like a whining child nervous for a doctor's appointment.

He laughed. "Well, the last time I checked, you do."

My jaw dropped. "*What?* How would you know!"

"You dozed off for a second during *Princess Diaries*," he smiled.

Kill me. I groaned through my hands. "I'm sleeping outside."

He laughed again. "They were cute, tiny snores. Don't worry."

"You're horrible at lying," I muttered, but couldn't help but laugh once hearing him snort.

He pressed a kiss to my temple, causing my laughter to die down, pulling me into his arms. I rested my head against his chest and breathed in the smell of his clean soap as the beat of my heart came to a slow rhythm.

My muscles relaxed and the lights turned off and my mind lulled. I dreamt of running across the beach in my orange dress collecting seashells in the sand as Levi kicked his shoes off. He spoke in French, and it sounded the same as the tune of a piano during a waltz. "I've never felt this conscious of the beat of my heart before, it was like it was sleeping without you," he whispered.

I swore it was real. The sun was warm, and the breeze was just right.

I woke up the next morning holding onto that sunshine.

40

I was weaker than I thought

"What's this?" I asked. When I reentered the room after finishing straightening my hair and applying some light make up. There was a garment bag on the bed that wasn't there before.

"A dress," Levi responded, tying his tie. He looked so professional in the black suit I had altered for him weeks ago; his legs looking longer than usual, and his curls organized in a glamorous fashion. Maybe I *was* good at my job.

I unzipped the garment bag and confirmed that it wasn't the dress I packed. Panic spread across my chest like a rash—*did I somehow pack the wrong dress? I've never even seen this dress before.*

"I bought it for you," Levi intercepted my dread. He completely stopped what he was doing, leaving the tie hanging half-done around his neck as he leaned against the wall watching me.

"You bought me a dress?" I asked with confusion.

"I wanted to repay you for altering my suit. You never let me pay you," he responded, a quiet look in his eyes, weighing my reaction.

"I … it's beautiful. You bought this for me?" I questioned. It

Liana Cincotti

was beautiful. A dress the shade of pomegranate juice with small white flowers printed into it. It was strapless with an A-line fit, and a mid-calf length.

"Of course I did."

Out of habit, I flipped the collar of the dress forward to check the size, but instead of a tag, there was a small, embroidered daisy. "I've never seen this logo before." And I've seen thousands of logos and tags.

He cleared his throat. "That's because I sewed it in."

My eyes widened. "You did this?"

"I thought I'd put my sewing skills to practice again. I wanted you to have something that was just yours. Which now that I'm saying it, sounds ridiculous, because you design clothes for a living—"

I crushed him in a hug before he could continue, squeezing every muscle in his back. He released a laugh of relief.

"Maybe you can pack it for Paris."

I instantly deflated. Paris. *He seemed pretty happy*, Bella had said.

"Yeah, maybe," I slowly pulled away.

"I did make us dinner reservations for the day we got there."

My heart stopped and my head whipped up. "What?"

"I'm coming to Paris with you."

"You're going to fly in with me?" I asked with hope.

"No, baby. I'm moving to Paris with you."

"You're joking." My spine was taut, and my hands were shaking. Was he kidding? Was he trying to make me laugh? Because I was about to tear down the middle with tears of joy.

"If I was joking, then why did I just tell *The New York Times* that I'll be moving to Paris?"

My stomach dropped and my hands hit my mouth. "You got the job?" *He got the job!* A heartbeat later, the rest of his words sunk in. "You turned the job down?" I asked in disbelief. "Why did you turn the job down?"

"My professor offered me a position in France. He read my book and wants me to teach French literature at an American school with him," he explained.

"Levi, *that's incredible*." I smiled with all of the happiness bottled in my body. He looked relieved at my reaction. Until— "But the girls," I said. *Rhea and Claire were his whole world.* He couldn't go to Paris. They needed him. *He* needed them.

Surprise grew between the space of his eyebrows. "Sarah and Jeff are moving back into the city—they got an apartment. It was a surprise wedding gift from her father-in-law. They'll take care of the girls when my mom can't. Sarah told me last night."

Hope escaped from under the rock of my heart and flooded my lungs. "So they'll be taken care of? You'd actually be able to come with me? Why would you want to come with me?"

He took a step forward. My hair moved out of the way to make room for his large hand on my jaw as if by his command. "Because when you find out the person you've been in love with for your entire life loves you back, you'll spend the rest of your life making up for lost time."

My heart was beating against my chest at the pace of a hundred drums. Hope bloomed on his face like a gorgeous tulip as he registered my love for him. Of course, I couldn't hide it, especially not now. He wanted to go to Paris. *He had a position in Paris.* He turned down the position with *The New York Times.* Rhea and Claire would be taken care of.

He was beaming at all the same things. I threw myself at him, wrapping my arms around his neck as his came around my body.

"We're going to Paris, baby."

41

Why can I still hear your voice when you're not here?

Today was Dad's birthday, and I was on my way to the cemetery before my senior exhibit this week. It was the first time I had visited him since the year he passed. It wasn't my idea to go, but rather Mandy's. When I returned from the wedding this week, she gave me a shoebox full of trinkets that were from Paris, all things Dad purchased when he visited Mom. One of them being mint sewing needles that matched the ones I used in my sewing kit that he gifted me.

It was one of the first real things I had seen of his in a long time. Proof that he existed and traveled and purchased things for himself not realizing that one day they'd just be things again, no longer his.

No one tells you how much losing someone feels like inheriting a dream. Because that's what thinking of him felt like: a dream. For him to have been here for decades, and then to only exist in my pictures and memories. I'd like to imagine that if I hadn't developed object permanence as a child, then maybe my mind would've had an easier time accepting that he wasn't here anymore.

I hadn't realized how much I was … avoiding this until I arrived at the cemetery, frozen in the parking lot. Should I have brought something? I always saw people bring beautiful bouquets and flags.

Mandy told me to talk to him, that's all. But that was a lot easier in an email than talking to a headstone that was supposed to sum up the entire life of your father. I didn't say that, of course. I simply got out of the car and walked on the path through the other headstones until I found him.

My throat tightened up. Looking down at the plot of grass in front of me, all I could picture was his bright smile. The one that made his eyes small, and his cheeks swollen when Mom accidently cracked her eggs into the trash instead of the bowl at least once a week. Or the time I was practicing softball in the backyard and sent a softball through the window, and he laughed so hard because I managed to land it in our bathroom trash barrel. Or when I got a C in the home ed class on sewing in middle school and he held onto me as I hiccupped with tears. When I told him he'd get better soon, holding his hand over the hospital bed as the skin on his hands became thinner and his cheeks hollowed out. Even when sick, he still managed to make the nurses laugh.

The muscles in my throat were wound up like rope, and my eyes collected and lost tears like a broken, ceramic tub. My hands shook and my knees buckled, hitting the hot grass. *He's dead. He's been dead for years, and I never came and saw him because I was too scared of the past.*

I opened my emails on my phone to where a folder of drafts sat. *Hi Dad,* they all started. Before I had another chance to think it over, I selected them all and clicked delete.

Picking Daisies on Sundays

For a split moment, I regretted it. But then I looked back up where our last name was etched in stone. The beauty he gave that name even when he was suffering. My skin was oily as I wiped away the last of my tears and pressed my hand against the gravestone, as if there were some shred of him in there.

"Happy Birthday," I whispered.

The grass brushing the skin on my legs and the humid wind knotting my hair became friends as I sat there talking to him, telling him how much I missed him, and why I hadn't visited, and why I wouldn't be again for a while.

My grief didn't disappear after my visit. It'd never magically disappear, that's not how grief worked. I didn't leave the cemetery with a smile on my face or closure. But it felt like I'd conquered step one. I was learning how to face the things I couldn't control, and how to let them go. How to not only hurt with my whole hurt, but how to feel with it, and accept those feelings. To not brush off my insecurities and concerns and sadness, but to exist with it and then face it. I was learning.

I imagined this was how Sarah felt the day of her wedding last week: so nervous she could feel bile in her throat. Making sure all my models had on the correct shoes that went with their dresses, and adjusting zippers and buttons, along with making sure I looked okay, which was the worst part of all. Why did I decide to participate in my own showing again? Oh, yeah, because Ethan sucked—I'd make clothes for myself if I want to. When I said it like that, it started to feel worth it again.

Fortunately, I wasn't the only nervous one. Sandra, Camille,

Lexi, and Vera were all equally as nervous. Even though they weren't wearing one of their project pieces, they'd still have to walk out at the end with their models to be applauded and credited for their work. It made me feel better to have them here, brushing my shoulder as they walked by and prepared for the same thing.

"Hi gorgeous." I turned and found Levi several feet behind me with a bouquet of daisies. My heart melted.

I ran into his arms. "You bought me flowers." I pouted.

"Of course I did." He stepped back and took in my dress. It was the color of clementines, appearing as sunlight that came in through windows and hit a white wall. It had the perfect summer glow to pair with my lighter dresses.

It felt weird saying it, but I was really proud of it, no matter how simple it was. I didn't feel ashamed either to say that I felt beautiful. My shoulders looked strong, my legs appeared long, and my brown eyes looked brighter.

"Nervous?"

"I was actually thinking of escaping out the back, want to help?" I gave him a childish smile.

He laughed but recognized the true nerves in my eyes. He leaned towards me and pushed one of the thin straps off my shoulder, kissing my collarbone. It made me shiver. I grabbed onto his bicep to keep from tipping backwards. I could feel the other girls watching, ogling. It happened often when I was with Levi; it was hard to miss his presence.

"You're going to kill it, darling. Knock them out of the park."

I smiled with my lips pressed together and leaned onto the balls of my feet to reach his lips. They tasted like coffee, and I indulged in it.

"I didn't say kill me," he groaned against my lips.

It made me laugh.

But that's what I did when I walked out with the rest of the models: I knocked them out of the park. My legs felt shaky as I followed them out and I felt the hot lights beaming down on my shoulders. But the people I found cheering me on was enough of a distraction, because I almost burst out into tears. Gabe, Jia, Mom, Mandy, Levi, Rhea, Claire, Trish, *Josh*, girls from *Look of the Week* and Sandra, Camille, Lexi, and Vera peeking their heads out from behind the curtains clapping and hollering.

My skin radiated with the warmth of their love. Happiness and joy riddled my smile and hurt my cheeks. The only person that wasn't here, was watching from above. And I was confident that he'd be so proud of me. I was so proud of me.

I bowed as my models left the runway, and I smiled a smile that was brighter than a field of daisies.

Epilogue

I once was poison ivy, but now I'm your daisy.
— Don't Blame Me, Taylor Swift

At sixteen, I fell in love with Levi when he drove me home from work, letting me sleep in the passenger's seat, despite only being a short walk away. I fell in love with him when he twirled his finger around strands of my hair while we talked in the cafeteria, like it was an unquestionable habit. I fell in love with him as I watched him bake for his sisters and chased them around the living room during movie nights.

I fell in love with him for who he was.

At twenty-two, I fell in love with him because of how he made me feel.

The light hand touches, stolen glances, and compliments that sounded like verses. The handmade gifts and gestures, like the glass daisy bracelet he'd made me for my eighteenth birthday, and he had one that matched. ("I wore it every day until I saw you in the bar that day. I didn't want you to think I was crazy, so I hid it under long sleeves," he had said. I kissed him in response.) Never making me feel sorry or insecure or weak. For making me feel beautiful and wanted and *desired*. He didn't just notice me in a crowded room, but he sought me out.

We hadn't stopped telling each other stories we kept secret since Sarah's wedding. While sitting on the turf of one of Claire's soccer games this summer, I told him when I saw him kiss someone for the first time and how I wanted to vomit.

"That's why you hated Jennifer O'Brien?" he had asked with a laugh.

"I did not hate her!" I had argued.

"You hit her mailbox," he said deadpanned. That was unfortunately true, but it wasn't on purpose. She and Cora Messing just happened to live on the same street and fell victim to my lack of peripheral vision whilst driving.

When we took a trip to the beach in June, he twisted one of his rings off his fingers and dropped it in my palm as he applied sunscreen. He admitted that the two rings he wore every day as a set weren't meant to be worn together.

"I bought this for you for graduation; it matched the gold earrings you wore all the time." Obviously, we weren't speaking at the time, so he wore mine too. I looked down at my hand now in class, where his ring sat on my finger.

Despite living together now in Paris, we didn't see each other as often as we had anticipated. Most of the times that I didn't have class or work, Levi was teaching. He taught two afternoon classes and then stayed for office hours, coming back home late at night, planting a kiss on my cheek before sliding into bed with me. We still spent time together trying new restaurants, visiting bookstores, cooking breakfast together, and discovering new pieces of Paris every day.

Liana Cincotti

Paris was as beautiful as I hoped it would be. Of course, there were the influxes of cigarette smoke in certain side streets and a ludicrous amount of traffic at night that made it impossible to take a cab anywhere, paired with the constant concern of pick pocketers around the metro. But every city had its blemishes; I'd lived in New York City for four years!

Paris had these gorgeous lights that twinkled above the bridges along the Seine River, desserts that melted in your mouth, and architecture on every street that was worthy of painting. Levi and I visited the Eiffel Tower every night for a week straight when we arrived just to see it sparkle for five minutes. It was so breathtaking that we were completely silent as everyone around us ran to take pictures. I even dropped half of my chocolate croissant that was in my hand.

I hadn't even mentioned the fashion yet! Everyone here had a sense of fashion, regardless of their age. My orientation for ESMOD was a few weeks ago and everyone dressed like they could be caught by paparazzi. Fortunately, everyone spoke English too.

Levi's been tutoring me in the language all summer, but I was nowhere near capable of having a conversation yet. It made my heart race with anxiety to think about it, but apparently, I wasn't the only one concerned.

I met a few other girls—Kenz, Misha, and Anna—at orientation from the New York area who knew no French either. We went out for coffee after and voiced our shared worries about it and it was *fun*. We laughed and shared numbers and took the metro back together. Relief washed over me like an ocean; *I had made friends*.

It was a genuine concern I had when boarding my flight weeks ago: what if I couldn't make friends? But I was doing this to push myself out of my comfort zone. I couldn't continue to go through life dreaming and never moving forward. I had to do the scary stuff to get to the good stuff, just like Dad said.

It was overwhelming to realize what a commitment I had made moving to a place where I had no family and no understanding of the language. But I was taking it day by day, and it hasn't failed me yet. Knowing that I had friends and family coming here to experience some of Paris's sparkle with me made it easier when thinking of the future too.

Jia would be arriving in a few weeks to pick up some pieces for a client that's attending next year's Met Gala—yes, she's finally going! I've never seen someone so excited to take an eight hour flight to shop for earrings before.

Gabe said that him and Oliver would fly out in October. Oliver, Levi's favorite roommate, was around a lot this summer when we got together with Jia and Gabe, and they hit it off! No more dating apps for Gabe. Then Vera, Daya, and Sandra were planning on coming in May for a big "girl's trip." And my mom and Mandy would be here in March for fashion week. It made me so happy that I jumped in place every time I thought about it.

"Now, I wanted to wait until the end of class because I know none of you will be able to focus once I tell you. You've all been asking for weeks about fashion week," my professor, from *London*—I *know*, so cool—spoke as she walked around the room. There were about fifty of us in the class falling asleep because of how late the class started, but we were all wide awake now.

Paris. Frickin. Fashion. Week. Every fashion student's dream.

Since it was mentioned at orientation a month ago, we had all been poking at the professors for a confirmation.

"I am excited to tell you that you'll all be invited to at least one show." She clapped her hands together with a smile. My head whipped around to Anna, who sat behind me, to give her a *can you believe this?!* look. She shrieked with joy, as did many of the students in the room. Everyone back home was going to *freak out*.

The professor sighed, but smiled, satisfied with our response. "Details will be released in the coming weeks. Class dismissed." She waved her hand.

Anna, Kenz, Misha, and I jumped from our seats and tackled one another in the hallway. What were we going to wear? Which designer do you think we'll see? What *celebrities* do you think we'll see? They were all topics of conversation as we walked out of the building into the cool night air.

"I'm making a Pinterest board for each designer ASAP," Anna announced.

"That sounds a little excessive," Kenz laughed.

"I refuse to get caught in the back of a paparazzi photo and *not* go viral for what I'm wearing," Anna replied.

"I think you'll be—oh my gosh," Misha had begun speaking and then halted.

"What is it?" I asked.

She fanned her face. "Your boyfriend is just so hot; it catches me off guard every damn time."

I followed her gaze to— "Levi!" I ran across the crosswalk and jumped into his arms almost knocking him backwards. He was in his work clothes: a sweater, slacks, and his leather satchel over his shoulder. His arms wrapped around me as my legs wrapped around him. His head buried itself in my neck.

"Hi Daisy," he exhaled like it was his first breath of air all day.

I pressed a kiss to his neck and felt him shiver. "You finished work early," I said with joy, moving back to see his face.

"I know PDA is popular in France but that doesn't mean you need to join in!" Misha shouted from across the street making us both laugh.

He pressed a quick kiss to my lips that made me lightheaded, squeezing my hip before putting me down. "I did. I thought it'd been a while since we spent a Sunday night together."

I beamed at him. My heart was jumping in my chest at the sight of the handsome, loving man in front of me. A thousand flower petals falling to the bottom of my stomach.

"That sounds perfect."

"Ready to go home?" he asked.

"With you, always."

Chapter 23
(Levi's Version)

One moment, we were dancing—her soft hand on the back of my neck and I was telling her she looked beautiful—and then I was left in the middle of the room alone. She was trotting away in her heels with a distressed look while I stood there speechless thinking over and over, *what did I just do?*

I went too far; I made her uncomfortable. Already asking her to pretend to be my girlfriend and hold my hand and spend time around my family every Sunday—that was *a lot*. And then I go ahead and tell her how she looks as if this relationship was real. *Idiot.*

My feet started moving in the direction of the stairs before I could further my list of internal insults. I rushed down the steps and out the front door. *Please be here, please be here.* One sweeping glance and I found her getting into a cab.

"Dani!" I shouted, running down the grand steps. She turned, *she turned.* My heart ached watching her lack of hesitation as she stepped away from the cab and came towards me. I felt overwhelmed watching her striking figure move towards me, meeting me halfway up the stairs. She looked so gorgeous. Her dress touched every curve on her body and her lips held this natural color of pomegranate juice. If she knew what it did to me, she'd be horrified.

But she looked bothered, and it was my fault. I did that.

She turned away as I asked her what I did, what I could do to fix it. My hands gravitated towards her by habit without me even realizing it, lifting her face up. She was crying, and it felt like I was shot in the heart with an arrow.

"Hey, hey, hey, no, no, no, don't cry. What'd I miss? What's wrong?" Words were tumbling out. All I could think of was: *how do I stop her crying? How do I take her sadness and make it mine?*

"I'm not beautiful, Vi," her voice cracked, along with my strength.

How… how could she not think she was beautiful? How could that be possible when she was the most gorgeous woman I'd ever seen. It couldn't be real, and I questioned it aloud. And then she tried making a joke, *a joke*, and it almost would've made me smile if it weren't for the fact that my heart was cracking down the middle.

The only thing I knew to say next was the truth, and it rolled out like dice in a crowded casino. "Everywhere we go, people are"—*I am*—"infatuated by you, looking at you and yearning to talk to you. I… I am infatuated by you." My heart was burning behind my ribcage. I had never gotten this close to telling her the truth. But she didn't believe me; I could see it in her eyes.

"Every time I see you, I think about …" My words fell short, because I had no idea what else I could say to make her believe me.

But seeing her upset when I spoke to Brianna—a past

student—Dani almost looked jealous, and the hope that gave me, the switch that went off in my head that said *maybe she feels something too?* Well, it was enough of a kick in the ass to try.

I didn't know what I was thinking. All I knew was that I was an absolute idiot for doing it. To look at her like this when she wasn't mine, and yet still kiss her.

I told myself no weeks ago when I saw her in the bar with that short hair and joyous smile on her face. I told myself no when I saw her at Senior Prom with Jeremiah Sullivan. To kiss her would be to obliterate all the self-control I had been harnessing since sophomore year of high school.

But when I saw her in that dress, and she looked up at me in that ballroom with those full lips and brown eyes, and then ran out of my arms. I couldn't let her go again.

So, I leaned in and kissed her. And when I felt her lips press against mine, I lost all that self-control. She was kissing me, and her hands found their way into my hair, and they were tugging on strands, and it was making me go wild. *Fuck.*

Ses lèvres étaient si douces. Oh my god, I was going insane. Listening to podcasts in French as I fell asleep had come to haunt me because I couldn't even think straight to the point that I was thinking gibberish in another language. This was what she'd done to me, what's she's always done to me. And *kissing her*, kissing her felt like night swimming in a summer ocean.

Oh. Oh *God*. "*Daisy*," I moaned. *My Daisy*. The way her hands gripped my hair and the way her waist felt under my grip. It was home, she was *home*.

How did you tell someone that you wanted this every day, every morning, hour, and night of your life? I was pathetic. If she knew just how weak I was when she dragged her hand up the back of my neck, let alone when she kissed me, she'd be horrified. Seeing her with Ethan earlier made me want to rip my eyes out. Having to watch as some man flirted with her and pretending that it didn't flood my chest with jealously was like standing on hot coals.

She dragged her tongue across my bottom lip, and I must've groaned because she pulled me in closer—no, held onto me tighter. Was I imagining it, or did she want this as much as I have these past years?

The small sounds she was making between our lips were ripping me apart inside. I couldn't get enough of her. I cradled the back of her neck, tipping her head backwards to get full access of her jaw and kiss every spot.

She gasped and clung onto my arms. She smelled like vanilla and roses, and I wanted it all. I'd get on my knees and worship her if I could have this every day. Her hips my altar and her lips my religion.

I didn't even know what I was saying before it was coming out of my mouth. "You intoxicate me, Daisy. The scent of flowers lingers on you everywhere you go, and I always want to follow."

She felt tense under my hand. *Jesus, why couldn't I say something normal?* I'd been in love with her since I was sixteen, daydreaming about kissing her, and now I was fucking it up.

Then, as soon as I was pressing my lips against hers, she was pulling away.

I knew almost everything about her, every sign of anger, dissatisfaction, joy, and insecurity. But when she pulled away from me, I couldn't figure it out... and that terrified me. I couldn't read what she was feeling, meaning I couldn't fix it.

Her eyes roamed my face and then she pressed her hands against my chest. It was so light, but she could've pushed me over right there if she wanted to.

She started speaking but was quickly cut off by a girl behind me. I tried not to intrude, standing off to the side like a ghost as they spoke.

But then I heard her friend say:

"—Paris, babe! When will you leave?"

She applied to a university in Paris? She got in. She's going to Paris.

"Oh, I–I haven't made a decision yet on ESMOD actually," Daisy responded. She was nervous. The way she twisted the earrings in her ears and smiled. She … she didn't want me to know about this.

They finished their conversation, and the friend was gone. Everything after felt slow, but it happened so quickly that I couldn't react because all I could think about was that she was leaving *again*, she was going to move across the world and there was nothing I could do about it. I couldn't follow her there; as much as I wanted this relationship to be real, it didn't make it any less fake.

"Congratulations," I heard myself say with a smile.

Even if there was some slim chance she wanted me there as a friend, I couldn't leave. They needed me. Rhea and Claire. Who would do their hair, and make sure Claire had her inhaler packed for soccer practice, and double check the booster seat set-up, and remind Rhea to brush her teeth, and what if something happened and no one was with them? That thought alone made me want to vomit—

Her lips pressed against my cheek and her hand left mine. I don't even remember taking her hand. But just like that it was gone. And she was rushing down the stairs, her long dress dragging behind her like an ocean wave in a storm, leaving me stranded.

Acknowledgements

Writing is a truly terrifying and self-conscious process. Especially when you're self-publishing, because there's no one there to ensure that you don't throw away your entire manuscript just because you stayed up late one night after having a dream that it was the worst book ever written. It's a very lonely, terrifying process, similar to high school exams, but there's no definitive answer on whether or not you did good. But it's worth it (promise)!

I want to thank my (*takes a deep breath*) beautifully intelligent creative friend Megan Hemenway. If it weren't for you, I don't know if I would've finished editing my book without your friendship. Between you and the writing club we've started, I've found a true support system in this community.

To my amazing, sweet beta readers, Sofia Kaitlyn Ong and Veronica Wheat. You were my Gabe and Jia, helping me figure out what should stay in this story.

To Kenz, Misha, and Anna, who I couldn't not give a cameo to because we *did* go to Paris together and you *have* become my best friends. I'm beyond lucky to have you constantly instilling your confidence in me as a writer and friend; it keeps me going.

To my boyfriend Nick, who got stuck listening to every plotline, character arc, and worry I expressed. You never once complained, and only ever asked to hear more. Thank you for dealing with me throughout this process. You helped me put page numbers in this book, sat with me during dinner as I wrote down just one more idea, and always called me an author even when I couldn't look at myself as one. Much of the comedic banter in this story is because of the supportive relationship you've created where I could say stupid things and not feel insecure. You helped me grow the confidence I didn't have, much like Levi does for Daisy.

For the readers: I want to thank every one of you who has a read something of mine, purchased it for a friend, or reached out to tell me you enjoyed it. *You* are the reason I keep writing. It's very easy to read bad reviews and take them as truth. But your kind words, whether it's via a review or a direct message, always bring me to Nicholas Sparks-worthy tears. I'd bake you a million strawberry shortcakes and send you daisies if I could. Thank you, always. I love you to pieces.

Liana Cincotti creates characters and stories about romance, self-discovery, and travel for both teens and adults. She recently finished her Bachelor of Science in Marketing and Accounting at Merrimack College, and now works in Marketing and Communications.

On her best days, you can find her sharing tubs of cookie dough ice cream with her friends, meeting with her writing club on Wednesdays, or curling up in the corners of bookstores reading the newest romance.

Befriend her online @LianaCincotti or on her blog, www.WithLiana.com.

Made in United States
Orlando, FL
03 November 2024